SCALPI

by

Richard A. Brown, M.D.

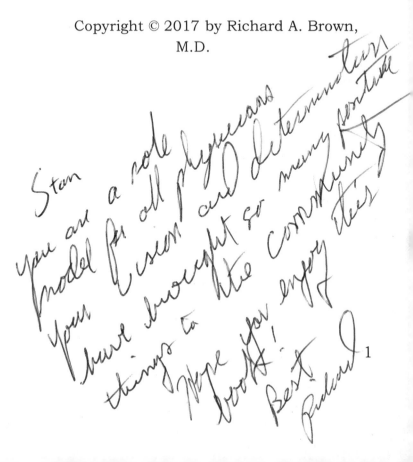

Stan

you are a role model for all physicians. Your vision and determination have brought so many positive things to the community. Hope you enjoy book!! Best, Richard

1

www.scalpelscut.com

Published by Sharp Knife Publishing

Cataloging-in-Publication Data is on file with the Library of Congress
TXu 2-061-945

ISBN-13: 978-0-9991291-0-4
Cover design by Emily Mahon
Cover photos: Shutterstock
Printed in the United States of America

Part I

NICK

A Bad January in Boston

The partially dismembered victim lay motionless on the narrow slab. He was alive, but paralyzed. A woman, shrouded in green, cleansed the body for the ritual event. Standing by, a masked man, holding a razor-sharp knife, waited impatiently. Then, without ceremony, he began.

Earlier That Day

The new year was not starting well. There Nick sat, hand strapped to the elegant wooden butcher block. It was one of the few wedding gifts his ex had left behind. She'd smile if she understood what it was about to be used for. She still hated him that much. A mahogany clock ticked loudly. He'd spent hours designing it, finding just the right wood, and ultimately building it. Now the noise was torturing him. He wanted to smash the damn thing into a million pieces. Rain splattered against the windows. It was a miserable day outside and in.

Three prison-hardened men surrounded Nick Mahaffey. Escape was impossible. He'd already pleaded with them. Useless words spoken to an uncaring audience. The largest of the enforcers talked to him like he was delivering lines from a play, "Mahaffey, it's simple—you threatened the Cooperative, and so you must be punished. I apologize for the violence, but it is necessary." Slowly the man removed his coat and folded it neatly on the chair. Nick's trained eyes locked on the distinctive tattoo adorning his tormentor's forearm. A fanged clown smiled savagely, holding a large knife in his hand. Skewered on the knife was a bleeding human heart. As the behemoth picked up the object lying on the table, Nick watched with horror.

In an instant the newly sharpened meat cleaver separated fingers from hand. Nick screamed. The branchless appendage felt like it was exploding.

Cyrus gathered the four white-and-red sausages, meticulously wrapping each in sterile gauze soaked in balanced salt solution. He then placed the quartet in a clear plastic bag, which, in turn, was nestled in a second, ice-filled container.

He resumed his lecture. "I'm going to give you a chance to get your fingers sewn back on. That is my personal gift to you. Nobody from the Cooperative said I couldn't return the digits once I cut them off. I read about replantation surgery on the Internet and verified the proper storage technique for amputations. Hopefully, it's accurate. Sometimes the information isn't as precise as I'd like. The articles say you'll be a good candidate—multiple fingers, sharp cuts, you don't smoke, you're not too old. An

6

ambulance will arrive shortly. Tell them the obvious—you suffered an unfortunate accident with a saw. Lucca will do his best with the dressing. I took the liberty of acquiring the materials from a pharmacy. It should suffice for the moment. I'm going on my way now. Don't make the Cooperative summon me again. Be wise."

With that Cyrus disappeared. Armaceo and Lucca Luciano, the psychopathic cretins the Cooperative had sent to help, lingered for a few extra moments to gloat as they finished the bandage. Clients "accidently" died in their hands on a regular basis. Once Cyrus was out of sight, Armaceo gripped Nick's injured hand forcefully, taking great pleasure in the severe pain created by the sadistic act. "Mahaffey, youah a lucky mothahfuckah. If it'd been up to me I'da cut off yah nutsack and stuffed it down yah fuckin' throat."

Nick was relieved to see the two depart without the threatened alteration to his standard-issue manhood. He remained stunned. The huge maniac had partially dismembered him without hesitation. Yet the man still gave him an opportunity to have the fingers replanted. If the reality wasn't what it was, he would've been impressed. Unfortunately, his fingers were sitting in a bag, and successful replant or not, his livelihood was a thing of the past.

CYRUS

Cyrus made the required call to the Cooperative to report that the job was complete. That's what they paid him to do. Get the job done. His patrons knew he wouldn't terminate anybody, but Cyrus' size and knife skills made him a valued commodity. He was a busy man.

Cyrus hopped on Boston's famous T and took the Green Line back to his St. Stephen Street apartment by the Prudential Center. Most of the time he kept to himself, but there was a young lady he had noticed in his art class. They'd exchanged a few words, though nothing substantial. She intrigued him. Intense, petite, athletic, and exotic looking. He'd decided to create a "chance" meeting if he could. *Despite this crap weather, maybe today will be the day,* Cyrus thought to himself. He'd heard her say she lived close by. It was easy enough to stake out the area. Out loud he said, "After all, what else do I have to do?"

There was one major problem. He was awful with women. They seemed to have a sixth sense for his violent side. The ones who liked him weren't the ones he preferred. Cyrus tried to compensate by refining his speech and making himself into someone he could never be.

Inevitably something bad would happen. That was part of the reason he had washed out after just a year of physician's assistant school. One of his classmates reported Cyrus to the dean for stalking her. It wasn't the first time. The leader of the Cooperative, the queen of darkness herself, somehow found out, and used the information as a recruitment tool. This happened even before the Cooperative *was* the Cooperative. Several state sponsored vacations followed. That hadn't helped his cause. Now here he was, a decade later, still doing her bidding.

TESS

Fast-Forward to Middle March
"Hey, Tess, what's the matter?" Axel shouted, with more than a few hints of beer on his breath. "Aren't you coming out with us? We've planned this St. Patty's Day costume party for a month!"

Tess Risdall groaned, watching the computer whiz kid stomp through the apartment wearing a highlighter-green BRO, DO YOU EVEN LIFT? tank top and dripping hair gel everywhere. Never mind that it was twenty-two degrees outside; Axel sought out any and every opportunity to show off his biceps. He ran his fingers through his greasy locks to set what Tess assumed was supposed to be his "look." Despite Axel Syndergaard's off-the-chart IQ, the fact that he had gotten into Harvard with the social skills of a two-year-old amazed her. She wanted to tell him he didn't need to don a costume to be a douchebag, but settled for glaring at him instead.

He was undeterred. "Aw, what's the matter? No love for big A tonight?"

Axel's continued romantic interest was bothersome in and of itself, but knowing that she couldn't make it to the party was worse. Her costume was perfect—a pulsating green jellyfish complete with long, blinking strands of light. She and her lifelong accomplice and current roommate Jessica had worked on their outfits for weeks. Then boom, no party. Unfortunately, there wasn't a choice. A cadaver was waiting, and for a struggling first-year student, that call had to be answered.

Her professor, Dr. Bianka Messi, had strongly implored that she come in to complete the dissection on this of all evenings; Dr. Messi was going to function as a personal tutor. Bianka was a friend of her parents, but Tess still thought it was strange that she would want to meet on a Friday night. Rescheduling was not a realistic choice. Tess was traveling to her college roommate's wedding in Maine the next morning. At first she had reconsidered her RSVP. The Bowdoin College friends would understand if she had to decide between missing the wedding or tanking a vital class. But even more than a passing anatomy grade, she realized she needed to see her people again. Tess's closest friends described her as complex, but they understood her. Right now, that connection was essential. So, in her mind, there was no alternative but to go to the anatomy lab tonight and miss the big party.

Dr. Messi was a mentor. She knew Tess was having some trouble and wanted to do what she could to help. The C on the micropathology test had set off a small panic. Tess hadn't gotten a grade that bad since elementary school. The teacher thought girls should have better handwriting and handed her a D. If the woman had known then that her pupil was going to be a doctor, perhaps she might have been less severe. The stakes were much higher now.

"C'mon, Tess, it'll be a great time," Axel piped up again hopefully. "Do that cadaver crap afterward. Your stiff isn't going anywhere."

She directed a vicious stare at her nemesis. "Axel, some of us in this class actually have to work hard. From this point forward, I am rescinding your right to speak. When you have the ability to say something reasonable I'll reconsider." With that the conversation ended. Axel shrugged off Tess' umpteenth rebuff without apparent psychological injury and grabbed another beer from the fridge.

Jessica pulled her into the alcove. "Tess, do you always have to be so difficult? Axel's not a bad guy. He just wants you to have some fun. That's not so terrible. He doesn't know anything about your micro test or the wedding. Why don't you give him a break? He really likes you." She paused. "Plus, you just come off looking mean."

Tess thought about what her roommate said. It was true. Still, she couldn't summon the words for an apology. All she could manage was "You guys have fun" as Jessica turned to leave with Axel and the rest of the group.

Tess felt deflated. Jessica wasn't suggesting something unreasonable. The first year of medical school is like being adopted into a new family. Support is critical but tenuous. She constantly wondered where she belonged. Many of her classmates, like Axel, seemed akin to the superheroes from Marvel comic books. One was training for the Olympic decathlon—nothing special. Another had been working on rocket engines chosen by NASA for extended space travel—no big deal. They continued to do these things *and* conquer the demands of medical school. The fact that these people could pull it all off with such seeming ease made her crazy.

Tess knew she was smart, but she felt amazing in precisely zero ways. Friends constantly complimented her on her painting, but she thought they were just being nice. She played club field hockey, danced, and at one point made every campus security screen at Bowdoin play Bugs Bunny cartoons simultaneously. In no world were those accomplishments in the same category as working on the space program.

Tess remained convinced that the intervention of the Bowdoin president, Avram Friedlander, was the primary reason she was where she now was. President Friedlander enjoyed hanging out with his flock. In turn, the students universally considered him to be wonderful. She and the president had bonded instantly during her freshman year after a conversation focusing on the brilliant insanity of *Catch-22*. A job at his office followed.

Over the next four years Tess had performed various tasks—welcoming VIPs, speaking to parent groups, hosting students. She was asked to stay on after graduation in a more formal role. The offer was tempting, but she felt she owed it to herself to reach beyond the friendly confines of the Bowdoin campus. Tess relocated to Boston to conduct research and spent three years creating a citywide communications care bridge for oncology patients. She felt the work distinguished her, but not as academically special.

Originally, she was slated to go to Emory Medical School. She had convinced herself that the heat and humidity wouldn't be a problem, and that she'd have no trouble adjusting to the South. Then it happened: The chairman of the department of medicine's kid wigged out at the last minute. A spot opened up at Harvard, and Tess got in off the waiting list. It was one of the happiest days of her life. Georgia was in the rearview mirror. Now, she was in the thick of it, and things weren't as peachy in Boston.

As Tess studied the four open anatomy books on her table, she tried to remember that moment of euphoria. The multidisciplinary approach was helpful, but too often overwhelming. She was rapidly growing to appreciate that medicine entails layer upon layer of complexity. Just when she thought she understood something, she'd find out that a controversy existed and what she thought was right wasn't necessarily true. Even something as seemingly straightforward as anatomy could be that way. The variations in the nerve and blood supply to the hand were ridiculous. She thought to herself, *I'm never going to learn this. I should just call Bianka and tell her not to waste her time.* Then Tess yelled at herself for indulging in self-pity, and resolved to kill the anatomy test. With newfound determination, she bundled up and set out on the journey to the land of the dead.

* * * * *

Cyrus followed carefully from a distance. He was frustrated. After that first mildly successful night, all the subsequent attempts he'd made to connect had failed. More than two months had passed, but he'd decided Tess was still exactly the type of woman he wanted—definitely worth the extra effort it would take to finally get her. Although he was tracking Tess, he decided that the information he'd read about the five different types of stalkers didn't apply to him at all. His situation was unique. He'd been told more than once that he had "issues." Cyrus thought to himself, *Screw all those quacks; I like Tess. Why shouldn't I follow her?*

VJ

The wet cold seeped through Tess' North Face jacket as she hurried, taking the dark shortcut to the anatomy lab. "Why didn't I put on my heavy parka?" she muttered as she tripped over a large tree limb. "Damn," she swore. A few days ago, the bomb cyclone had raged. Half the city was ravaged. The medical school hadn't been spared. Finally, Tess navigated around the fallen branch and made it to the entrance.

As she grasped the door handle, Tess jammed her index finger. Completely agitated, shaking her hand in pain, she yelled, "Asshole motherfucker." A woman walking her dog on the sidewalk turned and glared. Tess smiled apologetically while thinking, *Bitch,* and simultaneously asking herself, *Is there someone else standing near that lady?* For some time now she'd had the sense of being watched. Spooked, Tess hastily ran inside and climbed the stairs to the fourth floor of the education building. Her boots created a squeak with each step. It was otherwise dead quiet. No lights were on above.

Suddenly, there was a loud grinding noise like someone was moving furniture. She called out, "Bianka, is that you?" No response. Tess freaked for a second, thinking that 24/7 access had its good and bad points. She made a mental note to avoid coming to the lab at night again. When she reached her destination, she stared at the door. Tess fingered the cold, round handle then hesitated. Finally, taking a deep breath, she turned the knob and entered.

Row after row of embalmed bodies wrapped in plastic greeted her in the cavernous room. Modern-day mummies. Anatomical charts were the only wall decorations. Her team's cadaver, Orville, waited motionless on the closest dissecting table. They weren't supposed to name the specimens, but every group did. Tonight, the familiarity calmed her down.

The place was always too hot or too cold. Too cold was the flavor du jour—even colder than normal.

Tess couldn't escape the odor. Nothing tickles the nostrils quite like formaldehyde. Dissection tools were strewn about the tables. The windows were frosted. Searching for the lights, she noticed that a window was open and wondered where Bianka was.

At that moment, a singsong voice called out. "Tess, do you mind closing that? I needed some air, but I'm having trouble getting up. My knee is talking to me big-time."

Tess whirled around as she yelled, "Who the fuck are you?!" She dove toward one of the tables and grabbed a scalpel. Alarm bells were going off in her head. Whoever this was definitely didn't belong here. "I'll slice your throat in two seconds," she threatened as she held up the knife as menacingly as possible. The lights were still off. Tess could only see the outline of a body slumped down on a chair near the wall. At least it didn't look anything like the person she thought was stalking her. The apparently reanimated cadaver across the room was new territory for her. She had been under the false belief that speaking to the dead, let alone conversing with them, usually had to wait until the latter part of the second-year curriculum.

The odd voice said, "Tess, try to calm down. Believe me, I'm not a threat to you or anyone else right now. Bianka isn't coming tonight. I'm standing in for her. Everything is going to be OK—really, don't worry."

"Did Axel send you here to mess with me?" she asked, still absolutely committed to using the blade in her hand if necessary.

"The only Axels I know live on cars or in Sweden," the raspy voice responded. "Is he a friend of yours?"

"So you think this is a joke?" Tess asked as she closed her eyes and forced herself to take several deep breaths. The preclinical instructors had told her that was helpful—that and swearing. If Axel was behind this, she was going to disembowel him. Jessica wouldn't be able to stop her.

"Honestly, Tess, I don't know Axel, but I have to speak with you. Bianka was very kind to set up this meeting. I'm not really myself yet. I'll explain that. I promise." He coughed. "Damn anesthesia. You'd think the atelectasis would've cleared by now. I'm moving sort of slow, and, as I just mentioned, my knee is starting to hurt like hell. Too bad the Marcaine is wearing off so fast.

"Bianka is a close friend, and take my word for it—I can teach you the anatomy. We used to give this course as a team. I know this is lunacy, and you probably want to get out of here, but I'm going to ask you not to do that. I won't do anything to stop you if you want to go. There's a reason you're here and a reason I'm here with you. Trust me, I wish there was a better way to do this. There wasn't. I'm not a rapist or murderer. I'm not even a bad person. Here, I'm going to throw my wallet over to you. Check it out. I'm a hand surgeon at MRMC. Bianka said to tell you that Max will be thrilled to go to opening day at Fenway. I'm not sure what the significance of that statement is other than the obvious. But she suggested it would mean something to you and would let you know I really do know her well. Can you sit for a few minutes and talk to me?"

Tess relaxed slightly, despite her adrenaline still maxing out. The reference was to her brother, who had been desperate to go to opening day to see the Red Sox. He was under the impression that the family tickets had been earmarked for friends. Max lived nearby in Chestnut Hill and was always a gamer for sporting events. Tess had confided in Bianka that the tickets were his to use, and that she was going to surprise him.

The wallet belonging to the male voice landed near her feet. Considerably uncertain about the whole strange situation, she answered directly and concisely: "If you make one move toward me, I *will* slit your carotids."

He said, "Now, that would be unfortunate."

Tess finally located the light switch and had a better look at the mysterious visitor. The man was shaved bald, with a salt-and-pepper beard. He was wearing MRMC scrubs. She could see from his chest and arms that he wasn't a stranger to the gym. She looked through the wallet and found his medical license. Erik Samuel Brio was a member of the hand surgery department at Massachusetts Regional Medical Center. If anyone could teach her extremity anatomy, it would be him. Obviously, he had a different agenda.

Tess wondered why she wasn't already out the door. There was still plenty of time to go to the party. However, now that the man didn't appear to be a threat, her curiosity was piqued. She'd stay, at least for the time being. She did keep a distance, however, and the scalpel remained in her hand.

The sallow man tried unsuccessfully to stand, settled back in the chair, then opened his mouth to speak but coughed again instead. "Maybe I've contracted that Middle East respiratory syndrome," he said when he could. "I'll definitely have to get rid of that friggin' camel I keep at my townhouse. I knew bringing that thing back from Egypt was a bad idea."

He smiled and beckoned her to come closer. "You can put down the scalpel anytime. In your clinical judgment, do I look harmful? Come on, Tess, what do you see?"

She slowly placed the scalpel on the table next to her. "What do you want with me?" Tess asked. She walked closer to Dr. Brio, who was now virtually collapsed in his chair. "I'm staring at a guy who looks like he just woke up from a three-day bender. If you're a fresh post-op, maybe you'd be better off back in the post-anesthesia care unit. If you're dead, then there are probably a bunch of pathologists who would love to interview you."

"Very funny," he said, looking at Tess with cobalt-blue eyes. "I'm clearly not dead, at least not yet. So you saw from my hospital ID that I'm a hand surgeon. Are you thinking about pursuing anything surgical?"

She started to respond, "I don't know what . . . ," but he interrupted.

"Don't say no. Did you ever read *The House of God*? The author was completely wrong about some things. He said, 'The delivery of good medical care is to do as much nothing as possible.' There's a difference between internal medicine and surgery. Most of the time in the operating room, doing something is actually doing something. That said, there's nothing surgery can't sometimes make worse. Quite the dilemma."

Tess was surprised by the turn the conversation had just taken. She simply nodded yes.

The man continued, "I'm almost shocked you know the book. I suppose you figured out that it's not very politically correct. That's why I believe it should be on the required list for anyone who starts here. This PC garbage is way out of hand. You can't do or say anything these days without somebody getting their knickers in a twist. What'd you think of it?"

Regarding the man before her and remembering the eighth rule in the book—*they can always hurt you more*—Tess started to laugh. "One of the fourth-years handed it to me my first day of orientation. She said the book would give me perspective, particularly when I started my clinical rotations. I'm not sure how much of it is real, but it's pretty funny. All of my classmates know the rules of *The House of God* even if they haven't read it."

He nodded. "Take my word for it—the descriptions of hospital politics and the way things happen in the medical center are very accurate. So much of what you'll experience will seem completely insane. But I'm proud of you. Choosing to become a physician is difficult. The hours are tough, and you won't always feel appreciated. Still, it's an incredible privilege. Wait until you walk into the ICU for the first time. A family will be there desperate for you to help. Sometimes it will work out and sometimes it won't. When it does, you'll experience the greatest sense of fulfillment.

"By the way, everyone calls me VJ, but it isn't V-i-j-a-y. I suppose you figured out from my accent that I'm not exactly a native Bostonian. VJ is short for Viking Jew. I grew up near Stockholm. We Members of the Tribe are not usually thought of as seafaring, battle-axe-wielding adventurers, but when I was a resident, a friend gave me the nickname, and it stuck. People who haven't met me in person are surprised when they find out that I'm not from India."

Tess found another light and turned it on to see this VJ better. She said with more than a hint of sarcasm, "I'm not sure about all this. You're not a zombie, are you? There still seems to be a lot of that going around these days."

VJ seemed amused. "Actually, you're not that far off with your assessment. Of course I'm not the undead. I'm just now coming around. Walk over here and tug on my skin if you'd like.

Today is definitely weird. The soothsayer in *Julius Caesar* was right: 'Beware the ides of March.'" He paused, started to say something, but stopped and looked sheepish. Then finally he came out with it. "Do you happen to know if Duke beat Syracuse in the ACC tournament? Damn good teams, both of them. The spread was only two and a half. Duke lacks a true five, though, and they're playing in Greensboro, so it probably should have been more like four and a half."

Tess blew a gasket. "Come on! This is ridiculous. Here I am talking to a strange guy hanging out in the anatomy lab. You look like a train hit you. You haven't told me anything. You know, you have serious problems. You use Bianka to drag me here. Then you have the audacity to spew drivel about basketball games I don't care about. There's only a certain amount of bullshit I can process each day, and this isn't in today's quota. What's *wrong* with you?"

VJ collected himself. "Sorry, dissociative thought. It's an ongoing problem. Please give me just a small bit of leeway. Before I go on, Tess, I want to tell you how sorry I am about your parents. Bianka mentioned the accident. She didn't give me all the details, but I know a drunk driver was involved. It must have been awful."

Tess stared at VJ, stinging from the unexpected comment. "We're *not* talking about my parents."

24

VJ acknowledged her directive with a soulful look, then continued, "Got it. By the way, don't worry, I promise to make absolutely sure you know everything you need to know about this anatomy section. I did mention I used to help teach the course, didn't I? My brain is still a little foggy."

"You did," Tess said. She wondered who this guy was, all of a sudden bringing her family into the conversation. The reference to her mother and father had felt like someone stabbing her. It wasn't his fault. Tess could tell he was sincere. She'd pushed the horrible memory to a remote part of her brain to protect herself.

He said, "I'll cut to the chase. Bianka connected us because I have a completely absurd story that I need to tell you. You're going to wonder if you're having a dream or interviewing a patient on the psych ward. If all of it wasn't true, really, I wouldn't believe it myself. The thing is— it involves you directly." Sensing Tess' appropriate reticence, VJ added, "Plus, I promise to be your personal tutor in the future *anytime*, day or night. I just need you to stay and listen to me."

Tess considered what VJ said and weighed her options again. If she left, she could still make the party, but she wouldn't get any answers, and all hope of doing well on the anatomy test would be gone. If she stayed, she was obviously going to hear about something strange, apparently get some personal insight, and as a side benefit, ace the anatomy test *and* have help in the future. The last parts definitely worked.

Tess felt her phone vibrate and looked at the text. It was from Bianka. It read, So sorry! Misplaced my cell phone, couldn't find your number. Wanted to explain about VJ. He's my friend. Doesn't want anyone else to know you're meeting him. Important issues to discuss. Give him a chance. Her words clinched the deal, at least for the moment. Tess decided healthy skepticism was still in order. In her calmest voice, she said, "Well, Bianka just texted me. She says you're OK. I suspect you're well aware that you're playing on my insecurities about anatomy, but I promise to hear what you want to tell me. Seriously, though, I can't listen to you go off on a bunch of tangents. Also, put your money where your mouth is—take me through the anatomy of the carpal tunnel right now. I can't help but think I'm going to get grilled on it."

VJ suddenly sat up. "Please, please text Bianka and tell her you don't know who VJ is, that you arrived at the lab but nobody was here, and that you'll go over the material another time."

Tess looked at the man quizzically and said, "After all this? You really are out of your mind."

"Please, Tess," VJ pleaded. "Please do it. I'm going to explain, but it's critical that you do this now." His imploring sincerity pushed her to comply with the request. She sent Bianka the message.

Instantly Bianka shot back a text: Really?? Doesn't make sense. Tess remained puzzled by the deception. A few minutes later she felt her phone vibrate. Again, Bianka: Just found out something terrible happened to him. Can't explain right now. On the Cape. Know you are leaving town. Can you meet Monday?

Perplexed, Tess showed VJ the text. He glanced at the screen and said, "I'll explain—right now the world, including Bianka, thinks I'm dead. For me to stay alive, I need to keep everyone thinking exactly that. Tell her that you're OK with the change in plan."

Sensing that Tess might jump ship, even though he saw her sending off the requested reply, VJ quickly added, "Tess, let's get on this anatomy. When we finish, you can decide about the rest. Parts of the story will seem superfluous, disjointed, or inappropriate. It's going to take me a while to get to how you fit in. I mean possibly more than a few hours. I beg your indulgence. It's all relevant. When I finish, you'll understand. I sincerely appreciate that you're giving me a chance to try. Now, about the wrist and the carpal tunnel . . ."

Tess fidgeted, the wheels in her head turning. "So you really intend to keep me here for that long? This better be good; I mean damn good. And don't think for a second that I'm going to let you off the hook about helping me down the road."

A SURGEON'S TALE

Tess and VJ spent a healthy amount of time looking at the relevant nerves, arteries, and tendons in the wrist and palm. VJ mixed in the clinical importance of each structure with examples to make the information stick. He could see the lights of understanding go on in her eyes. She bumped fists with him and said, "All of a sudden I feel like a genius. You kept your word. You do know your stuff. And you can actually teach—that's a major feather in your cap."

He smiled and said, "*Qui docet discit*—who teaches, learns. Honestly, it was a tremendous pleasure."

Tess grinned in return. "It gives me some confidence that this tale of yours is possibly worth hearing. Remember the rules: You have to stay on point. I'll leave if you don't."

He had Tess' full attention now and wanted to blurt the whole story out at once. But the gory beginning seemed like the logical place to start. "It was only about two months ago and now, honestly, it feels like two years. I was headed home. It had been raining all day, but it was turning to snow. Windy like you wouldn't believe. Classic Boston. The cranes working on the new patient building at MRMC were shaking like trees. I don't know if you've seen them. They tower right over the side entrance to the hospital. If I don't use that door, I have to walk an extra half-mile to get home. When it's snowing hard, like it's been doing all this winter, those extra steps can be agony. Every time I walk there I wonder if those cranes are going to fall down and crush me.

"As an aside that's one of my great attributes—catastrophic thinking. Give me a situation and I'll always take a leap to the worst possible outcome. Somehow I think I'll be shielded from bad things happening, or be better prepared if and when they really do. It doesn't work like that."

"I agree," Tess said. "I actually do that, too. I manage to drive myself crazy, going in circles with that stuff. But focus," she said. "You promised."

He nodded, and resumed his story. "That afternoon I already had a lot on my mind. I was trying to prepare a talk. I had a patient threatening to sue me about something inane. On top of it all, I was still dealing with the aftermath of my live-in moving out. Apparently my priorities did not match hers. That she left shocked no one, least of all me."

Tess interrupted, "It's amazing that a woman wouldn't find your ruminations on basketball romantic. You should really try to find a higher-class person. By the way, why do I need to know this?"

"Part of my story is a little insight into who I am," he continued. "The good and the bad. It will help you understand how things have played out as they have. Anyway, about three minutes after I did finally get to my place, my phone rang. It was one of my partners, Nick. His voice sounded hollow, but very matter-of-fact. He said, 'VJ, this isn't good. I just cut the fingers off my right hand. I need you to do the replants.'

"'Funny, Nick,' I said. 'Listen, I've got a ton to do on this vascular insufficiency talk. Can I call you back?'

"A lot more emphatically, Nick repeated himself. 'VJ, I just cut off my fucking fingers with a saw.' There was a pause. 'I just texted you pictures!'

"Words were no longer needed. There was one shot of a Tupperware container filled with ice holding a bag with some bloodstained, gauze-wrapped objects, and another with Nick holding up a poorly dressed, clearly traumatized hand. 'Jesus Christ, Nick! How the hell did you do that? Are you at the hospital yet?'

"Nick said, 'No, VJ, but I can see the ambulance right now. I'll see you in five minutes.' Then he just hung up."

Tess practically jumped out of her chair. "I heard all about it! I remember that Friday really well. Holy shit! So it was you who did it! How was

Nick able to call you? Wouldn't he be passed out?"

VJ was startled. "For the record, most people who get their fingers cut off don't lose enough blood to go into shock. When I see them in the ER they have a lot of pain, but they're mostly just anxious about losing their body parts. Now *I'm* curious. I didn't realize that what's happening at MRMC filters down to the first-year med students."

"You're right," Tess answered. "But I have my own story. Do you want to finish, or do you want to hear it?"

He said, "Talk to me now. We're the only ones sitting here. What I have to say isn't going to be done anytime soon. So how did you know about this case?"

Tess turned her bracelet around her wrist, then said, "There's a short and a long version. Which do you want to hear?"

"Whatever you decide."

"I'll stick with the abridged story. That same night my roommate Jessica and I were supposed to go to dinner at this guy's apartment. He was in my art class, but I barely knew him. Jessica's mother fell and broke her wrist about an hour before we were supposed to go, so Jessica went to the ER to help her. I couldn't bail. I was responsible for us going in the first place. Jessica and I had been at the Rich Pour on Lansdowne Street, celebrating because I'd finally beaten her on a neurophysiology test. We drank a *lot* of those $5.50 beers. The dinner thing was spontaneous. We ran into this guy on our way back. He's huge. He appeared out of nowhere, almost like he had been waiting for us. I was pretty lit up. He invited us to come over, and I said yes.

"The guy was nice, but turned out to be kinda different. Plus, I wasn't myself. I told him a lot of things that I wouldn't normally tell anyone, including the bit about me wanting to kill that alcoholic asshole driver who ran into my parents. I could tell the guy really wanted to sleep with me, but he wasn't my type at all. I sort of ran out of his apartment, which also happens to be right down the street from me on St. Stephen.

"When I got back, Jessica clued me in about the adventure she'd had. Her mom needed emergency surgery because the fracture was coming through the skin. The problem was that there wasn't anyone initially available to do it. She said the hand surgeon on call was getting operated on himself because he'd cut his fingers off. That case had priority over everything else going on. Finally, they found another surgeon to take care of Jessica's mom. Of course, I didn't know any more than that until a minute ago. So yes, I remember that January night very clearly."

He looked at Tess. It was obvious from her face that there was a lot more to the story. As eager as he was to continue, he wanted to encourage her to talk freely. "Tess, that guy didn't do anything to you, did he?"

"No—not at all. He was actually a gentleman and a great chef. I watched him prepare the food. He was amazing with his knife. The problem was that he was trying too hard to impress me. Also, when he rolled up his sleeves, I saw this tattoo that gave me the creeps. About one second later, I decided that we didn't have a future. Going there was a mistake. I've been trying to avoid him ever since; I haven't been completely successful." Tess paused for a minute then abruptly said, "What happened with Nick?"

VJ took her cue that she was done with the subject. In his practice he was used to seeing tattoos on anything and everything, including a trauma patient covered with more than fifty swastikas. The coup de grace was the one on the head of his penis. VJ had become desensitized. But something else was tugging at him about the dinner guy. He wanted to ask Tess more, but decided to wait until she was ready. He went on with his story.

"When I realized I had to deal with four fingers off my friend, my sphincter tone went from baseline nuts to diamond-producing. I asked myself, *What kind of surgeon manages to cut off four digits?* I grabbed a coat, made a quick call to make sure that my dog and cat would be taken care of, and took off.

"My friend David Tuch says that hand surgeons earn the red badge of micro-courage doing replants. He's right. There are a million steps necessary to make them work. Also, it really helps to have a good team. There's no feeling like success, but failure is awful. With replants, there's very little in between. I've been on both sides too often. A replant can go south for many physiological reasons that have nothing to do with technique. Still, if the repairs aren't done right, there's definitely no chance they'll work. Patients depend on us to be at the top of our game, even if it's the middle of the night. Nick needed me perform.

"I was already at the point that I just wanted to be done the second I hit MRMC. The hospital is a crazy labyrinth. Finding a specific someone in the ER is usually an adventure. Miraculously, rather than the typical indifference from the nursing staff, I was met by an eager young lady who genuinely seemed to want to help me. I asked her if she was new. Of course she was. She led me to the bed holding my associate.

"When I saw Nick, the absolutely inconsolable desperation in his eyes said everything. As much as I wanted to blast him for his stupidity, I held back. Nick was still grasping the Tupperware container. He looked like a little boy holding his lunch. At least the fingers were perfectly maintained. The arrangement reminded me of Russian matryoshka dolls. I evaluated the fingers more closely. They didn't look at all like a saw got to them. There weren't the usual ground-up pieces of wood attached to the parts. Plus, the cuts were clean, and the skin and bone portions weren't chewed up in the least.

"I asked the nurse to leave us alone for a minute. As soon as she was gone, I said, 'So what really happened? You didn't do this with a Skilsaw. Both of us know that.'

"Nick stared at nothing for a minute, then began talking. 'The bottom line is that I reneged on a deal I made with a shadow group called the Cooperative. They're into billing fraud here at MRMC. Remember that ten-million-dollar work-comp kickback scheme in the news last year? I think the Cooperative is much, much bigger. They hired a big, tatted-up, surprisingly articulate dude to chop off half my hand with a meat cleaver. You know, just a routine day at the office. Incidentally, VJ, you can close your mouth anytime you want.

"'For right now, you've got to go along with my story. The history and physical and the operative report have to say that this was a saw accident. You have to take care of the dictation yourself, don't let the fellow do it. Can you take care of that for me?' I nodded my head to reassure my friend I would.

"This new wrinkle came totally out of left field and certainly did nothing to quell my anxiety. My mind jumped to some of the other recent 'accidents' that members of the MRMC staff had experienced. Was that actually what they were? Had Len Pedowitz's rope really broken while he was rock climbing? Did Beth Gregory hit an oil slick on her motorcycle? What actually happened to Sheila and Andy Magit's helicopter on their Hawaii vacation? Cheryl Ornstein and Gina Lambert both left the staff without a word. Everyone thought it was strange at the time, but just let it go. My concern quadrupled. I couldn't deal with those issues, so I shoved them into a different part of my brain and decided to focus on the task at hand. I called out to the orderly, 'Can you please take Dr. Mahaffey up to the OR now? It's time to get moving.'"

THE OPERATION

"I was running like a maniac to make sure everything was organized to begin the replantations. Then I got a call from pre-op. 'Dr. Brio, you need to come out here and put your initials on the surgical site before we can come back to the room. We have to verify which side you're operating on.' My eyes popped out of my head. At times like this I have to check my anger. I ran to pre-op and performed the mandatory scrawling of my initials on Nick's hand.

"He actually laughed. 'VJ, I tried to do it for you, but they busted me. That's all I need now—forget the fact that I'm never going to operate again; what happens if I get reported to the OR Nurse Review Committee? Then I'll be completely hosed.'

"'You know, Nick, I was thinking I might take the fingers off your left hand and move them to the right side and use the ones I've got here in the Tupperware for your left. Thank God the correct side is marked; otherwise I'd really have no idea what hand to do.' Fortunately, the nurse didn't hear me. My sarcasm doesn't always ingratiate me with the staff."

Tess said empathetically, "Been there, done that."

VJ smiled at her and said, "Et tu, Brute?" then continued, "Nick laid his head down and didn't respond. The cocktail the anesthesiologist had slipped him was taking effect. After more requisite time-wasting, we started the tedious process of cleaning the wounds and tagging nerves, arteries, veins, and tendons. Nick's surgical career *was* over. Even in the best case, his dexterity and sensation would be significantly diminished. He knew it and I knew it. Still, 'To someone with nothing, a little is a lot,' as one of the gods of hand surgery once said. At that moment, Nick had almost nothing. So, the goal was to repair the fingers that were separated from my partner's body and to try to make him whole again. Afterward I'd get the answers to the other questions."

Tess cracked wryly, "If I could only be so lucky. Answers? What's an answer?"

"I'm getting there," he reassured her.

She smiled. "You're fine. I'm just reminding you about your promise."

"Thanks for the vote of C." VJ pressed on. "Here's how it went. Two teams—myself and one resident working on Nick's hand; Chi, the fellow, and another resident working to get the fingers ready. 'Chi, how's it look?' I inquired. 'How many veins do we have? Are they decent?'

"She looked up over her loupes." Tess glanced at VJ with questioning eyes. "You know, those surgical magnifying glasses we wear that make us look like we have telescopes coming out of our eyes. Anyway, Chi said, 'VJ, they're good. Are you sure he said it was a saw? It sure doesn't look that way.'

"I took a moment to contemplate the best response. 'Who knows what happened? Maybe Nick was too embarrassed to tell us he was practicing his sword-swallowing and messed up. Whatever. Here we are, and here these fingers are. Let's get them on and be done.'

"That seemed to placate Chi. Her hands are the best I've ever seen. Delicate and efficient. I'm honestly intimidated by her skill level. Whenever we operate together, I feel like the veteran pro athlete who is about to be displaced by the talented rookie. I've got game, but she's better. My only advantage is that I've been at it longer.

"I gently teased out arteries and nerves on the palm side of the digits and the veins on the top part. Veins are like tissue paper. Repairing them is often an adventure. Fortunately, Nick's were downright perfect—one small ray of sunlight. The straight cut of the arteries, nerves, tendons, and bones was also going to make the rest easier. One quick chop, and boom—four fingers off just like that.

"I shortened the bones, then fixed them. Taking some of the length away eliminates any tension on the nerve, venous, and arterial repairs. Like I said a minute ago, bad technique, bad outcomes. Next came the extensor and flexor tendons. If you ever do this stuff, don't rush through the tendon repairs. If they don't glide, even a viable finger will be worthless.

"Once those steps were completed, we brought the operating microscope back in to do the hardest work repairing the arteries, veins, and nerves. The microscope is like a large beast that has to be tamed. The focus and zoom controls need to be checked, the lens height has to be positioned. The boom needs to get rolled in. If microscope issues interfere with doing the case, it's a nightmare.

"The routine was the same: Hit the pistol grip button. Zoom in with the microscope. Hit the pistol grip again. Focus. Place the sutures. Zoom out. Focus. Tie them. I must have repeated the process a hundred times. My contacts were dry, and I began to struggle to see anything. 'Cindy, I'm dying here. Can you get some balanced salt solution and pour it in my eyes? The Sahara Desert isn't this dry.' Cindy and I have worked together for years. She's a dedicated nurse who knows what I want before I ask most of the time. In a flash, she was back with the eye-saving fluid. I was resuscitated.

"'VJ, I can't believe you actually wanted me to do something reasonable,' Cindy said. 'Are you sure you don't want to have me call the Chinese embassy and report Chi for smuggling?' There was a groan from across the microscope.

"Medical hazing is a long and honored tradition. On Chi's second day we played a small prank. I had one of my cardiothoracic surgery colleagues call into the OR and ask for Chi. In perfect Cantonese, he demanded to know how long she had been illegally moving medical equipment into the country. We really had her going for a minute."

Tess almost shouted at me. "You really did that? It's sort of funny, but not very nice. This whole deal tonight better not be some kind of more elaborate practical joke! Tell me this second it's not or your life will not be worth living!"

VJ quickly provided reassurance. "Trust me, Tess, I only wish this was some kind of ruse. By that night, Chi had forgiven me. But she's still probably waiting for just the right moment to exact her revenge. Got to watch the quiet ones.

"With my eyes in better shape we started back to work on the replants. It's funny how hours and hours can go by and not that much seems to happen. That night, music played, and occasionally I heard it. The anesthesiologist engaged the nurses in conversation. While I was concentrating, I had no idea what was going on around me. At times the team's chatter trickled into my brain when I was at a particularly difficult spot. With more edge in my voice than I wanted, I asked that they suspend their discussion until later. Since it was early in the morning and there were no other trauma cases, the rest of the OR was still. I could sense it. Eventually, three fingers were done. I was mentally digging to finish the fourth. The eyepieces of the microscope were eroding the flesh around my eye sockets, and my butt felt like I'd just ridden two hundred miles on a new bike saddle. My neck was sore, and I had a headache. I just wanted to be finished and take a rest. In some parts of the world, there are people, usually women, who are trained to perform the task of reconnecting the vessels and nerves. They're not physicians, but incredibly gifted human seamstresses. Conceptually, it makes sense. Right about then I would've loved to import one of them to finish Nick's operation. Unfortunately, it wasn't a choice. I asked Chi if she could hold down the fort for a few minutes.

"A quick visit to the head, cold water on my face, and I was back. The clock ticked on. When it's late, or in this case early, I get even more irritable. When the last vessel was repaired, I watched tiny rivulets of blood seep like apparitions from the small life-giving vessels. We closed the skin, and I felt overwhelming relief. It was over—or so I hoped. The bulky dressing went on, and we took Nick to the surgical ICU to watch him closely. If the replants went south, I wanted to know immediately. I'd hate myself if it happened, but I've done enough replants to anticipate anything that man and God together might dish out. A million different things can cause failure. Clots in the arteries, clots in the veins, circulating devils that induce the vessels to constrict. If a successful replant has to come back to the OR because it starts to fail, too often it stays failed. Nick didn't need that. I was too beat to contemplate the hardest part of the case—what to do to really help the man on the bed. So I just collapsed in the OR lounge and decompressed.

"These lounges are the same in every hospital I've ever set foot in. Soiled carpet flanked by peeling linoleum. Dilapidated furniture. Half-filled paper coffee cups sitting around, left by someone days earlier. Packets of cheese, soy sauce, mustard, and red pepper flakes from take-out. Half opened plastic dishware/napkin combos. A weird smell that is a cross between stale food and fungus. Unwelcoming, particularly at five in the morning. I scrounged through the fridge and found some string cheese. I ate it for no other reason than that it was there. Two is always better than one, so I downed the second piece lying in the bin. I hoped that I wouldn't be the subject of a later administrative inquiry into the sudden loss of the string cheese supply at MRMC. Those can get rough.

"Still unable to move out of the chair, my mind drifted back to an event on rounds during my medical school pediatric rotation. Sitting in the middle of the table our group was occupying was a luscious triple chocolate cake. One of the nurses had made it for some unspecified occasion. After grilling us on a complex cardiopulmonary birth disorder for thirty minutes or so, the chief resident broke down. All he said was, 'Possession is ninety percent of the law.' Instantly, we devoured the cake. It was so wrong, and yes, we got in a ton of trouble. Tess, take it from someone who has learned the hard way, crossing nurses during your rotations, or for that matter, anytime, is a terrible idea. Hell hath no fury like an angry nurse. But I can still taste that chocolate cake slice. Infinitely better than age-indeterminate string cheese.

"Ultimately I summoned the energy to get up and leave. I didn't know where I was going, but I did manage to get out of the lounge. Meanwhile, the main OR was busily gearing up for another day of inefficiency, oblivious to the hours of suffering Chi, myself, and the rest of the team had endured. I wandered down the hallways. For reasons unclear to me, most of the hospital was getting dismantled. Everywhere I turned I was dodging monster cables that hung from the ceiling. Massive clear-hose gizmos were also attached. Eyesores and obstacles everywhere. Like roadwork during and after the Big Dig, apparently the project is scheduled to continue until the end of time. Once I successfully navigated my way through the gauntlet, I found a resident call room and crashed for an hour."

Tess was playing with her bracelet and looking like she might need a break herself. VJ said, "Do you want a rest? If you're hungry, I can offer you some gourmet string cheese, or perhaps chocolate cake?"

Tess gazed at the row of cadavers and then back at VJ. "As appealing as the idea sounds, I think I'll pass. But I'm wondering, after the case, did Chi say anything else about the mystery of the injury?"

VJ shook his head no. "Once I finish doing a tough replant, I immediately focus on what needs to be done to keep alive whatever we've put back on. I think it's the same for Chi. After it was clear that the replants were successful, Chi didn't ask me a thing. Plus, she was going to have her hands full working with one of my partners, Rachel Reich, the week after. Rachel's schedule makes mine look like a Disneyland ride. I don't think she had the luxury to concern herself further with how Nick's fingers came off. Next time Chi and I have the chance to see each other, if that can happen, I'll tell her everything I'm preparing to tell you."

Tess quipped, "How are you going to bribe her to stay and listen? Doesn't sound like you've got a huge reservoir of goodwill left. On a different note, I'm wondering what it's like to do a case like that, particularly on someone you work with. What happens when it doesn't go well?"

VJ said, "That answer's easy. Then I feel frustrated and totally inadequate. There's a reason so many of us control-freak, anal-retentive people specialize in hand surgery. We hate it when things don't go our way. As far as Chi goes, I suppose I'll have to wait for the next replant she does and just talk at her while she's doing it. She won't be able to escape."

Tess stood up and stretched for a second. "Lucky her. By the way, I heard everything you said, loud and clear, but replants still sound like a fun challenge. You do them, so they can't be too awful."

"I'm Jewish. I like the combination of pain and something to complain about. Ironically, replants were the reason I got interested in hand surgery in the first place. Duke has a great microvascular program and a terrific lab. You wouldn't believe the number of rat arteries I put together. You're right, though. I like proving to myself that I can still do the surgery and help the people I manage to help. But if you showed up tomorrow and told me that someone would take over my replant obligations, I'd offer you an all-expenses paid trip anywhere in the world."

Tess said, "You're on. I'm going to hold you to that on top of everything else."

VJ was pleased. "Nothing would give me greater pleasure—see, that's what I'm talking about. Here I am telling you how much I hate replants and at the same time suggesting that you follow the same career path. It's a strange yin/yang thing.

"But there are other issues, like seeing scheduled patients when you're mentally fried. After finishing Nick's case and getting that little bit of sleep, I still had to battle through the office.

"If you really do go into surgery, you'll learn that the world doesn't stop when you've been operating all night. The government put in work restrictions for residents, but those don't apply when you're done training. You just have to suck it up.

"As soon as I showed my face in the office, I was confronted by some guy wearing a blue blazer and a regimental tie. He started grilling me about the 'unfortunate' events surrounding Nick's injury. I just told him that I'd make sure that none of the other surgeons would go near a saw and suggested to him that he get lost. He didn't strike me as the sincere, compassionate type. The probability that the man was tied to the group responsible for Nick's fingers didn't escape me. I wasn't in the best frame of mind for what turned out to be a crushing load of patients that day.

"Fortunately, I deal mostly with reasonable people who just want to get better. Sometimes the only thing a person wants to know is what the problem is. It's not always necessary to do something. Surgery is never a good idea when the patient isn't bothered that much in the first place. On the other hand, if they're like my patient Octavius Redford, and they blow off three fingers fishing in the bay with quarter sticks of dynamite, then you don't have a lot of choices.

"The people you really have to watch out for, though, are the never-ops. They are very cunning and will sneak up on you. Converting a never-op into a pre-op and post-op will rapidly become a why-did-I-ever-op. There are some folks you simply cannot make better. They suck you into their pathological world and you're screwed. The medical-legal system here in the States sometimes prevents doctors from telling patients the absolute truth, which would be along the lines of 'I tried something that didn't work. I have no idea what is wrong with you or how to get you better, and the overwhelming likelihood is that no one else knows, either. I don't have all the answers. Sometimes I don't have any. You'd better leave soon or I'll try something else that only doubles your pain. Remember—there isn't any problem that surgery can't make worse.'"

Tess rolled her eyes. "VJ, I appreciate the insight. I do. But you're ranting a little. Tell me more about Nick and what happened. It sounds like you two are pretty close."

VJ acknowledged the admonishment and continued. "Nick and I met eight years ago. We're really different, but I love the guy. Nick's father died when he was two. He was the youngest of six and never had much. I was a lot luckier. He's a genuinely compassionate guy, but you'd never think that when you first meet him. Nick's pretty irreverent. No one's faster with a one-liner. It's really sad—until two months ago, he was a great surgeon. Slick as grits in the OR.

"That afternoon, after the replant, I ultimately did get done in the office. All I wanted to do was leave, but I still had to visit Nick in his room. Fortunately, none of the ICU nurses had called to tell me that Nick's fingers were blue. God love leeches—those bloodsucking creatures really help venous outflow. Early in my training, I learned that even the best replants die if the veins don't do their job of getting rid of the blood."

Tess looked at VJ like he had just suggested that she eat a bowl of cockroaches. "No way. You put leeches on people's hands? That's disgusting."

He smiled. "Yes we do. Leeches can be key. The staff loves them, too. Look in the hand journal. There are advertisements for medicinal leeches. If there's even the slightest chance that the veins might clot, I use them. Think about what happens when the blood can come in, but it can't get out. It's a disaster in the making. Nick probably didn't even need them. We were happy with the vein repairs, but I didn't want to take any chances. Remember this for your boards, though. Leeches can cause a very rare type of infection, so it's important to keep a close eye out if they're being used, and give prophylactic antibiotics. The next time I do a replant, I'll show you how the little guys do their thing."

Tess definitively answered, "I'll take a pass on that."

"Wish granted. Have you been in an ICU yet?" he asked. Tess shook her head no. He explained, "The second you walk into any ICU you're accosted by a cacophony of sound—beeps, alarms, whistles, you name it. It goes on 24/7. The staff is immune to it, but those noises drive me crazy."

"As if you weren't there already?"

"Ha. Ha," he said. "The door to Nick's room was open. His nurse, Jan, was inside. 'Are our little leech friends doing their job?' I asked. 'Would Dracula be jealous?'

"She gave me the stink-eye. 'VJ, these things are repulsive. I can't believe you make me do this.'

"All the indicators suggested things were going well. Thank God! Since the digits looked OK, I pulled up a chair and suggested to Jan that it would be fine for her to take a break. The convincing part didn't take much effort. I closed the sliding door, pondering how to get to the obvious question. Replant patients need to stay calm. If they get anxious, their bodies send out lots of chemical badness that cause the vessels to constrict, the opposite of what we want to happen. The patients are usually kept on enough meds to smooth the rough spots.

"'Jan's giving you plenty of Dilaudid, I hope,' I said to Nick. 'Take as much of that as you need. What's a little drug addiction among friends? Seriously, Nick, neither of us wants to see your fingers die.' I didn't want to dope him up too much, but my biggest concern was that the inevitable massive depression might cause him to do something unwise. Jan and all the nurses were keeping an extra-close eye on him. The medical world is a harsh place, but we try to protect our own.

"'Don't worry, VJ, I'm being a good boy,' Nick said, giving me the answer I was looking for. 'Jan's awesome. I should hang out here more often. Give me a second to get some water,' he said as he lifted the Styrofoam cup to his parched lips. Then, very seriously, he said, 'I'm going to tell you what you don't want to hear.'

"Although I knew Nick was tied up with some bad actors, I couldn't wrap my brain around the fact that my friend could be heavily into criminal activity. This was not the person I thought he was. 'Before you tell me anything, Nick, you need to hear this. Some guy who said he was from administration stopped by to ask me about what he called your "unfortunate" accident. I didn't recognize him. I shooed the little prick away, but I thought you should be aware.'

"Nick frowned. 'I can't say I'm surprised. It's not like I expected the Cooperative to disappear after they cut my fingers off. This fucked-up deal with them started about two years ago. I fixed a wrist fracture on a demented patient who fell out of his hospital bed. He was on the ward getting treated for congestive heart failure, going nowhere in a hurry. The day after I did the surgery, I got this strange call from a person in administration named Bob Smith. He wanted to know if I could meet him to talk about the radius fracture man. The whole thing made no sense to me, but I figured this wrist fracture man was some VIP whose family the administration wanted to squeeze for donation dollars.

"'Coincidentally, the dude I met was someone I'd seen a few times at the gym, though I'd never talked to him. He didn't look like a Bob Smith, more like a Pacific Islander. I'd be shocked if that's his real name. He's twice as big as the asshole who chopped off my fingers. He asked me all about what I thought of things at the hospital, who I thought were leaders, who in the department might be having personal issues, if I had ideas about areas to improve. We got into my own personal life and the divorce—somehow he knew all about it. My financial problems came up. He actually was very friendly, which is why I let my guard down. Still, the whole time I was trying to figure out what he was really doing talking to me. He eventually cut to the chase.

"'He asked if I could do him "the smallest favor."

"'Confirming what I thought, the patient had run out of Medicare-allowed in-patient time for his other problems. The family, who were big MRMC donors, wanted him to stay. So the guy asked me if I would keep the patient in-house for a couple of extra days for "issues pertaining to his radius fracture," as he put it. I didn't think it would be a big deal, so I said yes.

"'About a month later I was ripping through the garbage on the computer I was supposed to electronically sign. You know, the stuff we never usually check over at all. For some reason, I noticed that the radius fracture patient's name had an extra op note attached to him. Apparently, he had gone back to the OR for a carpal tunnel release. I figured that somehow or another he'd developed symptoms in the nursing home and they'd gotten the plastics team to take care of it. The funny thing was that my name was listed as the surgeon. There was also an assist on the case. I called Medical Records to tell them to fix it. I started to go through some of my other notes a little more carefully. There were a few more procedures listed that I had no memory of doing. I called the EMR people and made some choice remarks that I thought for sure might come back to bite me.

"'Lo and behold, the next day I got a call from Bob Smith. He arranged for us to meet. When I saw him, I started to get belligerent about what was going on. Once I calmed down, he apologized for the "mistakes" and assured me the problem would be solved. He played the good cop and spent a lot more time asking my opinions on everything from medicine to the Patriots. Three weeks later, on payday, I got extra. There was a handwritten note thanking me for being so understanding. I figured, what the hell, it's their money, I'll take it. That's how they got me. Committing fraud happens to be a felony offense. I just didn't realize at the time that I was doing it for them. The month after, I got a bigger check.'

"'Two hundred seventy-two billion, at least. That's how much insurance companies and the government get bilked out of every year. I looked it up one night. Amazing. I'm not sure what the Cooperative's take is, but compared to that number, who's going to miss it? Did you ever wonder where I got all the cash for the Lambo?'"

Tess had a disgusted look on her face. "Don't judge too harshly until you've been there," VJ said. "Nick felt that way, too, before it all started.

"'It's funny how addictive money gets,' Nick said next. 'Things we just want quickly become things we need. Nice clothes, nice restaurants, great seats at the game, bottle service at the clubs. The lifestyle became too easy. I got in deeper. The problem, my friend, is extrication. I picked out this nice little practice in Brunswick, Maine. There's a solo guy there, Benjamin Saito, looking for a partner. I had everything set to make the jump.'"

Tess' facial expression changed suddenly. "That's weird. I'm going to Brunswick tomorrow for the wedding. I don't personally know the guy you just mentioned, but he operated on one of my college classmates. I remember hearing about him at a party. He made that big an impression on my friend. Apparently, of all things he's an expert archer, rock climber and a total crack-up. He takes his patients out to do this stuff if they want after he fixes them. People living in Brunswick are friendly like that."

VJ responded with his own odd look. "Well, I guess both of us have an unusual connection to Ben Saito then. I didn't know about the archery or rock climbing parts. Doesn't surprise me though. He is definitely funny. I'll fill you in on all that soon. As you might have guessed, soon is a relative term.

"Just after Nick disclosed his plan to move to Maine, he looked at me sheepishly. 'By the way, I was going to tell you about that slight transition.' He held up his mutilated hand. 'Then the Cooperative did this. I mentioned that I wanted to leave. It's not like I was going to tell anyone about what I'd been up to. The message came from high command that I was to stay, doing exactly what I'd been doing. Clearly they were not too happy when I told them I was going no matter what they said. Once I argued about it, they obviously thought I became too much of a risk.'

"'Now, here I sit, completely screwed. Thank God I paid my disability policy last week. Thirty-three hundred bucks a year for that little piece of paper used to seem like a lot. Not now. Of course, actually getting that money might be an issue.'

"Nick stopped speaking for a minute and just stared at his hand. 'This was only a warning. My guess is that they want me to be an example to the others. If I just disappeared like Gina and Cheryl did, it wouldn't have the same dramatic effect. The others wouldn't know if it was just another strange *coincidence*. The Cooperative will be sure to let the right people understand why what happened to me happened.'

"I interrupted him. 'How many *others*? I'm not really on board with the idea of doing more four-digit replants on doctor friends.'

"Nick shrugged. 'I can't promise that you won't, VJ. Probably there are at least a hundred, maybe two hundred.'

"'Jesus Christ,' I said. 'What planet have I been on?'

57

"Nick looked wistfully at his hand. 'There's so much going on every day that neither of us ever dreamed was happening. You just got a small glimpse. My problem is what's coming down the pike. I have a nasty feeling that the Cooperative might decide to take the obvious next step. There's no way to be certain, but I'm just a little paranoid. The suit that approached you in the office was definitely checking up on me. Can't you just see the headline? SURGEON, DEPRESSED FROM CAREER-ENDING HAND INJURY, TAKES OWN LIFE. It's easy to believe, isn't it? I need to vanish for a while. VJ, do you still have any connections in Sweden? I think I have to get the hell out of here. Boston doesn't look great to me right now.'

"I kept my eyes focused on Nick's fingers. They were swollen, but still pink. The pulse oximeter, the device that measures oxygen saturation in tissue, was showing the desired numbers. To think that a four-digit replant for a surgeon would be the least of his problems. After a few minutes, I said, 'Nick, let me see what I can do. I have an idea. It might take some work, but I think that a musculoskeletal radiology fellowship in Malmö, Sweden, might work out. The chief of radiology there, Nils Abrahamson, was in the army with me. I'll bet he can get you at least a one-year spot at the hospital. It's going to be quite a change. You might actually learn something useful.

"'Copenhagen's close by. Terrific city. Good food. Great people. Even better nightlife. Everyone is tall, though. Drives me crazy. I feel like the circus midget. There's also the socialism issue. It's wonderful until they run out of other people's money to spend. You'll get used to it. By the way, how do you feel about French bulldogs? Believe it or not, half the city population seems to have one.'

"Nick was starting to laugh. 'VJ, if you can get me there safely I don't care if they keep a bunch of murderers from San Quentin as pets. How realistic a shot do I have?'

"The events of the past twenty-four hours suddenly caught up with me. I was no longer capable of meaningful conversation. 'Nick, I've got to go home and close my eyes. It sounds like you've got a brief reprieve. If they'd wanted to kill you, they'd have already done it—I think. Give me some time. I'll make some calls. I can't do it now, though. You might end up in Pakistan.'

"Nick grasped my wrist with his good hand. 'VJ, thanks. I know how much this sucks. If I could undo the whole thing . . .'

"I let him off the hook. 'Don't worry. I'll think of a way for you to pay me back. Maybe get me a lifetime supply of the best Swedish herring.'

"Nick and I had spent countless hours working together. I felt like he was a second brother. I was profoundly disappointed by his choices. Now he was going to pay for those choices for the rest of his life. A sensible person would walk away. But I felt I had no alternative than to try to help him. Interesting how certain decisions change your life forever."

Tess signaled for a stop. "Nick's story is awful. But I can't for the life of me figure out where I fit into all of this. I assume—well, just hope, at this point—that you're getting to that sometime soon. Clearly I don't know Nick, but I feel sorry for him. He threw away everything for some money. I'm fortunate I never had the kind of financial issues he did. I definitely don't know anything about the Cooperative. Please tell me you're not a part of that group now."

"The good news is I'm not. Yes, it isn't your fault, but you're involved. I'm sorry. I mentioned earlier that some of the details of this story will seem extraneous. They're not. Believe me, the pieces will fit together. I'm sorry it isn't so obvious how they do yet—they will. If you can just indulge me . . ."

Tess grudgingly acquiesced. "So, what happened next?"

THE COOPERATIVE

"I went home and slept. Thankfully there were no phone calls. I was dead to the world for twelve hours. Nick's story was scary. I couldn't fathom my naïveté about my own surroundings. I didn't feel I had a choice about moving forward, whether I was psychologically prepared or not. I remained absolutely committed to helping Nick, but I knew there might be a price to pay. Not acting would've been worse. I wouldn't be able to live with myself. A trip to my homeland is never unwise. There are always people I want to see. It was going to be cold, though. A few winter months in Sweden, and Nick might change his mind and decide to take his chances in Boston.

"How to engineer the travel scheme was spinning through my mind. I fabricated a trip to the Windy City, wondering if I'd be followed or if anyone could find out I wasn't really in Chicago. That's how it went for the next few days while I plotted strategy and proceeded with my contacts. I suddenly felt like the eyes and ears of unknown people might be focused on me, so I just followed my routine. No more Cooperative flunkies appeared. Things at MRMC hummed along as they always did, oblivious to the surrounding evil.

"But I was paranoid everywhere I went. Even when I ran into colleagues I'd known for years, I was suspicious. While Nick knew there were many others like him on the Cooperative's payroll, he didn't know who they were. The Cooperative was good at running the show without letting the co-conspirators know one another's identities, at least among the underlings.

"About a week after Nick's surgery, one of my orthopaedic associates, Chuck Danguerin, stood next to me in the locker room putting on his scrubs. We were friendly, but not friends. I was zoned out, trying to determine the best way to approach my patient's fracture. Chuck said, 'That's rough about Nick. He's pretty much fucked. I don't understand what he was doing in the first place. He should've been more careful.'

"The comment got me angry. I yelled at him. I never do that to other doctors. 'Chuck, what's wrong with you? The guy just cut his fingers off. It's not like he *tried* to do it.'

"Chuck's face didn't show the compassion I expected, but suddenly he was contrite. 'VJ, back off. Hey, I'm sorry. I know Nick's your friend. We all like him. I just think he could have been smarter.'

"I calmed down. 'It's OK, Chuck. I'm not myself. I'll see you later.' With that I made my way to the front desk to see if there was any hope my humerus fracture case would actually go. The patient's surgery had been cancelled three times already in the past five days. Either the woman's blood count was too low, her chemistries were problematic, or she had too much fluid in her lungs. She had 'This isn't going to go well and I'm probably going to die' written all over her. The problem is that it's not right to just sit back and let someone suffer when there is something that can actually be done. It's a true ethical dilemma. What level of risk is reasonable to assume? We want to fix people, and it doesn't sit well with any of us if we can't."

Tess jumped in. "How do you make those choices? What if someone doesn't make it?"

VJ readjusted his knee for the umpteenth time. "There is no good answer to that question. Before all this happened, I had a man with forearm and hip fractures die in the PACU. The cases only took an hour skin-to-skin. For the record, that means start to finish. He must have had a massive pulmonary embolism. He had Alzheimer's and was a no-code, but I felt terrible. Yet if I hadn't done the case, he would have had awful pain, developed pneumonia, and died anyway. Things don't always work out. But being paralyzed when decisions have to be made doesn't help anyone. Try to rely on sound medical principles, and never be afraid to ask for another opinion from someone you respect.

"Ironically, my discussion with Chuck ended up being the least frustrating thing that happened in the course of getting that woman's humerus fixed. Once I made it to the scheduling desk, I saw someone I didn't recognize. That's never a good sign. I said, 'Hi, I need to check on my fracture case. Can you get the small fragment set, the Jackson table and the image?'

"The person sitting in front of me said, 'Doctor . . . now, what's your name?'

"'It's Erik Brio. What's your name?'

"She said, 'My name is Fiona. How do you spell Brio?'

"'Fiona, how long have you been working at the OR?' She told me she'd just started that day. I asked, 'Is there anyone here to help you out?'

"Innocently, she told me, 'No, they just told me to handle things.'

"'Have you ever worked in the medical field before?'

"'No, Dr. Brio, I just finished high school.'"

Tess tried to smother a giggle. "There but for the grace of God . . ."

VJ concurred, "Obviously, someone thought it was a good plan to put the least experienced person just where that person could wreak the most havoc. Beaten, I responded, 'My guess, then, is that you're not familiar with small fragment sets and Jackson tables.'

"She said, 'No, Doctor, I haven't seen those before. Should I order them from Supply?'

"I took a deep breath and tried to be nicer. 'Fiona, those are things that are kept in the OR. Don't worry about it. I'll try to help get everything together.'

"I ended up being jerked around all day. A different person at the main OR front desk told me, 'We might have time at five. But it could be six, though, or maybe seven.' 'We aren't sure about radiology support.' 'The staff needs another break even after finishing a break just two minutes ago.' 'The instruments have to go through DEFCON Five decontamination after being exposed to air for three nanoseconds.' 'Three people called in sick.' 'Space aliens from the planet Zatar have arrived, and they are demanding to bump your case to do experiments on your crew.' And so on.

"The woman ultimately did get into the room and was successfully put to sleep. When I removed the original splint she got in the ER, I made a startling discovery. 'Hey, check this out,' I said to my anesthesiologist friend, Lige Moultrie Debois. 'Her skin looks like twisted taffy. When she fell, her arm must've done a complete rotation like a propeller. I've never seen this.'

"Lige's profound shock was displayed by a slightly lifted left eyebrow.

"I said, 'It's my fault—I didn't take the splint off until now because I thought it'd hurt her too much. Plus, I figured we'd get her here quicker.' I performed a reverse twist, and a

65

definitive crunch ensued. Now the skin looked as it should.

"Lige groaned. 'That was ugly.'

"I felt extremely blessed that the arm was viable, but the sense of well-being was short-lived. While I was struggling to hold the fracture together with my forceps and fingers, I said to the scrub tech, 'Rob, small frag reduction clamps, please.'"

Tess frowned, not understanding. VJ explained, "Reduction clamps are what we use to temporarily hold fracture pieces together while we put in the permanent screws or plates.

"Rob told me the unfortunate truth. 'VJ, they're still in the autoclave. Erika Fleming used them for the open ulna fracture she just fixed. I have the large fragment clamps.'

"I asked the computer-crazed circulator nurse engrossed in some act of accomplishing nothing to grab another set. You see, charting takes precedence over everything else. I'm really not kidding or exaggerating. It's the new paradigm. I couldn't rouse his attention. If the public had any idea that our government regulations force hospital nurses to minister to computers rather than patients, something might actually change. Let's say I'm not optimistic. That day I gave in and used the large fragment reduction clamps.

"Wrong choice. Not so calmly, I watched as the bone splintered into barrel staves. I know this will surprise you, but many vulgarities followed. 'VJ, are you OK?' Lige queried over his *Wall Street Journal*.

"I was totally exasperated and advised him, 'Lige, in about two seconds I'm going to destroy every bloody computer in this fucking hospital! Is that a problem?'

"Lige is a good ol' boy from Georgia. Smart as a whip. He knows when it's time to talk and when it's time to stay quiet. He gave me sage advice: 'Well, VJ, as appealing a plan as that is, why don't we get through this operation first?'

"I had to laugh. Deciding to forgo mayhem, I addressed the now less-easy fracture. When that challenge was over and only the layers of tissue were left to close, I felt liberated to talk freely. 'Lige, I heard the Pope may be thinking about resigning. I've decided to throw my hat in the ring. What do you think?'

"Lige's face fell into a grin. 'Well, VJ, I kind of like the idea of a Swedish-Jewish Pope. It's a perfect fit. Does that mean you won't be gracing us with your presence after your assured victory?'

"I answered, 'No, you're going to have to keep putting up with me. I figured I could sort of do a traveling Pope thing.'

"Just as I was about to describe my ideas for Popettes, Chuck Danguerin wandered into the room. My sense of temporary relaxation instantly evaporated. It seemed I was seeing him everywhere. The Cooperative popped into my mind. He said he was waiting for his case to start, so he decided to visit. Surgeons do that, but I wondered if he was sent to test me—see if I might be a risk. Chuck glanced at the destroyed humerus. 'Hey, VJ, how's it going? How'd ya fix it?'

"I responded, 'Well, Chuck, that's not such a simple answer. Would that be before or after I blew the thing apart? Hopefully it's stable now. Her bone is sand. The image shots are over there by the computer if you want to take a look.'

"Chuck looked at the pictures. 'VJ, what are you bitching about? These look great. By the way, do you know how lucky you are to even get this image to function? My case got delayed thirty-five minutes today because the circulator entered "foot" instead of "tibia" into the system. The new electronic medical record shut down and wouldn't let us take pictures. The guy in X-ray said he was busy and couldn't come over. It's ridiculous! At this point, I'd rather have someone inject me with the Ebola virus than deal with this bullshit EMR.'

"Suddenly, I felt like an angel, not Darth Vader, had sent Chuck in. 'You're preaching to the choir.' This moment of pleasure lasted only until I heard what Chuck said next.

"'Well, there's one thing it's good for— billing. Finally, we're getting back some of what we deserve. You just press a button and presto, we get paid. The people in Accounting are eating it up.' With that, he left to do his scope. I pondered the near-certainty that the reach of the Cooperative was limitless, and made yet another mental note to avoid Danguerin at all costs.

"Finally, the last stitch was buried. As I put on the dressing, Lige skillfully extubated the woman and said, 'Let's get this patient to the PACU before something truly unfortunate happens.'

"We were all happy with that plan, but I couldn't resist one last jab. 'Who changed the name of the recovery room to post-anesthesia care unit? PACU is a stupid name. It doesn't mean anything to most people.'

"Lige, along with everyone else, disregarded me. They'd had enough for one day."

"Will wonders never cease?" Tess remarked, but she had been listening carefully.

She scooted her chair closer and scanned the silent anatomy lab. "VJ, it sounds like you're conflicted even in the best of times. I'll give you the ordeal with Nick. Still . . . I thought I had anxieties. Now I'm just saying, if an experienced surgeon is still having these problems, what will it be like for me? Are you sure you chose the right profession? I mean, you must have some good reason for wanting to do what you do."

"You got a minute?" VJ answered.

Tess rolled her eyes. "Like I'm going anywhere now."

"Tess, suffice it to say that it's still the best thing for me to do with myself. It works, on some strange cosmic level. Stories like the one I just told you about the lady with the humerus happen not infrequently. About half the time I'm completely frustrated, and I want to run as far and as fast as I can. But the other half of the time, when things click . . . there's just nothing else like it in the world."

She frowned. "I know I'm about to open up another can of worms with this question, but how do you deal with call? I mean, you have to do it a lot."

VJ laughed. "Call is no different for me today than when I started as an intern. I hate it while I'm doing it and am elated when it's over. Despite these inner frustrations, I believe if I stop taking call I'll have to give up my man card. Surgical training demands buy-in to the max. It's an interesting love/hate relationship with what I do and who I am. Anxiety defines me too. So I'm probably not the right person to be an orthopod. When I'm getting bombarded, I get demoralized. It feels like people are out in the world intentionally doing absurd things to hurt themselves as a way to specifically punish me. 'You say you were backing up the car and didn't realize that your wife was standing there, so you fractured both of her femurs?' 'That thirty-foot ladder looked awfully inviting after you had a six-pack, so you just had to climb it? The fall had to be great fun until the part where everything broke.'

"I have to stop and remind myself that I chose this path. I struggle with the desire and responsibility to fix the people who need to be fixed and the problem of sometimes being a total slug and just wanting to tell everyone to stop bothering me.

"The hard part is remembering that for most patients, particularly the ones I see in the ER, this is the first time they're hearing about a medical problem. Whatever I've had to deal with before that moment is irrelevant. I can't tell you how many times I've had to stop and remember something so obvious. I get short with people, and they don't deserve it. Probably the most important thing my fellowship director taught me was to always leave someone with something genuinely positive, even in the worst circumstances."

Tess got up and wandered to a nearby dissection table. She picked up a scalpel and twirled it in her hand. "VJ, I appreciate everything you're telling me. I know the difference between the ideal of what I'm going to do and the reality of what I'm going to do. I like the concept of having one of these in my hand. I guess it's the way some people feel about holding a gun. I've been to the range, and while .45s are quite a rush, I can take shooting or leave it. I'm totally on board with medicine, though. I know that this training is going to be a battle and that it doesn't ever stop. But I'm still really excited about doing it."

VJ smiled. "Tess, you're going to be a great doctor. I didn't realize you can also handle a gun. I'm impressed."

She flashed her own sly smile and replied with a slight edge in her voice, "VJ, there are a *lot* of things you don't know about me. I'm not the Goody-Two-shoes you might think I am."

VJ acknowledged her comments. "Tess, all of us have skeletons in our closets. Look, I recognize that a lot of what I'm telling you sounds pretty cynical. Despite that, when you have a patient sincerely tell you that you've helped them, it's the best. I just got an e-mail from an epidemiologist I did a tibial plateau fracture on in Sierra Lakes a year ago. I work there part-time, which I'll tell you more about. Anyway, a few weeks ago this woman, Nancy Siegel, finished a half-marathon in under two hours. I'm so proud of her. Those kinds of stories are what make medicine great. It sounds corny, but it's true."

Tess put the knife down carefully and returned to her chair. "I appreciate your confidence. Now, all I have to do is convince my professors that I've got the right stuff."

VJ regarded the intense young person sitting across from him. "Trust me. You'll have no problem doing that."

TESS' JOURNEY

VJ couldn't help asking: "So what did make you decide to go into medicine?"

"That's an interesting question," Tess replied. "Somehow, I always thought I might be a doctor—almost like I was programmed to do it. A few things happened that pushed me. When we were undergrads, Jessica and I spent a semester abroad together in Copenhagen. We went on one of those hut-to-hut hiking trips in Norway and went to the place where they filmed part of the second *Star Wars* movie, Hardangerjøkulen glacier by Finse. In the movie, they called it the ice planet Hoth. It was totally cool to be there. You probably know how beautiful the area is— streams, falls, mountains."

"It's incredible." VJ nodded. "I've been there, too."

Tess continued, "About a mile before we got to the hut, a storm rolled in. The path was a river in nothing flat. Jessica slipped on some rocks and fell down hard. Her wrist was jacked up. I had taken an EMT class during freshman year, so I decided to grab her forearm and snap it back in place. I'll tell you something weird: I liked the sound the bone made when it went back in. Jessica was stunned. 'Did you just do that?' was all she could say. The whole deal was automatic. I felt detached in an odd way. Then all of a sudden, I didn't. Has that ever happened to you?"

"Absolutely." VJ nodded. "It's just the beginning. You'll learn to do so many things you have to do without thinking about it, it'll become second nature." I thought about that for a moment, then added, "The problem comes when you accidently help someone die. You'll forget an order, make the wrong decision, misinterpret lab data. It happens to everyone in medicine. That'll be the test. The challenge is to maintain balance. Most of the time, it's incredibly hard."

A cold breeze from the still partially open window blew through the room. Tess shivered and rubbed her forearms, inadvertently catching her bracelet. "Perfect, something else for me to worry about." She wrinkled her nose and said, "Phew. I thought the fresh air would help. This lab still reeks."

"Truer words were never spoken," VJ replied. "But let's get back to your story, Tess. What happened next?"

Choosing to ignore the smell, Tess went on, "We certainly weren't going anywhere that night. It was autumn and way too dark and slippery. The cabin was clean and stocked with food and wood. I started a fire and made tea. Fortunately, I had aspirin in my backpack. That's great stuff. I always keep a bottle on me.

Jessica wasn't comfortable, but she didn't suffer. I felt guilty because it was me who had pushed the trip. Jessica would have none of it. All she could say was how thankful she was that I did what I did.

"The next morning was awful. Hard, cold, stinging rain that wouldn't let up for a second. I was soaked and freezing. Those rivers became torrents. Honestly, I thought both of us might die from either a fall or hypothermia. Finally, we made it back to a town and the nearest hospital. I met this really tall, blond orthopaedic resident, Lasse Tangen. After he put on the cast, and despite the fact that he looked beat, Lasse sat down and took time with me. I remember clearly what he said; it was really sweet and sincere.

"'Tess, you should skip college and go directly into ortho training. You did a better job than half the first-years. Are you going to be a doctor?'

"I immediately told him yes. It was the first time I ever heard those words come out of my mouth." VJ raised an eyebrow at her, and Tess blushed. "I'm not going to lie—Lasse was pretty great, too. And yes, we still e-mail. Who knows? There may be a Norwegian in my future. What would you think of that?"

VJ laughed. "Are you kidding, those oil-rich slackers are employing half of Sweden now. They have more money than they know what to do with. Did everything work out with Jessica?"

"She did fantastic! The whole experience turned me on. I'd been toying with the pre-med idea. When I was in high school, I found a book on a sale rack called *The Making of a Surgeon*. It was seriously dated, but it made being a doctor seem special. I read it in a day. The author talked over and over about hard work. I've never been afraid of that. My issue was whether I had the right stuff." She hesitated. "I'm still not convinced. For a while I thought—*too long, too hard, too much to give up, too expensive*. But there was this voice inside that said, 'You can do this.' Lasse gave me the push I needed. Helping Jessica made me feel good. That worked for me. Organic chemistry wasn't exactly a picnic, but I made it through all the other prerequisites well enough to be talking to you right now."

"Tess," VJ said, "I really like the Hamsa bracelet you've been playing with this whole time. Are those Eilat stones?"

Now self-conscious, Tess took her hand away from the jewelry. "You busted me. I fiddle with it all the time. My type A personality, I guess. You're right about the stones. My mom gave the bracelet to me after she gave a lecture in Israel." She held the bracelet up. "It's supposed to watch over me, and in a way, it does. Every time I look at it, I think about her."

He asked, "What was your mom like?"

"Intelligent and direct. Everyone always knew where they stood with her. You're a basketball fan, but she was a baseball *fanatic*. We have those family box seats at Fenway that Max is going to get. My grandfather passed them down. I like going, and it's cool to be able to treat people. Most of the time, though, my parents brought friends or academic visitors. Only in Boston can two physicists discuss the intricacies of chaos theory and simultaneously analyze the statistical probabilities of scoring after a one-out sacrifice bunt with the seven-hitter coming to bat—both conversations going on with equal passion. That's one of the things I loved most about my mom—her passion. I miss that. Sometimes it got out of hand. Like when she'd yell at our dad for spoiling me or Max.

"Normally, my dad was a pretty quiet guy. When Mom started in on him, he'd patiently wait out the storm. Then he'd lay out a perfectly logical argument about why he was right. One of my first memories is making a snowman with him in the front yard. I was about three. We worked on the face until it was exactly the way I wanted it. He was so patient and precise. That's why Dad was such a successful law professor—orderly thinking. I always envied that, because it's so hard for me to do."

Tess' eyes flashed suddenly, and with *Exorcist*-worthy rage, she said, "The guy who killed them was a piece-of-shit, dirtbag, motherfucker. He hit them the day after he got out of jail early for good behavior. What an irony—good behavior my ass. He died in the accident too, but whenever I think of him, I want him to die again."

Neither of them said anything for a minute. Finally, VJ offered what solace he could. "Tess, there's no explanation for what happened to your parents. I do know they would be really proud of who you are and what you're doing. It's hard to imagine, but it will get a little easier over time."

Tess looked at him and was visibly more calm. "I know that's true. It's just the getting there that's been hard. I'm ready to listen again. What else have you got?"

"You sure?"

She put her hand reassuringly on his good leg. "Absolutely."

He resumed his tale. "Here's what happened. A few days after that adventure with the humerus, I woke up and saw that my urine looked pink. I knew that meant blood. I immediately convinced myself of the worst—that I had the big C. Remember the penchant for catastrophic thinking I mentioned. Well this timing was particularly bad. I couldn't believe I had to worry about my plumbing while I was trying to smuggle Nick out of the country. I was also doing my best to ignore the reality that there were people out there who might not wish me the best if they even vaguely suspected I knew what I knew. It was very surreal.

"Milo Marconi, my urologist and supposed friend, put his finger where no man's finger belongs. I was glad to hear that I didn't have any lumps. Just after he finished, he said, 'I went to see Nick in the ICU. He seems to be doing OK. He told me you did a good job and only messed up two of the digits. Sort of ironic that a hand surgeon gets his fingers cut off. I hope whatever he was making in his wood shop was worth it. He just threw away his whole career. By the way, VJ, you're not off the hook yet. You have to come back tomorrow for the real fun.'

"This time I didn't get mad—just paranoid. Chuck, now Milo. It wasn't what they said, but how they said it. That conversation was on my mind when I return the next day for the cystoscopy. Milo strolled in. Before I had a chance to say a word he started. Tube up the urethra to look at the bladder. I don't recommend it. Finally, I said, 'Milo, don't take your frustration with your ex out on me! What the hell are you doing with that instrument?'

"Milo carried on, ignoring me entirely while he did his thing. When he finished, he lectured me: 'VJ, everything looked fine. I'm not quite sure what happened. Probably you got too dehydrated in the OR. I want to check your urine, though, in a couple of months. Tell Brandie to set you up an appointment now. I don't want you to blow this off.'

"I was relieved. My neurotic worries were addressed for the moment. I'd come up with some new ones to replace them soon. I put on my clothes, washed my hands, and shook Milo's hand. 'Thanks, man, I really appreciate it. Next time should I just leave a tip on the counter?'

"He laughed. 'VJ, get out of here. I'll see you Thursday night at the board meeting.'

"Before I left, I decided to probe a little bit. I sort of jokingly said, 'Hey, Milo, how do you like the new EMR? It's driving me nuts.'

"Milo said, 'I hate it. It takes me forever to do anything. At least it's making the billing easier. You wait. They'll probably charge you triple for what I just did.'

"Essentially the same words about billing, a second time. I was spooked. I needed to get out of the hospital as soon as I could. I was thinking about the movie where people were replaced by aliens. I had no idea who I could trust and who I couldn't. I needed to get some reassurance and love quickly, so I went straight back to my townhouse.

"On the way home, though, I looked around several times to see if anyone was following me. I was particularly on the lookout for a big guy with a meat cleaver. Unfortunately, this was just the beginning of feeling threatened. It's truly horrible. Fortunately, the second I walked through the door that night, Vikka greeted me with kisses. She's totally gorgeous—

80

all forty-five pounds of her. Vikka's my tricolored Aussie shepherd. I got Vikka from a breeder my brother knows. It's not politically correct. An eco-friendly, low-carbon-footprint rescue dog would have warmed the hearts of all the tree-huggers I hang out with. That didn't work for me. I wasn't up for a used one. But don't worry, Tess, I donate regularly to the Humane Society."

Tess harrumphed. "VJ, are you intentionally trying to piss me off? Honestly—I grew up with a rescue Corgi. Grace was as perfect a dog as you could have. Don't give me this trash talk about used dogs. Your leash is getting shorter."

VJ absorbed the reprimand. "My apologies. This is who I am. People don't always care for me, but they all love Vikka. They flock to her. Everyone says the same thing. 'Oh! She's *so* pretty! Can I pet her? She's *so* soft. She smells like blueberries.' Vikka's a stomach on legs. She'll look straight at someone and cock her head just slightly. At that point it's over for whoever's petting her. Vikka gets a treat. In fact, I need to have a long talk with her about that. If I allow her to get fat, I'll have no one to blame but me.

"Vikka's a terrific companion who always seems to know when I need TLC. I feel really guilty when I'm gone. That happens a lot. Fortunately, my neighbor has two kids who live to help with Vikka. They'd do it for free if I needed them to. But I worked out a deal that I pay them big bucks as long as they put half in the bank. Definitely win-win.

"Just before the whole fiasco with Nick started I'd been in Chicago giving a talk and working on the self-assessment test we 'hand weenies' take every year.

"Have you been to the Art Institute of Chicago? Great place. Those still-life pictures of fruit are pure crap, but so much of the rest is wonderful. I saw a Renoir painting of an upscale courtesan at the end of her workday. He captured her world completely. That's why I detest Picasso. I don't care what I read, or what anyone tells me. I'm convinced there's an art historian conspiracy. They can make up whatever they need to. Enough people will buy in because they're afraid to admit that what they are looking at makes no sense whatsoever. Tess, you're staring at me with those disapproving eyes."

Tess responded, "First of all, yet again you are getting way off track. But I happen to like Picasso. Just because your brain isn't developed enough to comprehend subtlety doesn't mean it's not possible for others."

VJ held up his hands in surrender. "I guess that means I shouldn't tell you what I think of most modern art. Not related, but for the sake of completeness, a cat also occupies my townhouse. It was never my cat. My niece,

Arielle, left her with me, and I was stuck. I didn't care for the name Brinkley, so I called the cat Cat. Cat is a calico, which makes her perfectly color-coordinated with Vikka. Cat lives in a small space upstairs and leaves Vikka and me alone. It works for the three of us. My ex-girlfriend never really understood the relationship. Then again, I really don't think she got me at all. She told me to make myself more emotionally available, communicate better, and make people, rather than sports, sex, and surgery, my priority. Doing those things even in the short run is a challenge. It's like giving up chocolate chip cookies and M&M's to lose weight. There's a certain appeal to doing it, but who really wants to?"

Tess jumped in, shaking her bracelet. "I hear that kind of feedback from people, too. It drives me crazy. I think my sarcasm and cursing are misleading. It's not that I'm heartless, it's that most people are too obtuse to understand my brand of humor."

He laughed. "Tell me about it. You now have a virtually comprehensive picture of my home life. Well, not one hundred percent. I have a black thumb with plants. Never ask me to take care of your plants. I can kill them by just being in the same room with them."

Tess regarded him now with kinder eyes. "All right, VJ, we've now established that you like animals but can't relate to women. You also seem to have an uncanny knack for making a short story long and losing focus. I'll humor you. Go on."

VJ proceeded as instructed. "That morning Vikka needed a walk, and I needed fresh air. I set off for the Charles, trying unsuccessfully to put the Cooperative out of my brain.

"I tried to avoid getting hit by the various runners and cyclists by staying close to the water. Just as I passed the Esplanade, Vikka ran ahead, ripping the leash out of my hand. She saw Kolya. Do you know him?"

Tess shook her head no.

"He's Bianka's Aussie merle—two different-colored eyes and a crazy coat. That dog can find trouble anywhere. If I don't watch every second, Vikka will get into whatever mess Kolya starts. Once the dogs met, Bianka popped up smiling from behind a tree. I gave her a hug. 'What a nice surprise. Of course, now I have no chance to meet the person I'm destined to share my life with.'

"She went on, unfazed. 'Tough, you'll have to do that some other time. I want some company.'"

Tess jumped up. "So that's when you two cooked up this plan?"

He shook his head no and told Tess the truth. "At that moment, I didn't have the slightest idea you existed."

"You're holding back," Tess snapped. "Bianka wouldn't have sent me here otherwise."

84

"Trust is a wonderful thing," he responded. "Bianka trusts me completely because I'm her friend. Both of us thought it was a good idea for me to speak to you privately. She knows some important information, but not the part about the Cooperative, and definitely not the part about me being still above ground. It was critical to keep her in the dark about those facts. That's why you had to tell her I didn't show up."

Tess asked, "OK, what's your connection to Bianka? I'm out of here if you tell me you're having an affair with her. I think her husband would be even more upset."

VJ reassured her. "Fortunately, you and Anthony have nothing to worry about. We really are just very close friends. I can tell her anything, and I do. As you know, she's a pretty special person. Before I moved to Charles River Landing, we lived almost next door in Beacon Hill. I'm pretty sure I even met your parents once at a get-together she had. She told me how much respect she had for them personally and professionally. She said that her brother and your mom were colleagues at MIT and that's how all of you got to know each other. The academic world here is so interconnected, it's almost scary."

Tess nodded. "My parents thought a lot of her, too. That's for sure. She recruited me for one of her studies and then got me to get some of my classmates. Very crafty, that one. Does she get you to do stuff for her, too?"

"Funny you should bring that up," he replied. "Indeed she has. The two dogs got to be buddies in obedience class. When she needs help with Kolya, who do you think she calls first? Moi, of course. Aussies go nuts if they're cooped up all day. My breeder forced me to sign an oath in blood that Vikka wouldn't be left alone in the house for more than five hours. Honestly, it's the main reason I moved next to the hospital. Beside the neighbor kids, I have a list of people on the exercise and entertain Vikka payroll. Bianka and I run into each other on walks all the time.

"That day we wandered to the edge of the riverbank. The sunlight was dancing over those small waves the boats make. Despite the cold, people were still sailing. Usually strolls like this turn into a therapy session for both of us. This was one of the few occasions I didn't feel at ease telling Bianka what I was thinking about.

"She called me on it. 'How are things, VJ? You seem totally distracted. I didn't even catch you staring at the gorgeous brunette who just ran by.'

"'You're kidding me,' I said. 'I'm really slipping. Life's been a bit strange for the past few weeks. What's up with you?'

"Bianka protested. 'You can't make a statement like that and then just ask me how I am.'

"'Last night I had to go to a hospital fund-raiser,' I answered, trying to divert the conversation. 'Oh my, what an experience. Speaker after speaker making grand pronouncements about how wonderful MRMC is. I'd like to see them spend one week in the trenches. I've been thinking about what they want us to do to get people to donate. It might be nice if some of the money would go toward getting more efficient, responsible staff in the hospital. We're overwhelmed with professional time-wasters who think that lengthy, worthless meetings are the solution to all problems. No accountability whatsoever.'

"Bianka nodded and shrugged her shoulders as if to say, *What else is new?* I plowed ahead. 'But my biggest problem right now is that Nick is out and my call doubled. I'm not sleeping because people keep waking me up. Even when I'm asleep, I'm stressed. Last night I had a dream that I was doing a replant, but the case was being done in a restaurant. The server kept interrupting surgery to refill my water glass. Talk about messed up. I can't concentrate because I'm not sleeping. I'm grumpy, so people keep getting mad at me. As a sleepy, unfocused, grouchy single person, I'm relatively worthless.'

"Bianka grabbed my hand. 'You need some serious R&R. I hope you're planning to come to our party tonight.' I had forgotten all about it. 'You'll know some people, like Chuck Danguerin.

He hangs out with Anthony. You can talk shop if you fail in the mingling department. You'll have fun.'

"Chuck's name got my attention, but I thought about my nonexistent social calendar. Despite what I told you about trying to avoid him at all costs, I figured I could still probably have fun. I committed to a yes."

Tess frowned. "What's the deal with this Danguerin guy? Did his connection to Anthony raise any red flags?"

"Tess, don't rush to conclusions. Even now, the only thing I can pin on Danguerin is that he made one or two possibly wrong comments. Today, I'd be suspicious of my mother if she was alive. Plus, Anthony's a really good guy, and he has nothing to do with the hospital. Look, I'm tight with Nick, and I didn't have the slightest idea what *he* was into. I'll tell you something that you probably don't know. Maybe that will make you feel better.

"Bianka met Anthony in Vegas when she was at a meeting. She noticed him not just because he's attractive, but because he happened to be leading a group of first graders off a yellow school bus into the casino. No one had ever seen anything like that before. Bianka told me she had to find out who this guy was. She tracked down the casino manager and grabbed a business card of Anthony's. He was a known entity in the casino as a part-time food reviewer. He'd started a program called First Grade Food Critics when he was part of Teach for America. The kids he brought from his school were about to have the coolest experience of their lives. Bianka said she fell in love with him the minute she saw him with the children. A year later they got married. Bianka was entrenched here, so he made the jump to Boston with her. Pretty cool story, right?"

Tess looked skeptical. "You make it sound as if they're living happily ever after. Are they?"

VJ regarded Tess carefully. He fished back. "Why do you ask? Is there something you know?"

"Not specifically. My parents made comments from time to time. Money has been a problem. I did hear that more than once. Teachers don't make that much, and Anthony seems to like nice things."

VJ sat back in the chair and contemplated the idea. "The place they have on the Cape has been a money sink—roof, deck, siding, windows. Bianka bitches to me about it all the time. Anthony loves to spend time there, and she doesn't. It's an ongoing problem. I do know how annoying it can be to have the constant outflow of dollars to fix things in a house, like the place I own now in Sierra Lakes. It's the death of a thousand cuts. Bianka also mentioned that Anthony doesn't like her doing her Sunday salsa dance class. He's away with the triathlon thing a lot, so I understand why he's frustrated. That said, she still seems happy—at least that's what she tells me. Look, Tess, no marriage is perfect. I've been there. They all require work. Take it from someone who has minimal quality experience in the sustained relationship arena."

Tess asked, "Before Anthony, was there ever anything more between you two?"

VJ answered honestly, "No. Sometimes when we're together walking the dogs, I wonder what might've been if we had met at a different time in our lives. *C'est la vie.* Our friendship just works. There are few people on the planet as special. I'll tell you something interesting about Bianka's family. I realize it's a breach of confidentiality, but I know she won't mind— particularly after tonight. Her mother is a big-time Marijuana grower. Apparently when Bianka was a teenager, everyone used to come to their place to light up. On top of that, her mother makes edibles. She tried to come down here one time to sell to all of Bianka's friends—sort of like a Tupperware party. Bianka threw an absolute fit. If you ever want to tweak her a little bit, just ask her if her mom can score you some hash brownies."

By now Tess had almost completely let down her guard. "VJ, she's still my professor. Remember, my goal is to pass anatomy. But, hearing what you told me, I love her even more."

SWEDEN

"Bianka's dinner party turned out to be a wild one. Everyone cut loose—men and women. All that athletic training made for some extraordinary bodies on both sides. People dancing in the rafters half-naked. Anthony did a turn pole dancing. One of the women there who didn't know him thought he was a hired male stripper. She tried to pick him up; I practically fell down laughing. Most of the evening I was on the dance floor with anyone I could find. Chuck Danguerin was not one of those people. He said something to me about keeping my nose clean. I chose to steer clear of him for the rest of the night. Vodka kept mysteriously finding its way into my glass. Swedish pride, you know.

"Yet again, lack of sleep caught up to me. When I woke up I found myself at home. That was good. What was bad was that I felt like my brain and body were two separate entities. From the moment I started drinking, I knew better. Except I didn't know better. Interestingly, I was lying next to a woman who looked vaguely familiar, like a person you've seen at the coffee shop a time or two. Slowly, recognition of the time-space continuum returned. The mystery woman smiled, gave me a kiss, and said, 'Hey, you. That was really nice.' The words, though, sounded pretty hollow, like it was something she felt obligated to say. The other problem was that I was having an incredibly hard time remembering the experience and her name."

Tess shuddered. "I'm thinking I need a shower. VJ, why are you telling me about this? It's not an endearing story. Was the woman a secret agent or something? Do I know her? Is she coming here tonight, too?"

VJ came clean. "The answer to the first question is I'm not sure. Fortunately, I can't imagine you know her, and there is no chance she's coming to this party. Hear me out." Tess started to count down from ten. He spoke more quickly. "God intervened when she announced, 'I have to get up and make a little tinkle.' The actual words made me cringe, but it created an opportunity. While she was in the bathroom I had the chance to sneak a quick look in her gold sequined purse. Her driver's license said Brittany Jane Morgan. I was hoping she went by Brittany rather than Jane—that would be awkward if I guessed wrong. Something else caught my attention. It looked like an MRMC administration card. Before I had a chance to look more closely, I heard her returning from her urologic mission.

"With a wide smile, she said, 'I'm starved. Sex always does that to me. Do you like to cook? I'd offer, but unfortunately I suck at it.'

"Somehow that fact didn't surprise me. I wasn't getting a lot of the Susie Homemaker vibe. I was torn. I desperately wanted her to leave, but I also wanted to see if I could find out if her being in my townhouse was more than a coincidence. While I broke out one of those Village Mill goat cheese–and–spinach quiches I keep stashed in the freezer, I thought about the optimal way to probe.

"I asked Brittany how she knew Bianka and Anthony. Turns out she only knew *of* them. Danguerin brought her to the party. They were just 'friends.' Now I was really wondering if she was a Cooperative plant. Had I blabbed something to her about Nick? I couldn't imagine, but I didn't know for sure. I literally had no memory of any conversation with Brittany Morgan. I fished. I asked her about her work. Her eyes gave her away when she glanced immediately at her phone and told me she had to 'skedaddle.' I winced, and before I knew it, she was out the door. Nothing concrete, but nothing good. I wasn't happy."

Tess shuffled her feet as if about to get up. "VJ, I was just kidding about the spy part. Either she used you, you used her, or both of you used each other. No matter what, it's not a pretty tale. Seems like you could have made a better choice. I'm also concerned about your boy Danguerin. Have you talked to him since that night?"

"Yes, I've seen Danguerin. So far, the only thing he's drawn on me is a scalpel. In fact, he's the reason my knee is so sore right now. Ironically, the scope he did for me is probably the last thing on his mind. And no, that night wasn't my finest hour. I was stressed out of my mind. Can I beg for your forgiveness?"

Tess smiled. "Granted. OK, you misogynist pig, I'm giving you another pass. But your credit line is running low."

VJ explained his next set of choices. "With this new uncertainty about what the Cooperative might suspect about me, I pushed the calendar up on Nick's departure to immediate. He'd tasked me with the need to escape, and that was what was going to happen. I'd been working on the travel details to Sweden in conjunction with setting up Nick in Malmö. My job was to get him to Nils and give exactly no one the slightest idea about what we'd done. Nils was on board. He'd cleared the way for Nick to start training as a musculoskeletal radiologist.

"I informed Terri, my assistant, that I needed to go back to Chicago for surprise meetings about the Touching Hands overseas volunteer project. That's actually Sohardi Kozart's baby, but she didn't need to know the truth. I also suggested that there was a woman I needed to see. After throwing a complete fit about having to reschedule patients and surgeries, she relented, gave me a wink, and reassurance that she wouldn't bug me with the usual endless texts and e-mails. Terri wants me settled down.

"Thirty-six hours after my unfortunate encounter with Brittany Jane Morgan, Nick and I were headed out. As directed, he exited from the side door of the hospital and crossed the street to Charles River Landing. As soon as I spotted him, I said, 'Hey, buddy, how ya doing? A car should be waiting for us over by Government Center.'

"'Let's move,' he said, glancing around. 'Sweden calls.' We walked double-time through the sprawling building complex. If you're out late at night, all alone, it's spooky."

"It's worse when a cadaver starts to talk to you," Tess countered.

VJ grinned. "Point made. I'm actually hoping the next time we do this we'll be in a nicer place.

"While we walked, the wind was relentless. We almost got blown over. Nick seemed a bit out of it at first, which wasn't surprising, given the events. Finally, he clicked in. 'VJ, this no-luggage thing is awesome. I hate dragging bags to the airport. Very liberating. Maybe I'll do it more often.'

"I laughed. 'Let's hold off right now on "more often." It's better not to take any bags for a couple of reasons. First of all, they'd just lose them in Heathrow. The last two times I went through there, I didn't see my stuff for days. I ended up giving a talk in a long-sleeve black Asics running shirt I bought last minute. More importantly, I figured if someone is keeping an eye on us, then it's less likely they'll figure we're blowing outta here. Who goes to the airport without luggage?'"

Tess raised her hand, student-style. "Um, would that be people who are sneaking out of town?"

VJ disregarded the remark. "'Also,' I pointed out to Nick, 'we're taking nine separate legs, with a couple of days in between in Norway and again in Stockholm. JetBlue to JFK, BA to Heathrow, Air Berlin to Berlin, Norwegian Air to Bergen, train to Oslo, Finnair to Helsinki, SAS to Stockholm, SAS to Copenhagen, hired car to Malmö.' The multiple flights were an added hedge in case my encounter with the 'tinkle' woman had tipped off the Cooperative. I hadn't mentioned that detail to Nick. Nothing useful would be accomplished by me making him more paranoid and knowing what an idiot I was. His eyes already suggested he was about to jump out of his skin.

"'Thank God. I love flying,' Nick said with more than a tinge of sarcasm.

"To needle Nick a little and try to lighten the moment, I said, 'I hope you like fish. Particularly herring. They haven't really figured out the recipe for other things yet.'

"Nick looked disgusted. 'Herring? That stuff gives me the heebie-jeebies. It's just gross.'

"I laughed. 'Don't worry, you'll love it! We'll get you some taco-flavored sauce and you're going to scarf it down like nobody's business. Put on your big-boy pants. There isn't a choice. Parts of this scenery change won't be so bad. Winter isn't that much worse than in Boston. It does get dark pretty early. That Irish-Scottish background of yours should help you hold your own in the drinking department.'

"Nick smiled. 'I'm more than happy to show your Swedish friends a thing or two about real alcohol ingestion. By the way, you sound like a CIA agent.'

"'Dude, it's in the genes,' I replied. 'You have no idea what my mom had to do just to make it through medical school. Want to know the best part? I booked this whole trip through a friend in the hospital accounting department. A safe one. I'm going to get billed, but it won't happen for a while, and he worked it out so it'll just get deducted from my salary. Even if one of those goons accesses our credit cards, there won't be tracks. That reminds me—did you pull out the cash? You're going to need it until you get established there.'

"Nick replied, 'Of course. Norwegian kroner, Swedish kronor, euros. What does a Big Mac cost over there—twenty bucks? What's up with that? At least the fish sandwich should be less. Why can't you be a Mexijew? It'd be closer and a hell of a lot cheaper to live in Mexico. Instead you're smuggling me into this perfect fish country where everyone is smart, beautiful, and happy. How will I survive that?'

"'My friends are going to take care of you. They even found an Irish pub for you to hang out in.'

"Nick relaxed. 'VJ, you've thought of everything. Can I start now on one of those drinks you're talking about?'"

Tess interjected, "Not a bad idea. Did you bring a flask tonight? I could definitely handle a shot."

"In due time," VJ answered.

"Are we thinking next year?" Tess asked.

"I'm thinking tomorrow might be better. I definitely needed one that night when we hit Logan and stood in the line waiting to get checked in. The online option was not functioning. A single, slack-jawed agent endlessly pecked on his keyboard without even glancing at any of us. Something was happening, but nothing valuable. After ten minutes of no progress, my patience expired. By yelling from the line, I determined our flight had been cancelled. The agent continued to bang on his keyboard. I decided that throwing him against the wall would not further our travel needs. I glanced up to the departure screen and saw another flight to New York. We actually got on the plane. Once we hit the ground, Nick and I both kept an eye out for anyone who looked like they were watching us too closely. Seemingly in the clear, we made the run to the international terminal.

"Business class on British Airways is good—not as good as Lufthansa, but more than adequate. KLM is nice too. They hand out these little liquor-filled replica houses. There are multiple types. Frequent flyers collect them. Not me. About the last thing on earth that I want is to be stopped by customs to see if I'm smuggling heroin in one of those things. Last time I flew with KLM I gave mine to the guy next to me. Later I saw him getting shaken down. Score one for me.

"On the flight over the pond, I intentionally separated Nick from me by ten rows. I ended up having a bizarre conversation with the woman next to me. I'm actually a pretty conservative person and not into weird stuff. The lady asked to borrow my portable phone battery charger. While I was closing my eyes, I heard some really strange sounds coming from her phone. The woman was watching a porn movie starring four people—herself and three guys."

Tess just groaned. "I give up. You're hopeless."

VJ acknowledged Tess' disapproval. "No kidding. The woman saw me glancing at the screen and volunteered that she was a prostitute at a famous chicken ranch in Nevada. She'd won Hooker of the Month and was on a free trip to Europe. She accomplished this by taking care of an average of twelve clients a day. The money she was making for her work makes my salary look stupid. I can't lie: I was fascinated by the woman, so I pumped her for information about the whole industry. It was definitely more interesting than watching movies. The woman was very proud of her accomplishments—who was I to judge?"

Tess interjected, "I trust you're not planning a site visit to that ranch."

He replied, "No, of course not. Tess, the point is there's a whole other world out there that most of us know nothing about. The Cooperative. Hooker competitions. Bizarre.

"Once off the plane, we were herded to the trains in Heathrow. No matter what time of day it is, the international connecting train is stuffed to the max. After three checks and a search by a man who certainly looked to me like a known terrorist, our zigzag around Europe commenced. I was a little sad that we couldn't really spend significant time in the places we were landing, but I made one concession. I thought it'd be smart to break up the trip, so I settled on Oslo. Hans-Martin, the son of an anesthesiologist friend from Norway, was conveniently going out of town for a few weeks and was kind enough to let us hang at his place.

100

"The travel respite gave us some time to review our plans for the umpteenth time. I also pumped Nick for information. 'So tell me more about the fine people who did this to you.'

"Nick got agitated. 'Well, they didn't give me their business cards or invite me to friend them on Facebook. There were three guys. Two looked like they were straight out of *The Godfather*. The third guy was big, with long hair in a ponytail. He was the one with the charming tattoo. You want to know the weirdest thing—he was amazingly polite. He was also pretty good with that cleaver. Seemed like he'd had a lot of practice. The other two deferred to him. I heard them discuss someone named Rick a couple of times. He wasn't one of them. This Rick fella seemed to be the guy that no one had any interest in pissing off. I'm wondering if he's the Bob Smith who roped me in in the first place. You know, the huge dude over in the administration buildings. Be careful if you ever come across him. That's the extent of what I can tell you. Still, if I saw their pictures, I'd definitely know them—particularly the golden-tongued Neanderthal. The next time I see him, I'm going to have to have a .500 Magnum. Biggest handgun made. Shoots 50-caliber bullets. That's about the only way I'd be able to take him down.'"

Tess' face darkened. She muttered to herself, "Jesus Christ," then she grabbed VJ's wrist and interrupted. "Wait, did Nick say anything more specific about that tattoo?"

VJ answered, "The truth is I should have asked, but I didn't. Nick didn't know his name, either. What's bothering you, Tess?"

Gravely serious, she said, "Oh, nothing of significance. Just that the dinner guy I told you about may be a homicidal maniac. That he lives right by me, and that right now that fact scares the shit out of me. VJ, I need to know more about that tattoo. How hard is it to get information from Nick?"

"I have to route through a third party, but I should be able to get an answer pretty quickly. Certainly no later than Monday."

Tess was all business. "Do it, VJ. Find out if meat cleaver man had a killer clown tattooed on his forearm. What else did Nick tell you?"

VJ confessed, "Unfortunately, very little more. Not that it's any real solace, but if your guy and Nick's are the same person, he seems to have a bizarre sense of honor and decency."

Tess acidly said, "That'll definitely make me sleep better. I don't have a choice at the moment, so we'll put that issue on the back burner. Thank God I'm leaving town tomorrow— or is it today by now?"

VJ tried to do a better job of reassurance. "Tess, trust me, we'll get this worked out. I've gotten much better at eliminating problems that need to be eliminated."

She arched her eyebrows. "I'm not quite sure how to interpret that, but I'll take it at face value. So what did you and Nick do in Oslo?"

"Well, I didn't see any harm in showing Nick the city. We wandered around near the royal palace and found ourselves inside the National Gallery. Edvard Munch has a huge exhibit there. There's a reason that *The Scream* is one of the most expensive art pieces in the world. It's special in a good way—unlike Picasso's *artwork*. Sorry, Tess, I had to say that. As we viewed the painting, I looked over at Nick. 'Hey, is that how you felt when you decided you wanted me to do your fingers?'

"Nick smiled painfully. 'Yeah, I guess so. Who would have thought a few weeks ago that you and I would be discussing Edvard Munch in the middle of Oslo? By the way, did you see that blonde with the short boots and jeans?'

"'That's the Nick I know.' The ironic thing was that Nick really wasn't going to be Nick anymore. What wasn't yet clear, though, was who he was to become.

"After the Norwegian interlude, the passage through Helsinki to Stockholm was easy. The minute we landed, I felt an immediate rush. Although I'd voluntarily moved myself and two of my family members to the States—"

"Them I'd like to hear about—can't imagine they're normal," Tess interrupted.

"Sorry to disappoint you, but honestly they're wonderful. I'll tell you more in due time."

"This year?"

VJ again ignored the reproach. "*As I was saying,* returning home always produces special inner happiness. I corralled Nick and led him to the train while I filled him in with some critical data. 'This takes only twenty minutes to get to City Center. I'll bet you didn't know that Arlanda Airport has a fifty-year record of never closing. The roads and bike lanes are cleared no matter how much snow there is. We Swedes have "snowhow." That's what you're about to buy into. Lame American excuse-making has no place here. While we're in Stockholm, I'm going to introduce you to some folks that you can connect with whenever you need to. Each of them is high quality. After a couple of days, we'll fly to Copenhagen and drive over the border to your new home in Malmö.'

"On the first day in Stockholm everything actually went just the way I wanted it to. We were lucky—it was unseasonably warm, so we were able to wander the city. I tried to get Nick indoctrinated into Swedish culture as fast as humanly possible. Although it wasn't hard to fall back into the rhythm of Stockholm life, it felt foreign to me. My focus remained Nick's needs. Still, it was odd to come to terms with my own transition.

"I'd found out that one of my med school classmates had a younger sister who was a hand therapist in Malmö. I gave her a call and made sure that Nick would be able to put in rehab time. He was going to need it. Those fingers were already getting stiff. I was hoping she'd introduce him to some people in the community, too.

"I was also able to communicate with Sharon, my neighbor growing up. She's best friends with my sister, Kari, who lives with her husband in Israel. Despite knowing me her entire life, Sharon continues to speak to me. I waited to reach Stockholm before trying to see if she could be the link between myself and Nick. I figured the less spoken about in Boston, the better. Sharon was amazingly receptive when I asked for her help. She told me, 'VJ, if you need it, I'll do it. Period.' She's the connection who's going to reach out to Nick to help us with tattoo man's identity."

This time without sarcasm, Tess said, "VJ, you're a fortunate person. I know you were doing all this for Nick, but you were calling in a lot of favors. What if people had said no?"

He shrugged. "Then I would have followed a different plan. Normally, I hate asking anyone to do anything for me. It's just not my nature. I always like being in the plus column in that department. This time I didn't have a choice. My friends realized that, so they made it easy. But yes, I consider myself very fortunate.

"On the second day, we went to Gamla Stan, the old town where the palace sits. The weather had turned. It was frigid walking around, so we ducked into the Nobel Museum. Bad idea. I felt a hand on my shoulder. It wasn't Nick. It was my personal stream team doctor, Milo Marconi. He did seem genuinely surprised to see us. Milo asked the obvious: 'What on earth are you two doing here?'"

Tess quickly asked. "Did you totally freak?"

VJ nodded. "Inside I was going nuts. I was mad at myself for being in such a public place. I didn't think Milo was tailing us, but no matter what, our cover was blown. At least Stockholm wasn't our final destination. I decided on the best story I could come up with quickly.

"I said, 'Interesting you should ask. I was scheduled to go to Chicago, but with the storm there, the meeting got cancelled. A family friend here in Stockholm has been sick. Last minute, I thought now would be the right time to come.'

"Nick jumped into the conversation. 'VJ told me what he was doing. I've just been moping around Boston, so I tagged along. The post-op visits are easier this way.'

"Milo still looked puzzled. 'Nick, I'm really sorry about what happened to you. This might be a weird question to ask two hand surgeons, but are you sure Sweden is the place to be with relatively fresh replants? It's pretty cold here.

Aren't you worried about those vessels clamping down?'

"I took over the conversation. 'No worries, Milo—look at the boy's gloves. They're heated. I ordered them for him day one after we put those fingers back on. It's not like Boston isn't cold as hell. You haven't told us, though—what are *you* doing here?'

"'I'm giving a talk for the European Association of Urology. It's their international meeting. I thought I mentioned it to you, VJ. I'm talking about the collagenase you use for Dupuytren's. It's working pretty well on the Peyronie's patients.'

"I said to myself, *No, you didn't fucking 'mention' that to me or I wouldn't be fucking walking around here!*

"Milo stuck out his hand. 'Gotta run, guys. My talk's in a couple of hours. Have fun. Nick, try to stay out of trouble. You too, VJ.'

"Nick and I looked at each other. I motioned to him to join me at an isolated area of the museum to ask him the obvious. 'Is he part of the Cooperative?'

"Nick looked frustrated beyond belief. 'I have no idea. I do know I don't like what I just heard. Didn't you say you were suspicious of him?'

"I sighed. 'Yes, I did. Here's the deal, Nick. We have a few choices. We can put you on a plane to somewhere else and see what happens, or we can do what we planned. Let's say the Cooperative does get tipped off. Malmö is way off the grid. Nobody will track you there. My situation is a little different. I feel like a fighter jet flying into enemy territory that just got lit up by radar.'

"Nick put his arm around my shoulder. 'Sorry, VJ. I really am. Hopefully we're making a lot out of nothing. Let's go to Malmö. Is now a good time?'

"I said, 'Yes, it is. Change in plan, though, we have to hit up one of those friends you met for a ride directly there.'

"I checked the urology meeting program online. Milo's name was there. He was telling the truth. Running into each other was a complete and unlucky chance encounter. Nick and I split up temporarily and arranged to connect later. To the best of our knowledge, no one tailed either of us."

Tess was shaking her head in disbelief. "VJ, this doesn't sound very good."

VJ said, "No, no, it gets much better. We rolled into Malmö and went to the hospital to meet Nils. Nick looked around, took a deep breath, and said, 'Toto, this isn't Kansas.' Although the people on the inside are top drawer, the physical plant is not spectacular. Very institutional.

"A voice rang out. 'VJ, how are you?'

"Nils' hulking frame took up most of the doorway. He's a former Olympic crew gold medalist. I couldn't have been happier to see anyone. 'Nils, this is Nick. He is going to make a fine musculoskeletal radiology fellow. I know, I know. None of this makes any sense at all. Nick had a little difficulty with some unpleasant folks in our hometown. Malmö is the perfect place for him.'

"Nils stuck out his big paw, grasping Nick's functional left hand. 'No worries, we're going to take good care of you. VJ may be strange, but he picks good friends. The hospital keeps an apartment for visitors. You qualified. Maybe it would be best if we get you settled in. New country, new field, no problem—we'll start tomorrow.'

"Nils was no-nonsense. He piped up again. 'VJ, are you going to visit us this summer in Fjällbacka? I wrecked the speedboat last year. One of the islands got in the way. That cost me twenty-five thousand kroner. Fortunately, the sailboat's still fine. We caught some big lobsters. Ate them all.'

"Classic Nils. His little red beach cottage sits on the beautiful Swedish west coast. I love being there. When Nils is waterskiing, insignificant things like a small land mass won't stop him."

Tess shook her head. "I'll be sure to look him up the next time I'm in Malmö."

"You should. He'll treat you like a queen. When we got to Nick's new place, I tried to reassure him. 'Nick, don't worry. Nils is going to help you out. You don't have to make anything for dinner for at least a week. Your hand should be perfect by then. See, you've even got a new knife set here—very sharp, perfect for cutting and chopping anything.'

"Nick could only shake his head. 'You deserve to take my call.'

"I'd arranged for Nick to get cash delivered on a regular basis. He'd emptied a couple of accounts before we left. Credit cards were going to remain an absolute no-no. There was enough to keep him going, but he wasn't going to be relaxing in Monaco's casinos. My smile faded. 'Nick, I know that this whole deal sucks massively. You'll be OK. Like we decided, everything goes through Sharon. She'll get you whatever you need. Anything I find out in Boston, you'll get from her.'

"Ultimately, proper goodbyes were said, and I left Nick to his at least temporarily safer life. Mine, not so much. I went back."

THE PROPOSITION

Tess weighed in. "Wait, VJ. You went through this elaborate plan to take Nick to Malmö because you were worried you might be followed; you probably got ID'd anyway, but then you just went right back. It's not like the people who cut off his fingers had gone to South America to set up shop. It doesn't make complete sense."

VJ nodded. "I knew there might be danger, but I didn't really process it as I should have. Mental frailty and wishful thinking. Yes, the smarter move would have been to pack up Vikka, the cat subleaser, and spirit away the lot of us. But I had a nice life in Boston. Job, friends, family. Stockholm is still the greatest city on earth, but it's not home anymore. When we were in Sweden, that reality hit me almost as hard as the sight of Nick's fingers in the bag. I had to come back. My brother, Anders, is my anchor here. Kari's situation is Israel is good, she's terrific, but we're not that close."

"Oh, right, that family we were just talking about," Tess said. Then she looked serious. "Is Nick doing OK?"

"In a word, yes. Surviving."

"And you? How did it go when you got back?"

VJ shrugged. "For a short time, everything was just hunky-dory. Clinic went as it always did. Call continued to suck. The main OR challenged me in new and creative ways. In short, I was happy doing the VJ thing. I went out to dinner with Anders and his husband, Jacques, and caught up. They've been together for eleven years and are truly a perfect couple. A Frenchman and a Swede in Boston. Who wouldn't want to hang out with them? They filled me in on the music scene. Anders was a hot item locally and was booked solid in town. For me, that was great: It forced me to get out at night to go to his shows. Nonmedical activities are very healthy. I started to feel normal. Nick's problems were gently fading into the rearview mirror. I tricked myself into believing that we'd achieved success.

"On a surprisingly pretty Sunday afternoon I was walking out the back door of the hospital after finishing a straightforward both-bone forearm fracture. One incision, two plates, twelve screws, boom and out. I was feeling good. The ER was clear, and I had at least a few hours to be a real person. A run by the Charles with Vikka seemed like the perfect thing to do.

"Two well-groomed gentlemen suddenly appeared and persuaded me that we should speak. The stocky, muscled guy with the eye patch seemed particularly menacing. We sat down.

"I was surrounded by the pair on the bench and immediately felt like the new prison bitch. On my left sat the eye-patch guy. When he shifted and his coat opened, I noticed a Smith and Wesson .38 caliber. To anyone passing by, we must have looked like a very cozy group— three men, possibly a research team, going over lab values that might someday save lives. Not exactly.

"The larger of the two, wearing the sharp black coat and turtleneck, began: 'Dr. Brio, we have some very interesting information to discuss with you. Our sources tell us you recently had a nice trip to Sweden with Dr. Mahaffey. The Cooperative assumes he explained to you how we work. At the moment, we don't know where you placed him. Our assumption is that he's hidden somewhere there. Given time and energy, we can find him, but Mahaffey seems to not be saying anything to anyone, so we don't care to devote the resources. You're here as a substitute.'

"Then they shared with me a number of doctored operative reports with my name attached. 'Look at this as a new opportunity,' Mr. Dapper Dresser offered. 'If you do the right thing, you'll make a lot of money. If you decide to speak out, then let's face it, with what we've got on you, you're likely to do jail time. That'd be an ill-advised plan. We've got friends in most of those places. You'd be unhappy.'

"He pulled an envelope from his pocket and withdrew a number of photographs from it before going on. 'But if you are the fall-on-your-own-sword type of individual, then you should consider the health of your family. These pictures of Anders and Jacques, are very nice. I've seen him play. He's really quite good. Isn't that his front door and the club where his last gig was? That's you, too. It's good that you're such a supportive brother. As far as your sister Kari goes, we're not looking at her at this time. Israel is harder for us to cover. Perhaps in the future.'

"To myself I muttered, 'Yea, good luck with that.' Outwardly, I just nodded. I did resolve to find the best way possible to destroy Milo Marconi. The instructions were clear: If they saw Anders get on a plane, train, the T, car, boat, motorcycle, or horse-drawn buggy that was going anywhere away from the city, then he and I were both going to have problems.

"The eye-patch dude glared at me. 'Hand surgeons are easy to replace,' the other one added. 'Family, not so much. Don't underestimate us. We're thorough. The Cooperative takes pride in it. By the way, don't worry about the surgical assist you'll see listed on your operative notes. Those add-ons bring in a lot more cash than you can imagine. Too bad you're not a spine surgeon. That's where the big money is.' I immediately catalogued my spine colleagues, wondering who the dirty ones were.

"Before they left, they gave me the rundown of the Cooperative's plans for me. Now I'd done it. I'd gotten deep into a mess I saw no obvious way out of. I liked my fingers and loved my family. I was mad as hell, but I was also really scared.

"After sitting for a few minutes to calm down, I debated my choices. The Swedish army, medical school, internship, residency, and the every-other-night-on-call-for-a-year hand fellowship introduced me to dealing with problems. This situation was different. I was being directly threatened, along with Anders. Unfortunately, Tess, the Good Decisions for Busy Decision Makers course I took at university didn't include the part about threats of bodily harm. Amazing, right? All I could think about was what I should say to Anders. I also had to warn Kari. That Anders was suddenly the unknowing prisoner of a clandestine group who cared not a bit whether he lived or died? I felt utterly demoralized."

Tess gasped. "This story is getting worse by the second. I can't imagine having Max be at risk for something I'm involved with. It doesn't sound like you had many options."

VJ responded, "I didn't. Under the pretext of an on-call schedule change, I asked Anders to let me know if he planned to leave the city at all.

He was used to me popping up at his gigs, so the request didn't seem disingenuous. Fortunately, he had no plans to go anywhere further than the North End for a few months. Navigating the disaster at hand now became the first order of business."

Tess had a look of incomprehension on her face. "Jesus, VJ, what a disaster. You're here telling me about it, so you must have figured a way out."

VJ answered honestly: "Maybe."

Her eyebrows flew up again. "*Maybe? Maybe* doesn't pay the bulldog."

He said, "A lot has happened in between then and now."

Tess acquiesced. "OK, let's have it."

VJ explained, "Here goes. When all this went down, I couldn't just do things the way the Cooperative wanted me to. I literally tore up their checks and blatantly disregarded their representatives. But I didn't say anything to anyone, and I didn't change any of the records they doctored. I played along just enough. Unquestionably, I knew what I was doing was dangerous, but my hardwiring wouldn't let me bend over and just take it.

"It seemed like every time I turned a corner in the hospital, someone who looked like they worked for the Cooperative was there to remind me that they were watching. For the first time, the OR was the one place I felt more relaxed. The stress of just trying to get a case started and finished was reassuring. Even the Cooperative was not strong enough to interfere with the predictable daily chaos of the main OR. Suddenly, I found any excuse to be there. The fellows and residents were stunned by my newfound love for skin-to-skin teaching."

Tess stopped him. "Well, at least someone was making out from this deal. With all that time you were spending there, did it at least get more efficient?"

VJ looked at her and, without the hint of a smile, said, "I have no words. Wait, check that. To again quote Rule VIII from *The House of God*, 'They can always hurt you more.'" Tess just shook her head.

He continued, "Eventually, each day I had to leave the safe confines of Bedlam. Nobody tried to hurt me. Either the money was too good, or they were worried that a second 'accidental' maiming in such a short time span would raise alarm bells, or they were toying with me. I wasn't sure which. My brain was still working double overtime to devise a way out.

"Finally, I told the person I was forced to check in with that I was leaving for my regularly scheduled work trip to Sierra Lakes in California. They had Anders as their ace in the hole, but I was still surprised when I didn't get more pushback. My handlers were acting almost reasonably. That alone gave me pause. These were not reasonable people."

Tess remarked with obvious curiosity, "Sierra Lakes? I've been wondering about your connection since you mentioned it earlier. California seems pretty out of the way."

VJ explained, "I fell in love with the place after some friends from Duke took me there. It's a funky town with a ton of character. Killer snow most of the time. With Global Warming, who knows? Sierra Lakes doesn't have a hand surgeon within a hundred-mile radius, so it's a great place to be. I have a pretty busy elective practice. The last time I went, I saw eighty-three people in two days. When I have to take call, though, I fix anything broken—femurs, tibias, you name it. I've been working there for ten years.

"I decided to buy a house—it's wonderful, but definitely a money sink. A lightning strike took out the first owner. Such an odd thing to happen to a real person. I hadn't thought of it before: Perhaps the house is cursed. What's been going on with me isn't exactly standard issue.

"But if ever there was a time I needed a temporary escape from Boston to Sierra Lakes, it was at that moment. I didn't care if I worked every second I was there. That's not really true. I lie to myself all the time. I was looking forward to at least a few hours of mental relaxation skiing on the mountain."

THE CABAL

While VJ was contemplating his new life paradigm and the planned trip to Sierra Lakes, the people responsible for his conundrum were conferring about the very same topic in a nearby office. The striking, intense woman spoke to her partner. "Rick, Nick made us a lot of money. I still like the idea of having someone in the hand department. Do you think you can keep Brio under your thumb?"

Rick waited a moment before answering, indicating his own uncertainty. "The answer is—I think so. He's a wild card. It's not like he came to us. He's not prototypical. He's not an alcoholic, he doesn't do drugs, he's not getting a divorce, and he doesn't seem to care about buying expensive toys. But there's no way Brio's going to take any chances while we've got his brother on watch. That's our leverage point. Still, we're going to have to keep leaning on him pretty hard."

He shifted in his seat before continuing. "Unfortunately, we can't prevent him from leaving to give his talks and do his Sierra Lakes thing. If he suddenly cancels out on commitments, it's going to be noticed. We can't pretend he's sick—he's obviously not. People around the medical center asking questions is bad for business. We make money here because we've managed to stay under the radar. We're going to keep it that way."

A deep frown creased the woman's face as she rubbed her temples. "I don't like it. I don't. He's going to try to fuck us. I can feel it. I don't know how, but he will. Rick, you've got to be all over him. Maybe I'll send Brittany Morgan back to see him again. She's a bimbo, but useful for projects like this. If there's even the slightest suggestion that Brio's stepping out of line, I'm going to take care of the problem my way."

Rick was decidedly unhappy, but chose to say nothing further. He knew when to push and when not to. At this particular moment, the woman with the Mediterranean complexion and long, dark curly hair represented more of a danger to him than any hand surgeon. Rick had seen Petra agitated like this before. The source of that problem had died in a suspicious home fire. Brio would play ball. He'd make sure of it.

After Rick left, Petra straightened her computer keyboard, aligning it perfectly with the edge of her desk. She knew it was obsessive-compulsive, but could never prevent herself from doing it. With the task completed, Petra strode over to the large window and stared at the Charles River and the people scurrying below. That was where they were, and that was where they belonged. She had almost forgotten what it was like to be one of them—the people no one pays attention to. Growing up without a father and a rarely employed mother, Petra was no stranger to anonymity and want. Now the Cooperative funneled millions her way. Business couldn't be better.

Brio was a problem, though. He hadn't done anything stupid. He was being watched carefully. Still, he wasn't taking the money. *Just what I need, a holier-than-thou, bullshit Scandinavian socialist who's giving us the finger every chance he gets,* Petra thought. *I've already gotten to him once, and now, I might have to do it again.*

Rick approving Brio's Sierra Lakes work plan was like an angel walking up to Petra and saying, *Problem solved.* In that instant, she made her decision. She thought to herself, *Accidents happen in ski areas all the time. People disappear. A skier goes out of bounds, and search and rescue can't find him. Two years later, some shreds of cloth and bone show up, and everyone's happy the mysterious disappearance has been solved.* If Brio encountered a bit of misfortune on his own turf, it certainly wouldn't be traced back to Boston. It would be written off as a terrible coincidence that the hand surgeons from MRMC couldn't stay out of trouble. Beautiful in its simplicity. The setup was perfect.

Petra smiled. She had nothing against Brio personally. She knew he was an asset to MRMC.

121

But business was business, and he represented an ongoing risk. She owed it to herself to take care of it. Petra was aware of Brio's usual flight plan through LA. To be on the safe side she would make sure the hitters would route through Reno and drive down to Sierra Lakes. Those two were effective but not subtle. The last thing she needed was them to tip off their target.

Petra opened the door and commanded to her admin, "Agnes, get Lucca and Armaceo Luciano in here today. Clear a space on my schedule. We have to have a short conversation."

Cyrus wouldn't do hits. It was his personal rule. The Luciano brothers would do anything, to anyone, anytime, as long as the money was there. Petra pondered her decision. How had it come to pass that it became so easy to decide to end a person?

Getting raped by one of her mother's many boyfriends when she was twelve had been a defining moment. The man died a year later of sudden deceleration disease. Massive head trauma. His car struck the retaining wall at the bottom of Petra's street, and he flew through the windshield. The police determined that all the brake fluid was missing from the master cylinder. Very unfortunate for him. How that happened was unknown. A disgusting human being was dead. Petra moved on.

Part II

LURKING

Cyrus' patience was wearing thin. He asked himself, *Where is Tess? She's been in that building for hours.* Had she somehow slipped away without him seeing her? Was there an exit he didn't know about? Resolutely, he decided it was time to investigate. Picking the lock in seconds, Cyrus walked inside, silently searching for any sign of his mark. He just had to know where she was. He scanned the directory. Anatomy lab, fourth floor. During art class, Tess had mentioned to one of her friends the troubles she was having in anatomy. It had to be.

Slowly he ascended the staircase. As he approached the door, Cyrus heard what sounded like two voices. Even more carefully, he turned the doorknob. Peering quickly inside, he could see Tess and the figure of a man. At that instant both seemed to look his way. Immediately he pulled back and carefully retraced his steps. He thought, *Now who is that guy? I haven't seen him before.*

Cyrus decided that continuing to wait outside in the cold was a monumentally poor idea. As he made his way back home, he resolved to see what he could find out about the man Tess seemed to find so compelling.

ALERT

Tess startled. "Did you hear something?"

VJ said quietly, "I did."

Tess got out of her chair, picked up the scalpel, and went to the door. She opened it swiftly, to surprise any invaders.

VJ called to her, "Do you see anyone?"

Tess took a moment before answering, "No, I don't. Are you sure that no one else knows you're here—like someone from the Cooperative?"

"Other than four people I'd trust with my life—dead sure."

Tess came back to where he was sitting. "Well, no one from my party would show up. That is, except maybe Axel. It would be just like him to try to pull something." She anxiously looked back at the door. "I hope there isn't a problem. I'm deciding to not worry about it. It was probably someone cleaning. But, now, there is definitely no way in hell I'm leaving here anytime soon . . . You got want you want. I'm your hostage—happy? So you blew out of here to Sierra Lakes, right?"

VJ began again. "Yes, correct. But wait. Tess, I don't want *you* to worry. For the first time in months, I feel vaguely safe. After tonight I'm going to reengage in the battle, but I do think you can relax."

Tess laughed sardonically. "No one has ever used my name and 'relax' in the same sentence. I don't think I'm genetically programmed to do that."

VJ resumed. "The morning I left, Bianka was sweet enough to give me a ride to Logan. She'd mentioned something casually about wanting to speak to me. Before getting into the car, I scanned the traffic around us to see if I was being observed. She got out and gave me a big hug and a worried look. 'VJ, you've been acting odd lately, even for you. Do you still want to go to the airport, or would you prefer to stand around watching the cars drive by?'

"I meant to act nonchalant, but I practically barked at her, 'Relax, I'm fine.' She looked hurt, so I gently took her free hand. 'Bianka, you know how much I care about you. I always get this way when I have to visit my TSA friends.' The human touch helped, but it was obvious that she was aware there was something I wasn't telling her.

"She stared at me for a second and said, 'VJ, I've known you long enough to know when you're not being honest. You can tell me now or not. But don't insult me with that bullshit about the TSA.'

"I obliged her a little. 'OK, Bianka, there is something else, I admit. I really can't talk about it right now. If I tell you anything, it might put you at risk. You're going to have to trust me on this.'

"Bianka gave me a concerned look and said, 'Jesus, VJ, what are you into? I was going to talk to you seriously about something too, and I have to do it in person, not over the phone. Now seems like it definitely isn't the time for either of us. Let me know when you get back. For God's sake, VJ, be safe.'

"For the remaining minutes to Logan we just made mindless small talk, each of us hiding a big secret. When we got to the departure curb, I promised Bianka I'd call her. She gave me a small peck on the cheek and left wordlessly. *That went well,* I said to myself. All I could think was that she was going to split up with Anthony and here I was being a lousy—"

Tess interrupted. "Wait, VJ. How could you just leave when there was something so important she wanted to tell you? I feel so bad for her."

"Wait a second, Tess. Remember, I was pretty distracted by the Cooperative. Basically in fear for my life. Plus airports, particularly ours, really do make me stressed. What Bianka ultimately said was entirely different than what I initially thought."

Tess folded her arms across her chest and gestured for him to go on.

"I got in line with about the same enthusiasm as a man facing a firing squad. I stripped off my shoes, belt, and watch, and emptied my pockets of various pieces of paper. Despite the fact that there were a ton of people waiting to be screened, the TSA people didn't seem to be doing much of anything. I overheard a guy ahead in line say there'd been a skirmish with some angry passenger who wouldn't take the cast boot off her broken foot to go through screening. Something about a search for explosive residue. The note from her surgeon and the pins sticking out of her exposed toes apparently weren't good enough. Honestly, can you imagine?"

Tess nodded in agreement. "I know all about that. I understand theoretically why they have to do what they do, but still. When I was going to Europe, every inch of me got touched, and I do mean every inch. I'm going to apply for one of those global entry deals. You get TSA pre-check at every airport in the US. It's about a hundred bucks, but who cares, it'll be worth its weight in gold."

"I need to do that," VJ agreed. "Think how frustrated the TSA agents will be if most of the people don't need to be screened."

Tess asked, "Did you finally make your plane?"

"Yes," VJ said. "I did, but that's when it really started to get interesting. We were packed in tight. Just as we were ready to take off, the airplane stopped and the captain announced a 'short' delay. We waited. The inside vertical tail cone shroud indicator was broken. I didn't think we were ever going to get off the ground. We finally left after about an hour and a half. It kills me when that happens, because it always means I'm exhausted when I finally do make it to LA.

"Once we were in the air for a while, long enough for the flight attendants to offer us free drinks for not committing suicide during the delay, this funny guy sitting in the next seat gave me a nudge. 'This is awesome,' he said, raising his glass. 'It must be self-defense for the flight attendants. Can you imagine how pissed everyone would be if they weren't drunk?'

"I had to agree. I said, 'Did you see those two people sitting in front of us go to the bathroom? They haven't come back.'

"'New mile-high club members, no doubt,' the man cracked. 'I bet they just met in the airport. The idea isn't that appealing to me, though. Those bathrooms always smell pretty rank. Don't tell me it's your favorite thing to do.'

"I shook my head no. I really didn't feel like talking, so I opened up my hand journal. The plan completely backfired. The man said, 'That's an interesting way to do a four-corner fusion. I think it works just as well to leave out the triquetrum.' Then he launched into a long explanation of the way he did it and why.

"I did a double take. I knew or recognized almost all the hand surgeons in the area. The man stuck out his hand and introduced himself: 'How are you? I'm Benjamin Saito.' Yes, none other than the infamous Benjamin Saito who tried to steal Nick and operated on your friend.

Tess almost erupted. "Wow, you said you'd tell me how you met Dr. Saito *soon* and now you're really telling me about him. It's still even the same week. My faith is renewed."

VJ could only shake his head before proceeding. "At that moment, though, I couldn't place the name. 'Erik Brio. Call me VJ, everyone else does. I'm surprised we've never met before.'

"He smiled. 'I'm not. Those national meetings make me bonkers. It's always the same people saying the same thing: "I did a hundred of these, and they all worked great." Strange how those techniques don't always translate in real life. I hide in Maine. Brunswick, to be exact. I do my thing and try to make sure I'm helping my patients. Nobody in the academic world knows me. I suppose you're one of them. But my guess, looking at those crocodile boots of yours, is that you picked them up at the meeting in Austin. I did go to that one. Love the style. Got some myself at Allen's.'

"I knew instantly I liked this guy—straight shooter. I said to him, 'Guilty as charged on both accounts. Want to see the uppers?' With tremendous enthusiasm now I removed one boot and showed off the elaborate designs. He said, 'Nice. I'm digging those socks too. What are those graphics I'm looking at? Great White sharks?' I smiled. 'Indeed they are. Stance socks—best on the planet. When I give a talk, I tell people if there's one thing to take away, it's that they need to get some Stance socks. Perfect stocking stuffers too.' I elaborated further, 'Yes, I'm one of those university types you seem to care deeply for. I work at MRMC.'

"Benjamin became more animated. 'No shit? Your colleague Mahaffey was all set to join me. Then he goes and cuts off his fingers.'

"The minute he said it is when I remembered what Nick had told me about making the jump to Maine. 'I know something about that,' I confessed. 'I put them back on. Bad deal.'

"Benjamin shook his head understandingly. 'I tried a million times to reach him. I never got a response. What's he doing now?'

"I desperately wanted to change the subject. 'He's taking some time away. Nick told me he's going to stay with his sister in Colorado. Unfortunately, it looks like you're going to have to start searching for a new partner again.'

"Benjamin adjusted his seat, digesting the coincidence. 'So what takes you out to California, VJ?'

"'Sex, drugs, and rock 'n' roll—what else? No, believe or not, I work part-time in Sierra

Lakes. Sierra Summit Mountain is there. Terrific ski resort.'

"He said, 'I know about it, heard it's great, but never been there. Where exactly is it again?'

"'It's about three hundred miles northeast of LA. I go every six weeks or so. I know it seems silly to travel so far, but I love the place.'

"Benjamin took a last draw on his beer. 'Sounds cool. Is this delay going to make you miss your connecting flight?'

"My face lit up, partially from the vodka I'd downed and partially from the joy of being able to say no. 'Glad you asked. In fact, I'm not going to miss anything. I've learned to never take a flight from LA to Sierra Lakes. Half the time they get cancelled. Or even better, the plane will get within sight of the runway and then not land because the winds are too high. There's a town nearby where you could land almost anytime, but they don't want commercial airlines. If you can't land in Sierra Lakes, you have to fly back to LA. Do that a couple of times and I guarantee you'll never do it again.'

"My new best friend asked, 'So what do you do, rent a car?'

"I shook my head. 'No way! Dealing with those people on a regular basis drives me crazy. I picked up a used truck. I park it at a buddy's house who lives close to LAX. His kids use it most of the time. It's perfect. The thing is dinged up as hell, but who cares? It gets me to where I need to be, and I don't give a damn about what happens to it. So, Benjamin, what's your draw to the City of Angels?'

"He looked a little sad as he responded, 'Typical story. The ex-wife moved west when her new and improved husband got a better job. He went to USC for college and B school, so he has a million contacts. The dude is crushing it in the food and travel business. Fortunately, he's a superb guy. They met after we split. I go to LA a lot. Otherwise I wouldn't get to see Chase and Bertie enough. They're my kids. You got any children?'

"I shook my head no and switched back to what I'd just read in the *Journal of Hand Surgery*. The plane shuddered violently. Both of us reflexively grabbed our drinks. Gotta protect the important stuff. There we sat, two single hand surgeons, quaffing free alcohol, entertaining ourselves discussing surgical pearls while the airplane did its best to blast into bits. We were happier than pigs in mud. Doctors are strange that way. If there's a medical issue occupying my mind, it doesn't matter what else is happening around me. I'll stay focused."

Tess almost fell off her chair. "You're kidding me, right? You, focused?"

VJ gave her a smile. "I think I'll just continue and ignore that remark. After touchdown, I wished Benjamin good luck and Godspeed, promising to connect with him in the future, knowing it probably wouldn't happen. I grabbed my truck and booked to Sierra Lakes.

"When I got in, I could tell the weather was turning. The wind would soon whip up to ninety miles per hour over the ridges. No one would be skiing at the top for the next few days. We'd be lucky if the whole mountain didn't go on wind stop. Still, I felt wonderful. It was such a relief to be in a beautiful place with no one looking over my shoulder. The mountains have a quality to them that is unique. You know that?"

Tess nodded in agreement. "You don't have to convince me. If I have my way, I'm going to end up in northern Vermont or Maine. You should consider it yourself."

VJ smiled. "I look forward to being able to make that choice." Then he resumed his story. "While I was driving to my house, I decided to cruise by Jeffrey Burch's place. Burch was really the one responsible for me solidifying my gig in Sierra Lakes. At a lecture in Atlanta about mass casualty orthopaedic triage, Burch sat down next to me. He's about six-four, has a Marine buzz cut, and wears cowboy boots for every occasion. Hard to miss. We started talking. He told me Sierra Lakes desperately needed someone to do hand surgery, even part-time. I remembered how fun it had been when I was there the first time. He had me with the ask. *Who better than me?* I thought. It didn't take long to learn about Sierra cement and the afternoon Sierra Summit

Mountain wind. It can blow like you wouldn't believe. That said, Sierra Summit on its worst day is a thousand times better than ninety-nine percent of resorts.

"Tess, I have to tell you more about Jeff because he's not human. Forget that he does ultra-marathons and is a talented surgeon. In the immediate aftermath of 9/11, Jeff rushed to NYC to do anything he could to help out. He set up a fully operational MASH unit at Ground Zero. Another time Jeff was getting his team set for a five-day medical mission in Mexico when a typhoon wiped out half the Philippine Islands. Burch diverted the entire group there. They landed in an area that was toast, and then they were transported on Huey military choppers to an even more remote and desperate site. He also did a stint as a volunteer in a forward medical unit in Afghanistan. The man is totally insane. Complete FUBAR is Burch heaven."

Tess chimed in, "Sounds like this guy Burch is legit. I'd like to get in on one of his missions. Do you think I could work that out?"

VJ said, "Yes. That can happen. You might want to think about it, though. You could end up in the middle of the jungle with no supplies, or in a war zone."

Tess smiled mischievously and shrugged. "After tonight, that sounds like a day at the beach."

VJ could see he was making real progress winning her over, and plunged ahead. "So, I decided to just show up at Burch's house because he won't answer his phone even if the president is calling. I found Jeff outside working in the dark and cold on a new project. It was a large structure with what seemed to be a lot of insulation. 'Yo, Burch, whatcha workin' on—a spaceship?'

"He looked up and started laughing. 'VJ! You know, I was going to call you; I just got a little busy. This is my new winter hydroponic greenhouse. I'll tell you all about it.'

"I stopped him. 'Burch, when do I start call, and for how long?'

"Burch answered with a big fat smile: 'VJ, buddy, you're the show for the next week starting tomorrow morning. Slim and I are going to do some heli-skiing in Canada. We were there last year. To get to the good stuff we had to rope up and cross a couple of crevasses. A few hundred feet, pretty easy, but a ton of fun.'

"I gave him my there's-nothing-that-you-do-that-surprises-me-so-don't-even-try look. 'Burch, I don't care about you, but just make sure that you get Slim back here. The town really needs him.' Slim Stall is one of the two other full-time orthopaedic surgeons in town. The third musketeer, Reynaldo Bilmer, was off visiting his family in Texas.

"The weather we were starting to get was also hitting Canada. I didn't even consider asking if Burch thought venturing into the teeth of the oncoming system was a good idea. I knew the answer already. I said, 'Jeff, take care of yourself out there. I'm not taking your call if you and Slim buy it.'

"Burch laughed. 'Wait, I want to show you a new toy before you take off.'

"He brought out a Pelican case and opened it with absolute glee in his eyes. Inside was a sleek black instrument of death. He told me, 'This is a long-range precision weapon system—a .338 Lapua sniper rifle. It can get you up to fifteen hundred meters with the right ability. Now I don't need my .300 WinMag. Maybe I'll sell it to you cheap. How's the shooting going? You ready for the biathlon in March?'

"I said, 'Damn straight, Farmer John. I'll be lurking there the whole race and take you at the end.'

"Actually there wasn't a chance that I'd beat Burch. He's an animal, and I'm just me. Even if I thought I could match his shooting accuracy, Burch would destroy me with his conditioning. Any competition involving Burch was just to see who would come in second place."

Tess looked skeptical and pointed at VJ's knee. "Are you sure about second place?"

"I said that before my knee entered the equation. It's sort of curious—I did end up winning my own private biathlon. But more on that *soon*. Biathlon turned me on when I watched the Olympics as a kid. The evil Norwegians always seemed to triumph. I vowed to stand on that podium one day, listening to the Swedish national anthem, clutching the gold medal, gloating. Somewhere along the way I got sidetracked. Mostly as a direct result of my at-best-average athletic talent. I did learn to shoot pretty well, though. My skills got a lot better during my time in the army."

Tess interjected, "Do you hunt?"

"I'm not big on that," he answered. "Not for four-legged animals, at least." She gave him an odd look. Acknowledging her, he said, "I'm about to explain that."

BROTHERS MALEV

The Luciano brothers landed in Reno a day before wheels down for VJ in Los Angeles. They picked up the requisite supplies from their local contact. Taking C-4 explosives and weapons on the plane hadn't seemed to be a good idea. Then they started the drive to Sierra Lakes.

The road trip did nothing to put them in a generous mood. First there was the ice, then the wind, then the chains, then the whiteout. Highway Patrol shut down Route 395 thirty miles north of Sierra Lakes, near Bridgeport. The closure forced the Lucianos to cool their heels in a small hotel overnight. There was no working TV because the cable dish was buried in snow.

With nowhere to go, the only thing left to do was smoke, play cards, and get irritated with each other. The original hit they'd planned couldn't be set up. Petra had told them what she wanted, but they had decided together it wasn't going to happen her way. Kidnapping the Swedish douchebag and burying him in some out-of-the-way place near the ski slopes lacked flair. No, this one was going to be a statement hit. The Cooperative wasn't the only game in Boston seeking their skills.

Late the next afternoon, the highway finally opened. That clearance didn't prevent the Lucianos from running into a snowbank outside of Lee Vining. Digging out took an hour. When they did finally roll into Sierra Lakes, the brothers were seething. Nobody was going to get in their way.

VJ BACK IN THE SADDLE

"Once I finished my business with Burch, I tried to engage in my upcoming call responsibility. The good news was that the storm would probably keep a fair number of people off the mountain. I didn't mind taking care of things, but the volume of ski trauma can be overwhelming at times.

"I needed some form of stimulation that didn't involve thinking, so I decided to wander over to the Rib Rattler. It's my favorite restaurant and bar. Fortunately, it's across the street from my house, downstairs in the Miner's Lodge. The white stuff was starting to come down harder. My hood kept most of it off my neck. I've got this great bright red coat that I picked up at a summer sale. At the same time, I got a matching yellow parka. Usually I'm not big on loud colors, but they're helpful when people are trying to find me.

"Just as I was descending the lodge stairs, I heard two voices with distinctive heavy Boston accents behind me, yelling. I whipped my head around and shot a glance toward a pair of bulky men standing at the front checking in. Cowering behind the desk was a diminutive young woman with large glasses and Heidi braids. I couldn't precisely hear the words, but it was obvious they weren't kind. All I could think was how wrong it was for these two jerks to be unloading on this poor innocent. Junior Tulasasopo, the bouncer at the downstairs bar, happened to walk through at that moment. He inquired if he could offer assistance. Getting on the wrong side of an angry Samoan isn't smart politics. The shouting stopped. I took another moment to study the men from afar. They didn't strike me as skiers. Did I see a glint of something else in the waistband of the taller one? Was he packing? I decided I was being paranoid, but also decided to skip the beer and go home.

"As I got to my driveway I pressed the button on my garage door clicker and watched the garage door of the house next door open. I could only shake my head. We both got them installed by the same company around the same time, and they were apparently operating on the same frequency. It was hit or miss as to whether his garage door or mine would open. The neighbor then sold the house for cash to some porno king from LA. That slime bucket was never there. There was no sign of life now, so I didn't think it was a big deal. But yet again I promised myself I'd call the contractor to correct the problem.

"My house was covered in snow. If I didn't know I lived there, I wouldn't know I lived there. I chipped out the key box, punched in the code, and prayed the key would still be there. I always worried that whoever used it last would forget to put it back. Thank God, the little guy was nestled exactly where it was supposed to be. Breaking in is a huge pain, and with the house buried, impossible. There are a ton of stairs going up, and at eighty-one hundred feet, carrying stuff from the truck, I always lose my breath. There's an ARRESTO CARDIACO sign at the top. It's the signal you've made it and survived.

"Inside, I noticed the wet and peeling walls. Part of the ceiling was crumbling. There was a frozen river traveling down the railing. Another leak. Ice dams on the roof are my enemy. They cause these bloody leaks all the time. Steve, my house caretaker, does a wonderful job, but tithing to him gets old. I considered burning the whole place down that instant, but decided that was too radical an approach. Instead I selected my usual path—deal with it later. There's nothing in life I can't put off.

"Before I had the actual chance to delay the inevitable, the ringer on my phone sounded, which made me mad because I thought I'd shut the thing off. The familiar number of the Sierra Lakes County Hospital ER was on the screen. They knew I wasn't on call, but sensed I was in town. No doubt there was something tailored just for me. Uriah was on the line. Hearing from him is about as fun as a blowtorch to the face. The injury he was describing wasn't good. It's an odd dynamic. Someone wakes up with no idea that anything bad is going to happen. Fate intervenes, we meet, and our lives become connected.

"I listened to Uriah and shook my head. 'You're fucking with me, right—a full-house wrist?' I wasn't up for it. Though thrilled to be in Sierra Lakes, I was tired. Every tendon, nerve, and artery cut in the wrist meant a long night. I grabbed my surgical loupes, and drove the two miles to the hospital.

"When I walk through the doors at Sierra Lakes County Hospital, I get the sense that no time has passed since my last visit. It can be two weeks or two months. Everyone is always so friendly and happy to see me. Genuinely. What a difference from the usual reception I get back home. Long ago I determined that the perfect balance involved coming often enough to be of use, but not so often as to have people expect me to be there.

"There's also a peculiar gravitational pull. The closer I get to the facility, the more I'm drawn into the role of surgeon. On the slopes, I can hang out and be a doctor in the abstract. That luxury evaporates the second I enter. At that point, I become responsible."

Tess smirked, "Well that's one problem you don't have to worry about anymore. That is unless your malpractice covers dead guys."

VJ said, "We shall see. I was alive then, so I saw the guy in the ER, had him in the OR in a record twenty-five minutes, and went into power fix-it mode. When I get like this, I worry about the things coming out of my mouth. For me it can be lethal. The 'put brain in motion before mouth in gear' concept sometimes gets lost. I've been reported for everything from foul language to misunderstood jokes to commentary not considered appropriate for prime time."

Tess feigned surprise. "VJ, I've known you for only a few hours, and I'm shocked that you might say something out of bounds. I do that myself, though. My filter isn't as good as it should be."

VJ smiled. "Tess, take it from someone who has been smacked down too many times. Whatever sarcastic comment you may think is necessary at the moment, it will usually come back to bite you in some way. You're better off taking a few breaths, internally devising ways to harm the person you're frustrated with, and moving on."

Tess nodded. "That sounds healthy, if impossible. You do know you're unhinged, right?"

"Maybe so. Perfection eluded me a long time ago." Thinking for a minute, he added, "Speaking of that, I know you're going to think the next part of my story may be slightly inappropriate."

Her voice dripping with sarcasm, Tess deadpanned, "O.M.G. I can't fathom that."

"I have to, though. It's important."

146

Contrite, she mouthed the words "Sorry, VJ."

He backed off immediately. "No, Tess, that's on me. I'm impressed that you've stayed with me this long." But he could see that she was ready to listen. "That evening there was a nurse, Leila Akekawanzie, nearing the end of a three-month traveler rotation in the OR. Travelers are hired by the hospital to cover during busy times or if there's inadequate staffing. I'd met her briefly the last time I passed through. The case we did together was short, and I was distracted by a difficult patient I saw in the office, so we didn't get a chance to talk that much, but I hadn't forgotten her. I even thought there were a few sparks. Sometimes it's hard to tell if someone is being nice because that's just who they are, or if there's more to it.

"Leila has these laser-intense green eyes and a presence that's hard to quantify. It's calming. In the OR, when someone is wearing a mask and scrub hat, what you see in their eyes communicates so much. She turned out to be witty and smart, and did her job superbly. The day we had worked together was my last on that trip. When I saw her that evening in the OR, I was simultaneously relieved and thrilled. For a tough case, having a good team makes a major difference.

"A half hour into the mass of lacerated tendons, arteries, and nerves, I was asking the anesthesiologist a question about the patient's blood pressure, when with my other ear I overheard a conversation I wasn't supposed to be privy to. Leila whispered a little too loudly to a nurse friend who had come in with some supplies, 'He's peculiar, but he intrigues me. When I tied up his gown I noticed he's the perfect amount of muscular. You know he's got good hands. And those ice-blue eyes! There's something about him.'

"I thought, *Wow, here's an opportunity. Don't blow it by being you.*"

"Good advice," Tess said with a sniff.

"Meanwhile I continued to plow through what I had to get done. Tag 'em and repair 'em, tag 'em and repair 'em. Same precise routine. Once I'd finished the arteries, the deeper tendons, and the nerves and was starting to repair the superficial tendons, I used the opportunity to find out more about Leila. Don't get me wrong, this part of the operation is critically important, too. Still, it's something I can do while talking. You can learn a lot about someone during a case, especially a long one, and particularly during the evening and night. People tend to let their guard down. It'd be a perfect place to meet if it wasn't necessary to do the surgery itself. I started the discussion with an open-ended directive.

"'So, Leila, I didn't really get a chance to know you the last time we worked together. Tell me about yourself.'

"'Sure, Dr. Brio, but first, do you have enough 3-0 FiberWire? I didn't see any more packages in the supply room.'

"'Please call me VJ. Everyone else does. My mom was and always will be Dr. Brio. We're good with the FiberWire, thanks, unless I colossally mess up.'

"As the tendons came together, we discussed matters of life and love—sports, politics, climbing, cars, travel, friends, family. The conversation was easy and free-flowing. At some point, I asked, 'Do you have a significant other here in town?' I keep finding out about relationships about two sentences too late. Sierra Lakes is a small place.

"She didn't answer right away, likely considering how forthright to be, then curtly said, 'Not that it matters and not that it's your business, but no, at this moment I'm not seeing anyone. My piece of human garbage ex decided that he'd rather be with some rich bitch he met at a hospital fund-raiser. He's currently on my shit-for-life list. I'm still thinking about treating him to a full Lorena Bobbitt. Any more questions about my personal life?'

"I said, 'Guess I'll hold off on that for right now.' Naturally, I was a little blown away by the bitter admission. I should have been put off, but truthfully, I was intrigued by the revelation of her nonattached status. The ex was obviously a complete idiot to do what he did and not realize the gem he'd had. I reminded myself to push forward with the actual surgery. After waiting for a few minutes, I took a chance with one question. 'Leila, I'm sorry that you were not appreciated in the way you should've been. You sound Southern, but you don't look like a classic Southern belle.'

"She nodded. 'I will answer that. My dad was part of the JAG Corps in the service—you know, the military justice folks. He's originally from Cape Town. My grandfather's black, but he married a white woman. They immigrated to Atlanta when Dad was a kid—being a biracial couple in South Africa was a challenge back then. And now, too, for that matter. They decided their opportunities would be better here in the U.S. Then my dad met my mother when he was stationed in Seoul. My mother still won't speak to me in anything but Korean even though her English is perfect.'

"'So you're a one-woman melting pot.' Now I was even more interested. She went on to explain that her father was currently a partner in the city's largest and most prestigious law firm. Fortunately, they didn't do any plaintiff malpractice work. That would've been an absolute deal-breaker—*You see, sir, your daughter may be the most perfect person on the*

150

planet for me, and I'm mixed up in an absolute nightmare situation. However, you sue doctors, so your family is not good enough for me.

"Leila's mother was no slouch. Early on she developed a traveling nurse business. Not to Worry is now an industry powerhouse nationwide. Little did she realize that her own daughter would take such full advantage of the company she'd created. After more than a decade of living in Savannah with this man who turned out to be a lot less than perfect, Leila wanted to break away. Travel nursing was the way to do it. Before Sierra Lakes, she'd done three-month stints in San Diego, San Francisco, Los Angeles, and Santa Barbara. Smart, talented, and energetic is typically a winning formula in the medical world. Any world. She was a firebrand, yet elegant.

"While I was doing the multiple circumferential 6-0 Prolenes to tidy up the tendon repairs, Leila told a defining story about channeling her inner free spirit. When she reached the West Coast, she decided it'd be essential to learn to surf. She found a guru at the hospital, and every day for months they went to the beach until she had the skills that locals wouldn't laugh at.

"During a trip to Costa Rica, she and three friends made their way through the mountains and rivers to the coast. On the road outside of a place called Manuel Antonio, she saw a small sign that read SURFBOARDS FOR SALE, and made the driver stop.

"The proprietor was a small, very dark, age-indeterminate man with a huge smile. Juan proudly showed off his state-of-the-art surfboard shaper and cache of beautiful new rides. 'Would you like to rent one?' he queried. She sweet-talked her friends into letting her stay for three hours.

"Juan led her down the path to the beach, where she was immediately adopted by his pals. 'This river-mouth break is *maravilloso. Ten cuidado señiorita* . . . Be careful. *Crocodrilos* live there.'

"Leila did it anyway. As I have come to appreciate, when she decides to take on a challenge, no one gets in her way. Stubborn does not begin to describe her."

Tess broke in, "VJ, I sure hope you didn't screw it up with her. She definitely sounds like someone to hang out with. It seems like the only thing wrong with her is that she was interested in you."

He winced. "What was that I told you about sarcasm?"

Tess was unfazed. "VJ, I just call 'em like I see 'em." Then she laughed. "Did you ask her out when your case was done?"

VJ said, "It didn't go quite like that, but since you ask . . . Once the last of the repairs was performed, I finished closing the skin and

152

put on the splint. While walking out of the OR, I asked, 'Is there *anything* you're afraid of?'

"Suddenly serious, she whispered, 'Psychopaths.'

"Sensing a lot more behind that comment, I followed up. 'Did something happen during your psych rotation in nursing school?'

"She said, 'No, much earlier.' After a decided pause, she went on. 'When I was fourteen, a couple of men broke into our house to rob the place. We'd been away on vacation and came back early over the weekend because the weather at the beach was terrible. We found out later that home invaders had a connection in Dad's office and didn't think anyone would be home. My mother was in the backyard and walked in on the two creeps. For reasons that nobody understood, rather than run out of the house, the two decided that going after Mom would be a good plan. Unfortunately, her first few screams didn't get the attention of my father, who was in the basement. That's also the place where he keeps his guns. When Dad did hear something and finally got up the stairs, he saw one of them on top of her. My dad didn't ask any questions. He blew the side off of one guy's face and shot the other one in the abdomen. The Atlanta police had no problem with what happened. Neither did the DA. Neither did I.'

"I said, 'Jesus, that's awful. I don't really know how to respond. I'm so sorry that happened to your family.'

"She said, 'There's nothing to say. The guy who lived is still rotting in prison. I hope he dies there.'

"'Guess that sums it up,' I said. 'What should we talk about now? Charles Manson, perhaps? At least *he's* dead.' The tension broke. For the moment, we parted ways. I went into the PACU to battle the new EMR system, and Leila went to the cafeteria to grab a cup of coffee.

"Normally, even though the arteries I fix are a lot bigger than the ones I repaired in Nick's fingers, I spend a lot of time post-op worrying that they might clot and I'll have to come back. But at that point, it was about two in the morning and I was pretty beat. Yet I couldn't get Leila out of my mind. I thought, *Is it possible I've met the woman of my dreams at the worst conceivable time?*"

Tess studied VJ carefully. "You're right, she sounds great. But that story about her home invasion . . . Are you sure she's not some sort of Jekyll and Hyde herself looking for retribution? Teenagers are very impressionable. If she's one hundred percent wonderful, why wasn't she with someone new after that guy left her? How do you know there aren't unsolved murders in all these places she goes? If you think about it, it's the perfect cover. No pattern for the police to examine because each case is in a different location."

VJ was taken aback. "The truth is, Tess, nothing like that ever crossed my mind. And I thought *I* was paranoid. I have a feeling that if you get a chance to meet her, which I sincerely hope you do, you'll feel completely comfortable."

Tess smiled slyly and settled back in her chair. "I'm just messing with you, VJ. Leila sounds marvelous."

VJ said, "You know, you do have a little evil streak in you. Well, at least I'm glad you don't really think Leila is dangerous.

"I had to start office hours later that morning. When I come to Sierra Lakes I start early. I decided to bag the trip to my house and grab an empty bed in the hospital. Even though it's only a couple of miles, I couldn't mentally deal with skidding on the ice into a tree.

"I strolled down the hallway by the new patient wing while trying to scope out the best room to sleep in. At that exact moment, Leila rounded the corner with her fresh cup of coffee. I jumped back about ten feet when it hit my chest. In a flurry, she grabbed a towel from a cart and frantically started to dry me off. 'I'm so sorry! I can't believe I spilled that all over you. Your scrubs are soaked.'

"I gently clasped her hand. 'Leila, seriously, don't worry about it. They're easy to change.' Tess, I know you'll think I'm nuts, but

155

there was just something about how she held my hand back and the way she looked at me. I took a chance and gently gave her a kiss. No, she didn't knife me in the back. She kissed me right back. I felt like I was hit by a tidal wave.

"I heard another pair of footsteps coming down the hall and immediately let go of her waist. The scrub tech appeared within seconds and flashed a look. All she said was, 'Sleep well,' and continued on her way to the cafeteria.

"Leila shrugged off the comment. 'That won't be happening, but it might be nice to grab a fresh cup of coffee.' In the break room, I discovered what I couldn't see in the OR when her scrub bonnet was on—Leila had a beautiful, wild mane of long, tightly curled, jet-black hair. I'm constantly surprised by what people look like when they leave the OR and take off their masks and hats. The style fit her personality. We spent most of the remaining time before the start of office hours talking. I knew I'd be dog-tired, but it was worth it.

"I didn't tell her anything about the Cooperative. I thought I might save that for at least our first real date. We settled on having a late dinner. That would give me a few hours to sleep and try to be coherent. Tess, despite everything else going on, I was head over heels. There's only been one other time in the past when I'd felt this absolutely intense emotional bond. It didn't end up working out."

THE WRONG KIND OF PATIENT

"I thought about hiding from the world in the hospital room I borrowed. No one would discover me there for years. The great thing about any hospital is that it has everything you need—food, fresh scrubs, razors, shaving cream, soap, shampoo, combs, hot showers. After snatching an hour's nap, I cleaned up so I could see my patients. Slightly refreshed, I walked across the parking lot and up the stairs to the office. KD, the clinic coordinator, greeted me with a warm hello. 'Hey, Doc VJ, it's going to be pretty light today. It's a total whiteout on the 395, so the road is completely shut down again, north and south. The only people who can get here are the ones from town.' That was going to be about six patients. I was thrilled.

"Johan Villetta, the Sierra Lakes police chief, as solid a guy as the day is long, was sitting in the first room. Fair to everyone he meets. Of all the funny things, the man knows how to make cookies. They're revered by everyone who knows him. I wanted Johan to franchise them. We'd call them Top Cop Cookies. I thought it had a nice ring to it. A million dollars, easy. Johan's wife, Loraine, is the hand therapist at Sierra Lakes County Hospital. She's

157

an equally superb person. Loraine makes it possible for me to come in, do my thing, then leave knowing that my patients will get excellent follow-up care.

"Johan greeted me with a firm handshake and said, 'VJ, this damn trigger finger is acting up again. I'm on the run. I promise you I'll let you fix it, but can you just give me a quick injection?'

"'No worries,' I said. I whipped out the magical Jesus juice and the deed was done.

"Johan got up from his chair, slapped me on the back, and said, 'Thanks, the cookies are in the kitchen. Let's try to catch up. This storm is going to keep me pretty busy. Talk to Loraine. We'll have you over to dinner.'

"'Sounds great, Johan. Be safe out there. I'm on call, and the last thing you want is me fixing you up.'

"Johan laughed as he left. 'You got that right.'

"My next patient was definitely not of the same quality. He was an add-on who didn't want to fill out any of the standard intake forms. Perfect. Do the man a favor and get stung for it. Happens every day. I walked into the room. As I put out my hand to shake, I immediately recognized him as one of the pair from the check-in at the Miner's Lodge. Attempting to hide my revulsion, I said, 'Hi, I'm VJ. What kind of trouble are you having today?'

"The gruff-looking man said with a thick New England accent, 'Doc, mah elbow's been huahtin' heah on the side foah about two months. I'm just visitin', and it huaht moah aftah I picked up mah fuckin' suitcase. Is theyah anything yah can do?'

"After an exam, I decided he had tennis elbow, so I launched into my standard discussion of the topic, trying to ignore the obvious. The man sitting on the chair across from me seemed to be studying me carefully, but not really listening. The hair on my forearms stood on end. My personal alarm system lit up. In the calmest voice I could summon, I said, 'Is this your first time in Sierra Lakes?'

"He stared through me. 'Yeah, Doc, it is. Me and mah brothah might buy a restauhant heah. We came out heah togethah to look around. We like that bahbecue place—what do they call it, Rib Rattlah? Say, wheah do yah like to go to eat?'

"'That depends on the food you like,' I replied stiffly.

"'Just curious. Where aah yah going tonight?' he asked with too much interest.

"I said coldly, 'You know, I haven't decided yet. You should try Crazdi. Outstanding chef, excellent service. Let's get back to your elbow. Would you like a steroid shot?'

"With a malevolent smile he said, 'Nah, Doc, maybe I'll just take some Tylenol. Thanks for yah help. Maybe I'll see you latah.'"

Tess remarked, "That sounds dangerous."

VJ said simply, "It was. God intervened, and the office finished an hour later. Between the lack of sleep and the threat, my concentration was destroyed. I speculated why the man had come to check me out. Likely his arrogance persuaded him I'd be an easy mark. He probably didn't realize I'd seen him at the hotel, or perhaps he just wanted to torment me. The visit was definitely unnerving. As I told you, I'd been surprised the Cooperative let me go. It was as if they wanted me to head west. It hit me that Sierra Lakes was exactly the place to have me disappear. I was so focused on escaping Boston, I never considered the possibility I might be playing directly into their hands.

"I had to leave the cocoon of the hospital and get my stuff from home. The stakes of this game seemed increasingly clear. I was being hunted. Maybe they just wanted to keep tabs on me, maybe they wanted to hurt me, maybe they wanted to do worse. It was impossible to know. It wasn't like I could ask anyone and find out. I had to formulate a plan. I thought that evacuating my house as soon as possible would be the first logical step. I made a quick call to my friend Matt and asked if I could crash at his granny flat. I told him that I was having some unexpected work done at Chez VJ. Since that's a continuous state of affairs, Matt wasn't even vaguely surprised.

"I thought that there'd be safety in numbers. I decided to call Steve. 'Hey, buddy, it's VJ. I really want you to see the inside walls near the back of the house. They're disintegrating. Do you mind cruising over with me?'

"Steve said, 'VJ, sure. Now's probably a good time. I'm going to be plowing nonstop. Can we meet in ten minutes?'

"Once we were at the house, I intentionally talked louder than usual to be sure that anyone in the vicinity knew that I was there with someone. I walked Steve through to the back and let him check out the crumbling rear end. I really didn't hear a word he said. My mind was focused on what to do next. I grabbed all my stuff while Steve was deciding how much the job would cost me. Usually it's between ten and twenty million dollars.

"In addition to clothes, toiletries, and ski gear, there was one other important article that I wanted to snag. I found it nestled in my downstairs closet. While I was busy packing, Steve sauntered up behind me. I jumped. He looked at me strangely and asked, 'What're you doing with all of those bags and your ski stuff? You know, you do live here.' I told him a half-truth. 'When I'm on call, I never know how long I'm going to be at the hospital, and even if I have an hour break, sometimes I want to be able to run up to the mountain and get some turns in.'

"He shrugged. 'OK, whatever floats your boat.'

"My phone rang. I was thrilled to see it was Leila. When I told her that I was free, she suggested we get some sleep, then go snowshoeing, hang out, then dinner. Why not, I figured. The trolls from Boston certainly wouldn't be venturing into the wild—they probably wouldn't even be leaving the bar.

"I passed out for a while at Matt's, then Leila and I connected near Twin Lakes. Not that it surprised me, but Leila is tough as nails. She ran me into the ground after a couple of miles. She was fresh as a daisy. I took her to my favorite bench by Lake Marie. It sits at the end of a short path off the road. The view at any time of day is stunning. With the fresh snow, the frozen lake was pristine. Crystal Crag towered above us. In the summer and fall, it's a rock climbers' paradise. The peak reminds me of a monster, though. Last year I got the call about a guy who got hit by a boulder careening off the top. The rock almost bashed his partner's head, but he ducked at the last minute. He told me that his pal was holding on, but without warning the entire edge gave way. The guy I operated on was lucky it was just his femur that was blown apart. I was zoning out, thinking about the case, when Leila squeezed my arm. 'Where'd you go?'

"I explained and said, 'It never ceases to amaze me how the difference between living and dying can be so small. Almost always, in any series of events leading up to what ultimately happens, even a tiny change would completely alter the outcome. Like stopping to get a cup of coffee instead of going straight to the office. The coffee might cause you to get hit by a car or prevent you from getting hit. If the tail cone shroud indicator on my plane coming out hadn't been fixed, I wouldn't have gotten here. I wouldn't have spent this morning talking to one of the most special people I've ever met.'

"Leila snuggled closer. 'VJ, I'll bet you say that to all the girls. But if it means anything to you right now, I'm glad the tail cone shifter or whatever it was got fixed.'"

Tess snickered. "I was just thinking, if I'd done better on my anatomy test, I'd be partying with my friends right now and I might've never met you."

VJ looked at her seriously. "Actually not. This conversation *was* going to happen."

Tess nodded. "I was just kidding. I got that impression a couple of hours ago. So did you ever confess to Leila that you might be endangering her life?"

"Interesting question," he replied. "Right after our discussion about the finer points of airplane maintenance, Leila said, 'OK, so tell me the things you don't want me to know about you.'

"At that moment, a ray of sunshine momentarily broke through the clouds. It framed Leila with a glow I can't describe. I knew I didn't have a choice about being totally up-front with her.

"'Leila, there's the fact that I'm totally neurotic and worry about everything all the time. That's baseline. But there's something I *really* need to tell you about. Be ready to run as fast as you can.' Then I brought her up to date on everything I've told you so far."

"I hope you gave her the short version," Tess wise-cracked. Then, with compassion, she said, "I'm impressed, really. God knows where I fit into this, but it's getting interesting. What did you think she was going to say when you told her you thought people were trying to maim or kill you? *Did* she run?"

VJ stood up for a second, putting his weight on his good knee, and stared out the window into the darkness. The wind was blowing, causing tree branches to scrape against the windowpanes. The sound lent even more creepiness to spending the night in the anatomy lab. He turned back toward Tess, picking up the scalpel she'd threatened him with earlier. Admiring its sleek profile, he turned back toward her and admitted, "I love these. When used correctly, a scalpel's cut is so elegant. Incise too deep, and you're instantly in a world of hurt. Life is that way, right? So much is dependent on how skillfully you handle other people, stress, unexpected events." He laid the instrument back delicately on the table. "I'm really not sure what I expected Leila to say. There was no way I was going to hide what had to be a legitimate threat. I didn't know for sure that the man I saw in the office and his partner really were after me. But to think otherwise would have been naïve.

"Once I finished telling Leila about the Boston guys, I said, 'Now, here I am. Here we are. It's hard to believe these goons came all the way out here to play in the snow and buy barbecue restaurants. My guess is that the Cooperative wants me out of the picture, and whoever's in charge probably thinks this is the perfect place to take care of business. They're right. If I go to the police, my brother will be killed and I'll end up in jail, or dead, or both. No happy ending. I need to get this fixed, and I'm already afraid that you might become a target, too. I can't have that.'

"We got up from the bench and started back down to where we were parked. She ran her hand through that gorgeous hair of hers and measured her words carefully. 'VJ, I honestly don't know what to say to you. I don't usually go out of my way to look for trouble. This sounds like a situation that is much bigger than you and me. Are you sure that someone like the FBI can't help? My dad is pretty connected. I'll call him this second if you want.'

"I put my arm around her waist and steered her back toward the path. 'Thanks for the offer. I wish he could help. I just can't take a chance that Anders might get hurt. I'll work it out.'

"Leila stared at me long and hard. Finally, she said, 'VJ, I need to think about this. Can we go back to town?'

"I answered, 'Leila, I'm just glad you still want to talk to me at all. At this exact moment, though, I've got to put something in my stomach. You have to be hungry, too. What do you say we get something to eat? I make an amazing grilled cheese sandwich. Plus, Johan gave me a bag of his Top Cop Cookies. I'll even let you have a couple.'"

Tess spoke up, "VJ, I can't even believe she was still willing to give you the time of day, much less think about helping you. Then again, you've successfully held me here this whole time. Must be something subliminal in the Swedish accent."

VJ grinned. "Alas, I'm discovered. It was part of my medical school training and the master Swedish plan to take over the planet. Too bad the technique doesn't work on the Cooperative.

"Back to that day. Once we grabbed the truck, we went back to Matt's place, and . . . I won't bore you with the details." Tess snorted. "In any case, we slept for what seemed like a month. Dinner never happened. Fortunately, I didn't get a single call from the ER. Everyone in town was buttoned up at home.

"About two in the morning I woke up and smelled toast. I looked down from the sleeping loft and saw Leila busily making scrambled eggs. She glanced up at me. 'Want something to eat? I'm famished.' The sliding glass door was virtually buried in snow from outside. At that moment, no one could get to us, literally or figuratively.

"I came down and pulled up a stool. 'Leila, I've only gotten to know you for about a day and I think I'm totally in love with you. Is that possible?'

"She smiled. 'Try the food first. You might not feel that way in five minutes.' We devoured the meal and then just sat for a while looking through the upper vaulted windows at the huge snowflakes continuing to fall. Before I went back to sleep, I felt content in a way that's impossible to describe. I've read that new love causes an endorphin rush. This was more than that. Leila was the person I'd been waiting all my life to meet."

VJ sat for a minute, seeming distracted, perhaps pondering the implications of what he had just said out loud.

Tess cleared her throat. "Um, VJ, I'm still here, in case you have forgotten. I can't figure out if I'm in the middle of a love story or some bizarre, quirky thriller."

He answered the question for her. "Actually, both. I'll admit, though, it is definitely not run-of-the-mill. The problem is that the ending of the book isn't written yet. Not even close."

Tess said, "So what you're leading up to really doesn't have a conclusion? But if I understand correctly, I somehow play a big part in this?"

VJ settled back in his chair. "Tess, this crazy series of events is like medical school. Without foundation and context, what follows won't make sense to you. I want you to understand all of it."

Tess sighed. "Patience is not my best virtue. However, if nothing else, the story continues to intrigue me, so go on."

"All my scheduled operative cases became storm casualties. Leila and I discussed a number of possible options moving forward. Probably it was a combination of stupidity and false confidence, but I felt that I had certain advantages being in Sierra Lakes. I knew the town and the people; the Boston guys didn't. I thought that, ironically, hanging around the ski area would be the smartest thing to do. In a storm, you can ski next to your twin brother and not know who it is. The snow was still falling, but the wind had died down enough that the mountain reopened. We both thought it would be nice to get out. Matt's place was near the least used of the entry points, Silver Springs. Getting on the slopes was easy. Within a few minutes we whipped up chair nine, a high-speed six, to Serpent's Tail.

"At the top, I said, 'Hey, are you up for some Type I fun?'

"Leila hesitated, then asked, 'What on earth are you talking about?'

"I explained, 'Type I fun involves going out and doing something that's a blast. Type II fun is what you have when you finish busting your butt to get up a mountain or running a marathon. "Proving you're a hard man" stuff. A lot of the things that you do are Type II even though you think they're Type I.'

"Leila said, 'VJ, that sounds way too complicated. How 'bout if I bust your butt right now? I think that'll be great fun.' With that, she took off, hitting the steep mogul field like a maniac.

"I had my K2 Hellbent powder skis. Love 'em. I scrambled to catch up, and finally passed Leila halfway down the run. Like an idiot I turned to gloat, promptly caught an edge, and did a full yard sale—skis and poles spread everywhere. For a second I didn't move. Leila skied over to see if I'd done the Cooperative's

169

work for them. I grabbed the neon-yellow coat she was wearing and pulled her down with me into the soft, deep powder.

"She said, 'VJ, skiing is much easier if you keep your skis on your feet.' With that, she mashed a big handful of snow in my face.

"I managed to stay upright for the next few runs. The wind gusts kicked up, and the top of the mountain closed. At least chair twenty-two was still running. Even if gale-force winds are pounding every other lift, it's frequently calm for most of the ride. That is, except for the last part, when it can feel like a hurricane. Despite my optimism, we were hammered by snow pellets. The tree skiing would make it worthwhile.

"Dark, angry clouds hung over the peaks that surrounded us like a cloak. Leila buried her head in my coat, and I forgot the weather. Once we got off the lift, we found completely untracked terrain. Our skis moved silently through the powder as we carved down the face and hit the forest. Floating over a fresh snow dump is virtually impossible to beat. I wanted this run to last forever; it was pure magic. Skiing takes us places we rarely experience otherwise. Outside in the woods, howling wind, driving snow. It's the essence of natural beauty."

Tess grumbled, "Sounds like another routine winter day in Boston to me."

VJ said, "Seriously, Tess, it's amazingly pretty. Something entertaining happened just as

170

we were getting ready to stop. The call of nature struck Leila. We were in a remote area not even vaguely close to the lodge. Out of nowhere a snowboarder whizzed by. He let out a shout when he got a full view of Leila as she was reorganizing her ski pants. She didn't seem startled. Apparently he was. He ran into a tree well and went down like a heap. It was my turn to find out if the kid was broken. He couldn't get up and get away fast enough. Before the words 'Are you OK?' could leave my mouth, he was gone.

"Leila asked, 'VJ, do you think he's going to recognize my coat if he sees me later?'

"I laughed. 'Leila, you just made his month. Judging by how quickly he blew out of here, I doubt he'd ever say anything to you.' I looked at my watch. It was already nearly four o'clock—closing time.

"We went back to the top of chair twenty-two for the final run and surveyed the mountain. It was bliss, a moment to hold on to. Leila grabbed my coat and said, 'Do you want to keep going or just hang around here being an old man?' With that she pushed me so I'd lose my balance, and took off. Leila seemed to effortlessly glide down. I followed her turns, focusing on the joy of her presence and my luck in finding her. It didn't stop me from converting the last half of the run back to chair fifteen into a balls-to-the-wall downhill race. Few sensations match racing down the mountain at breakneck speed.

"About thirty seconds or so after I made it to the bottom, Leila joined me. She took off her skis, put her arms around me, and said, 'You do know turning is an actual part of skiing. It can even be fun. Have you ever tried it?'

"I answered honestly, 'I don't believe in it. Why turn if you don't have to?'

"Once we got back, I took stock of our rations. There wasn't much food left in Matt's fridge, so I volunteered to hit the Goodfare Food Center. Leila came down hard against that choice. She was out the door before I had a chance to realize I'd lost the argument. While I thought it was even more unlikely that the Boston pair would be shopping for food than skiing in the backcountry, it was hard to disagree with her logic. I'd mentioned to her during the day that the one thing I make well, other than cereal, is spinach lasagna. When she returned with the food, I started constructing the meal. While prepping, I was talking and didn't hear any responses. I turned around and saw Leila asleep on the couch. Studying the way her chest rose and fell with each breath, I realized yet again how fortunate I was to have found her, and how much I wanted to keep her. Just before I was about to take the lasagna out of the oven, I felt two hands slip around my waist. I have to say, the sense of well-being I experienced at that moment will be something I'll always remember."

Tess couldn't hold back. "VJ, for God's sake, you were convinced someone at best was trying to hurt you, and you're goofing off playing house."

VJ shrugged his shoulders. "I know it's hard to understand. Don't get the wrong idea, my problems were on my mind. It's not like we weren't talking about solutions. We were. A perfect one wasn't obvious. Whether it was smart to do or not, I had to compartmentalize what was happening. Anyway, my hand was forced pretty quickly."

THE HITTERS

"The next morning I didn't have anything scheduled, and I'd forgotten a few things from my house. I figured this was as good or bad a time as any to swing by and pick them up. It also seemed reasonable to do a little recon. Maybe I was wrong about the whole thing. Maybe these guys were just a pair of knuckleheads with no designs on me and no connection with the Cooperative, but I certainly wasn't going to take any chances.

"The snow was coming down hard and blowing sideways. With the windchill, it was probably ten below. I bundled up, covering virtually every inch of my face. I borrowed Matt's all-black parka and face shield. I knew the Boston thugs were staying at the Miner's Lodge. The ongoing storm was likely making them go stir-crazy. If they weren't on the mountain, there wouldn't be that many places for them to venture. I wandered through the shops, looking for things I'd buy in the summer when they went on sale, but keeping my eyes open. After about an hour, I saw the men in their dark leather jackets as they emerged from the Starbucks. I tried to get close enough to hear snippets of their conversation without them noticing. So much for that. The shorter one glanced my way without any sign of recognition and said, 'Whatah yah looking at, yah fuckin' asswipe? Get the fuck outtah heah.'

"I did as I was told and walked quickly to the parking lot to grab the garage door clicker from my truck. It was my only way into the house, since I'd left my house keys at Matt's and had already removed the lockbox key."

Tess quizzically looked at me. "VJ, wouldn't it have made sense to just have your police friend Johan ask them questions and rattle their cages a little bit? Maybe scare them off."

VJ responded, "Perhaps. Obviously, I still didn't know if there was a plan to go after me or not. I remained convinced that anything I did to stir the pot might harm Anders. I decided to walk around the condos across the street. From that vantage point, I thought I would be able to tell if they were casing my place.

"There weren't any tracks from the driveway to the front door, but that didn't mean much. With the snow falling, anything would be covered in minutes. Seeing no one, I started up the recently plowed street. Even though I was trying to be careful, I found an ice patch under the snow with my boot, slipped, and fell hard on my forearm and hand—the one with the clicker in it. A thunderous explosion shook the ground. I looked up and saw the porno neighbor's garage blown to bits and his house on fire. Luckily, I was far enough away so I avoided getting hit by shrapnel. I looked myself over, decided I wasn't hurt, then got the hell out of there. I no longer cared the least bit about anything in the house.

"As I was cutting back around the condos, I heard sirens screaming. Blasts aren't common in Sierra Lakes. A big crowd formed within minutes. Two men standing near the front had a smug look on their faces. You can guess who they were. Then there was a murmur, and soon everyone standing there knew it was the porno king's house that was on fire. Apparently he was still in LA. I saw the smaller of my Boston friends slugging his brother. They'd gotten the wrong house and rigged my perverted neighbor's place. It was easy to understand, since the houses were so similar, and with all the snow, none of the addresses were visible. At the same time, it was pathetically funny. They'd had their chance and blown it—literally and figuratively. It was my turn."

Tess interjected, "Jesus, VJ, dirtbags trying to blow you up—that's pretty sobering. I can't believe it went down like that."

"Just as I described. The whole scene was totally nuts. It's one of the reasons I'm here tonight talking to you. I absolutely need you to understand the reality of all this. Those two were not playing games.

"Once I did get back to Matt's, Leila rushed up and gave me a hug the instant she saw my face. She could tell I was unnerved. But I was also massively pissed off. She said, 'I heard that explosion and all I could think was that you were hurt. You're bleeding. Were you there?' I hadn't even noticed blood running down my hand. The clicker must have dug into my palm when I fell.

"I sat on one of the kitchen chairs and invited her to do the same. 'Yes, I was there. The explosion was actually my fault.'

"As I explained, I watched Leila's face transition from concern to anger to resolve in a manner of minutes. She took my hand and looked directly into my eyes. She reached for my face, then gave me the most intense, passionate kiss I've ever experienced. Her words were deliberate. 'So what are we going to do now?'

"For a minute, I was actually speechless, if you can imagine that. I was trying to process what was happening. Ultimately I said, 'I'm not sure what to tell you. I did hear the part about *we*. What does *we* mean to you?'

"Leila didn't hesitate. '*We* means you and me. *We* means I intend to help you. *We* means we don't let the guys who are after you win. Jumping into this mess with you makes no sense. I know that. Maybe I'm crazy, but being with you seems right, VJ. Don't ask me why. I'm not an innocent. I've met good people and bad people. Getting on this train may be really idiotic and dangerous, but I'm willing to take the risk. So, I'll ask you again—what are *we* going to do now?'"

Tess looked excited. "So you did get her to help. Staggering that two guys trying to blow you up did the trick. That would normally scare any sane person away."

VJ stared in the distance. "You're right. Leila is hardly standard issue. There's no question that some of those events I told you about pushed her to help me. I'm really fortunate.

"As the morning turned into afternoon we talked a lot, but I had already decided on the only path that I thought I could take. 'Leila, settling my problem is going to require resolve and getting dirty. Extremely dirty. Gloves off, total war. I mean, there is no way to make these two guys go away without making them permanently go away. Are you sure you're on board for that?'

"But Leila was now as determined as I was to remove the threat posed by the two assassins. She almost looked through me with those green eyes of hers. 'VJ, if I were you, I'd refuse to look over my shoulder every second of the rest of my life. I'll support you, whatever it takes.'"

Tess had been listening intently. All of a sudden, she shot out of her chair. "Hold on, though, VJ. Are you saying what I think you're saying?"

He looked at her in all earnestness and said, "Pretty much, yes."

Tess sat down again. "I guess the Hippocratic Oath and the 'First, do no harm' thing both go out the window when someone's trying to kill you. You had to do what needed to be done. Still, I've never been involved in a conversation like this before. It feels more and more like *The Twilight Zone*."

VJ massaged his knee. "I was living it and I couldn't believe it. No one who isn't in the military or law enforcement should ever have to. This insanity became my reality."

Tess looked worried. "Should it be time for me to leave? You told me Bianka knows none of this—correct?"

"You're right," VJ answered. "I had to keep her in the dark. Your case is different. I won't hold you here, but I'm fairly comfortable and want you to listen to what comes next."

She settled in again. "So how *exactly* did you deal with those assassins? I'm not even going to ask how I fit in."

He took a deep breath. "Leila and I camped out for the rest of the day and evening in the house. We bounced ideas off each other and finally agreed on something we thought would work. For once, everything I learned in the military was going to be useful. Those instincts had taken over. To defend myself I had to go into battle. I also had the weirdest sense that Burch's guiding hand was on my shoulder.

"First thing the next morning I threw my cross-country skis into the back of the truck and drove to the hospital. I parked behind the ER and more or less snuck in through the side entrance to the office. The narrow pathway was flanked by seven-foot walls of snow on either side. I wore the borrowed black parka with a face mask to walk in, then changed to my bright red jacket once I entered the doors downstairs.

"While working through my short patient list, I told the whole staff that I'd be out in the Meadow after one o'clock. Of course, I wasn't positive, but I thought there was a high probability the killers would be trying to find me. I made it clear that texts would be OK if anyone needed me, particularly since I was still covering the ER. Funny thing, worrying about ER responsibilities while being engaged in a life-and-death situation. Once a doctor, always a doctor. Because of the weather, KD thought I was crazy to even think about going cross-country skiing. That said, she knew how obsessed I'd become and that changing my mind would be impossible. It's the Sierra way. I was definitely prepared and completely resolute.

"I had the elements and firepower on my side. I didn't relish what I envisioned happening, but the alternative—me taking two to the head or getting dismembered in another explosion—had even less appeal. I had no intention of making this an honorable fight. They needed to go, and I had to take them without anyone knowing, least of all them. My big backyard was perfect. I just needed to lure them there.

"For obvious reasons my concentration was poor that day. The highway was open again, so there were more people to see. I did my best to pretend that I was engaged in the conversations I was having. I wasn't successful. More than once, a patient asked me if I'd heard what they'd said. Thank God it wasn't a surgical day.

"My mind wandered. What would've happened if Nick hadn't called me that night? What if I hadn't answered my phone? I was tired of the whole thing. I'd called to let Leila know that the plan was moving forward. We'd agreed that if she didn't hear from me, she was to alert Nick, the Sierra Police Department, the Mono County sheriff's office, the Boston Police Department, and the FBI. Anders would get scooped up. All eyes would be on business at MRMC."

INTERNAL COMBUSTION

Having failed to take out Brio with the explosion, the Luciano brothers conspired to kill him with plan B. What plan B was had been the source of a daylong argument that at one point almost again led to blows between them. Ultimately, they decided to camp out by the orthopaedic clinic in their rental car and ambush the sneaky bastard. They'd already called the clinic and verified Brio was working. They were going to get him this time. It was just a matter of waiting. No doubt about it.

With the snow blowing sideways, seeing anything was a challenge. After they went through two packs of cigarettes, good fortune intervened. Lucca spotted a person who looked like Brio driving away from the vicinity of the hospital in a truck. They gunned the engine and started to follow. Their car smashed into a snowbank, but careened back onto the road. The Lucianos cared little about the new huge dent in the front fender. Now they had a matching set. They reacquired sight of Brio's truck at the four-way stop by the Goodfare Food Center. Lucca worked the action of the precision bolt gun lying across his lap.

VJ DROPS THE HAMMER

"Finally I was done. I left the hospital via the ER without seeing either of the men, then drove by the Goodfare, where the snow was creeping over the roof. Yellow signs were everywhere, warning of the danger of ice shedding onto people's heads. The tree branches carried a similar load. Walk in the wrong place and you were likely to never emerge. It was crazy—the weather, the situation, the plan—everything. I passed Jake's snowmobile rental. He had a huge banner outside making sure everyone knew there was something fun to do if the mountain was closed. I found a spot by Sherwood Creek Road and parked. The roaring wind whistling through the Meadow accentuated the sense of danger I was already feeling. Doubts started to creep in. I asked myself for the umpteenth time, *Is this the dumbest plot ever conceived?*

"The answer came quickly. I had all my ski equipment on and was ready to set out. A wind gust hit me and nearly knocked me down. At the same moment, the driver's-side window of my truck shattered from the bullet directed at me. Another shot followed almost immediately, taking out the side mirror. With my rifle slung across my shoulder, I took off across the parking lot into the Meadow like a bolt of lightning.

"My goggles fogged, and the snow collecting on them made seeing an adventure. Between the wind, the snow, and the goggles, I was getting a little disoriented, but I was flying. I lucked out. In that instant, the snow really started to dump. There was no way they'd be able to see two feet in front of themselves. Somehow I'd screwed it up, but they'd missed their shot—again. Either their poor aim or the wind had saved me. I'd convinced myself the contract killers were out of their league—city boys used to small firearms. I wasn't sure what they'd used to shoot at me.

"Now it was my turn. Mentally, I was as focused as I've ever been. I'd already figured they'd have to rent a snowmobile to come after me. Since I was tipped off, I knew they didn't have a choice. They had to get me now. If they bungled the kill again, they'd be finished in Boston—or worse. I had a good head start. I needed it to get ready.

"The snow briefly lightened up—thankfully. It was critical for the killers to find me. But the wind continued to be relentless, buffeting me, pounding my covered face with particles of debris. I'm used to blizzards from all the years in Stockholm and Boston. I still find them fascinating, though. There's a unique sense of solitude created by a storm. This wasn't one of those times.

"The roar of the snowmobile engine was considerably dampened by the elements, but I still picked up the distinctive sound. I skied to a place that was relatively open and hung my coat on a nearby tree as a decoy. I was now covered head to toe in combat winter whites—a remnant of my days in the Swedish military. I located my nest and settled in. There I watched with my binoculars. Soon the machine came into view. I actually laughed. Both of these guys were still wearing their black dress shoes. The rifle slung across the back-seat rider's shoulder answered the weapon question. I could tell it was a Remington 700 SPS in 6.5 Creedmore. A nice piece. I had to respect what it might do to me.

"From their shift in direction, I could tell the ruse was working. They were headed straight for the red jacket. The snowmobile stopped for a moment. I watched as the guy in the rear stepped off, gathered himself, and snapped off two rounds at my coat. I wasn't sure if the lack of response made them suspicious or not, but they got back on the Polaris and continued down the path I wanted them to take. Seeing the assassins try to kill me again extinguished the little voice in the back of my head saying I should find a different way to resolve this conflict.

"Out loud, I said to myself, 'There are a thousand ways to die in the Sierras. I'm just

going to help these guys with one of them.'
Maintaining my advantage was critical. I trained
my sight on the driver and steadied the gun. *This*
was the other item I made sure to take with me
that day I brought Steve to the house. I told
myself, *Breathe, slow and deep. Exhale. Ready,
ready—now squeeze the trigger.* Firing the .17
HMR, I had to be sure they were close enough.
The bullet caught the man just above his right
eye. His face ceased to exist. Pink mist. He was
no longer a problem for me or the penal system.

"The snowmobile twisted, and the other
hitter was thrown near the woods. He clearly had
little idea what was happening, but
understandably decided it wasn't good. Before I
could sight and get the next round off, he was in
cover. Now, I was the hunter and not the hunted.
This turn of the tables appealed to me.

"I knew the area well. Just behind the
stand of trees was another open space. I decided
to circle around and wait. With this amount of
snow he wasn't going to make better time in
street shoes than I would on cross-country skis.
I took my time and got mentally settled, just as I
do when I tackle a challenging case, like Nick's
replant. Lose your cool and you fail. Not today.
With a nice even pace, I worked my way through
the elements.

"The snow started up again and the
visibility got worse. I thought about just leaving
the guy out there alone. The overwhelming odds

were that that'd be enough. But I asked myself: If he did somehow get out alive, how safe would Anders be? Or would the guy call in a new army to come after me in Sierra Lakes? The obsessive-compulsive hand surgeon part of me screamed, *No—complete the task or you'll regret it forever.* I simply refused to accept the immediate threat. There was no way in hell this lowlife assassin was going to do anything but take a dirt nap, courtesy of me, thank you very much.

"As silently as possible, I skied to a small overlook where I figured I could best locate the prey I was now tracking. I waited. I started to get antsy, thinking I'd completely miscalculated. Then I detected movement. I raised my gun and aimed carefully, waiting just an instant more to be sure.

"Unfortunately, right then, one of the relentless blasts of wind knocked a large clump of snow onto the HMR barrel. The shot struck a tree just to the left of the man's head. He turned, and gunshots rang out now in my direction. I dove for cover. Though he was shooting wildly, the man still could've killed me. I cursed at myself for letting him back in the game. If I didn't take him out, it wouldn't be long before I'd be on the receiving end of the Remington. In fact, something was now stinging in my leg. I dropped down and saw him running back toward cover. I steadied the HMR and got the round off quickly.

"This time I didn't miss. I saw his left shoulder jerk backward. He fell to the ground, then struggled to get back on his feet. Just as he steadied himself, the next bullet entered the right side of his chest. Blood poured through his jacket. His future looked rosy and not, all at once. I knew he was toast. Slowly I walked toward the man, keeping my gun trained on him every second of the way.

"As I got close, I watched the blood continue to spread on his coat. He had the same look of terror that Nick must have had. The man seemed to decide that maybe I'd try to save him. At that point, the reality was that he was done. I peered at him through the slits in my face mask. 'Hurts, doesn't it?' I said. 'It's strange about lungs. You wouldn't think they'd be so painful. A lot of it is the rib fracture. Very densely innervated. Those intercostal nerves are a bitch when we put in chest tubes. I have a few questions. Who paid you to come? Was it Rick?'

"He panted for breath. 'Man, I don't know anything. The Cooperative gave us fifty K to kill you. My brother did the deal. That's it.'

"I had no reason to disbelieve him, nor did I think he was going to know anything more in the near or long term. The developing hemopneumothorax wasn't giving him a lot of time. The breaths grew shorter; his mouth was moving, but the words stopped. Then his mouth stopped moving, too. As a physician, I thought I should feel some element of remorse. I didn't. I was just numb and relieved. I won. They lost. This time. I could worry about other feelings later. With my immediate problem eliminated, I looked down at my leg. There was a stick impaling my calf. No bullet hole. I yanked it out, making a mental note to clean the wound later."

Tess' eyes were popping out of her head. "VJ, you really *did* off those two assholes. I mean, you *really did*. Holy shit!" She started pacing, then looked at him. "I don't blame you at all, you did what you had to do. But talking about it and actually doing it are two different things. It's hard to wrap my brain around." VJ held up a hand to say something, but she just shook her head and kept right on. "In case you're worried, no one I know will hear about what you just told me. Would I kill the guy who killed my parents to prevent him from killing them if I could? Yes, without hesitation. Still, it's probably not the message you want getting out there in social media—quasi-premeditated self-defense killing. It's an interesting question, but I don't think you want to test the courts on that issue."

VJ breathed a relieved sigh. "Tess, I had to tell you all this. I was hoping that you'd see it from my viewpoint. Something else happened to me about five years ago that pushed me. A patient I'd operated on for a wrist fracture became a paranoid schizophrenic. He decided that the plate I put in was a mark of the devil.

189

One day I was walking to my office and was treated to seeing DIE JEW KIKE! painted in bright yellow on the stairs. I got a restraining order, but there was nothing else I could do. There wasn't a day that I didn't look over my shoulder worrying that the guy would act on his threat. Too many doctors have really been killed by people like this. It just happened to some guy in the Midwest. That feeling of impotence is horrible. Eventually the schizophrenic patient moved across the country, so I was off the hook. Leaving this unfinished wasn't a choice."

Tess regarded VJ solemnly. "What did you do with them?"

"I'd planned for that. The blood would be covered by the new snow in under an hour. The casings lay in a three-foot arc to the right of where I shot. I gathered them up, but didn't worry too much about whether I might have missed one. It wasn't like no one else in Sierra Lakes had ever fired a gun. With all the biathletes and hunters, I'm shocked that we don't see an accidental shooting once a week in the ER.

"There was one small issue: I couldn't find the gun that the man fired at me. I figured he'd lost it in the snow after I nailed him. I've had the same problem finding skis in deep powder. Casings didn't worry me, but I couldn't exactly leave a big rifle sitting there. I finally felt what I was searching for with my ski pole and breathed a sigh of relief."

Tess frowned. "So, I'm thinking this through. You couldn't just leave them there. Even I know that would create too many questions when they were found."

VJ nodded. "You're absolutely right. Disposal of the two corpses and the incriminating bullets was the next planned step. They were all about to evaporate together. My original plan involved strapping them one at a time around my waist and towing them in snowboard bags I stashed on a small sled. The sled and the bags were left in the truck when I got fired on. The snowmobile solved my problem. The bigger assassin got slung over the passenger seat. I attached body two to the back of the Polaris WideTrak and hauled both at the same time. By now it was dark, so I was less concerned about being seen. The hospital incinerator for medical waste wasn't far. I figured Johnny, who ran the place, would have called it a day early.

"Jackpot. The incinerator site was deserted. The snowmobile's engine noise was a non-issue. Not only had Johnny absconded, he'd left the door open. He was reliably unreliable—a good guy, but Johnny and Jack Daniel's are close pals. I think everyone figures one day he's going to accidently disappear into that furnace himself.

"I rifled through the killers' wallets to see if there were contact numbers or anything else that might help me. I found the keycards to their room at the Miner's Lodge, still in their envelopes. Their names were Armaceo and Lucca Luciano. Brothers in crime and death. I set about the business of loading the bodies into the furnace. I struggled, but within a minute the Lucianos were finished, along with my bullet-ridden red coat. The irony of the two of them burning in the fires of hell was not lost on me. Ashes to ashes. Even if a couple of bone pieces remained, they'd never be seen.

"When I was satisfied the task was complete, I took the snowmobile back out and left it just a few hundred yards from my truck. I called Jake at Sierra Outdoor Adventures with my cell phone. My number comes up as no caller ID, so it was safe. Doing my best Boston accent, I growled, 'Yah rented us this piece ah shit that just stopped workin'. It's fuckin' wicked cold out here, yah fuckin' fuck. Come get this yahself. It's sittin' by the road.'

"Jake yelled back, 'Luciano, you moron. I knew you wouldn't know how to use a snow-go. Did the engine flood? If you just leave it, I'm going to charge you triple! What road?'

"I almost laughed as I said, 'Chahge whatevah you want, ass-dick, just pick it up.' I didn't care if Jake levied the freshly dead for a whole new snowmobile. The credit card folks would have to pick up the tab. Screw it. I'm not too fond of them, either. They never miss an opportunity to hose me. Do you think the Cooperative may also be running the airline, rental car, and credit card companies? You can't rule it out."

Tess commented, "Now you're bagging on the credit card people after you just told me you wasted two guys and promptly burned them to a crisp. You are absolutely the strangest, most unfocused person I've ever met." She glanced around the cavernous lab, rubbing her arms. Both of them were sitting in the worn-out roller chairs they'd claimed hours earlier. It hadn't gotten any warmer.

VJ found the edge of a table, pushed himself up on his good leg, and grabbed a lab jacket hanging nearby. As he handed it to her, he said, "It looks big, but it should help you warm up."

Tess thanked VJ, then asked, "I'm not judging. I'm asking. Does it bother you now that you killed two people?"

He answered sincerely, "You may be disappointed in me, but no, it doesn't. I've asked the same question to some of the military people I take care of. They've told me the same thing. They were doing what was necessary to protect their fellow troops and themselves. I look at this the same way."

Tess said, "I'm not disappointed—a little worried about hanging out with you, but not disappointed."

VJ's face softened. "By the way, I really don't want to have to do that again. I will if I have to, though. I'm not even a violent person. I have a bad temper, but I usually take out my aggression on inanimate objects like phones and doors."

Tess smiled. "I have that problem, too. So, what did you do next?"

"When I finally got to my truck, I was totally drained. Even though I knew that the best thing to do was to leave, I just sat there like a lump for a few minutes, watching the snowflakes drifting through the shattered window. I felt about the same way I did after doing Nick's replants. I'd already called Leila and told her that I was OK and that the other guys weren't. When I did get going, I don't think my brain was working yet. I almost drove directly into one of the unique Sierra Lakes snowplows. I refer to them as Plowasaurus Rex. Fortunately, I swerved at the last minute and avoided a pathetically ironic fate. Dodge the bullets of contract killers, die at the hands of a savage machine. These plows have menacing blades that grind through snow and anything else in their path. Once they build up momentum, forget stopping them. Cars, people, whatever. If it gets in the way, it's history.

"I managed to negotiate the rest of the short drive back to Matt's without hurting myself or anyone else. Leila was waiting on the porch, bundled up like an Eskimo. She didn't say anything. She didn't have to. I held her as tightly as I could. There was one more detail I needed to address before I could close the book on the Luciano brothers, but I decided it could wait.

"The next morning, I drove to my house, stopping the truck twenty yards away. I tested the clicker ten times to watch the garage door open and close without blowing up. I pulled in, carefully dodging the center support beams holding up the garage, as well as the stacked wood, bikes, canoe, sawhorse, and other items lying around. Most of the dents in my truck are the result of me not being able to do this. One day, I know I'm going to crash into that damn beam and the ceiling is going to come down on my head.

"I checked out the front door. It seemed OK. I spent about an hour going through the house to make sure nothing was booby-trapped. Once I was finally satisfied, I walked across the street to the Miner's Lodge to see if there was anything tying the Lucianos to me in their hotel room, and to simultaneously clear it out. I wanted it to look like they just decided to leave. What if the brothers were reported missing? The last thing I needed was someone from the sheriff or police department thinking the pair were still in town or that something had happened to them. Unfortunately, the final part of the room number got wiped out in the snow. I could tell the floor and the wing. I worried I was going to get screwed because I couldn't figure out which bloody room they were in.

"An idea came to me. I went up to the floor, found a house phone, and called the operator. Again, with my best Boston accent, I said, "Lucca Spahriglio, please."

"The operator rang the phone as requested. From the end of the hall, I could make out the general vicinity of the noise. I called the desk back to get them to ring the room again.

"I followed the noise. I was in a hallway with six rooms. Close enough. After trying multiple doors, the magic green light went on. Almost nothing was there—a couple of small bags, junk food, packs of cigarettes, condoms. Pathetic, really. Who'd they think they were going to find to sleep with here? Fortunately, it wasn't a problem I was going to have to worry about; it just intrigued me on an intellectual level. Their stuff would be easy to toss in the garbage dumpster. I'd already dismantled the Remington and distributed the components in multiple bins.

"Plane tickets were sitting on the small kitchen counter. I called the airline from their room phone and cancelled their reservations. It looked like they'd flown in to Reno, but intended to depart out of Sierra Lakes. My actions moved up their actual departure time, so their seats were now open. There were plenty of reasonable people who'd love to fill their airline seats. I caught myself in the absurdity of the situation. Here I'd killed two people, but I was assisting the travel needs of some visitors who would get a plane that probably wouldn't work or take off in the first place."

Tess applauded. "I'll give this to you, VJ. You're thorough. A lot of other things, too, but definitely thorough."

VJ said, "I'm telling you, Tess, life is like the operating room. If every step isn't taken correctly, the procedure fails. Even when it comes to axing murderers."

"I'll be sure to remember that during my surgical rotation." She smiled. "Any other pearls about snuffing people that you want to share?"

He grinned sardonically. "You should have it all now. You know the saying in medical school—see one, do one, teach one."

"Okay, I'll check that one off my list." Then she became very serious. "Those two guys were gone, but obviously the Cooperative still had to be after you. Or did they think you were dead?"

"You're one hundred percent right. I was dead, then I wasn't, then I was again. Actually, I wasn't officially dead until yesterday. But I'll get to that," he said, leaving Tess baffled. "The threat in Sierra Lakes was over, but living with the one here in Boston was now going to be completely untenable. Did you ever see that movie *The Fugitive*?"

Tess nodded.

VJ went on. "That's how I've felt. I wasn't going to get my life back until I settled things here. But it wasn't like I was in a rush. I still had no good idea what I was going to do next.

"I lucked out. For once Burch succumbed to the mortal world of reasonable decision-making. Rather than persisting through the blizzard, he'd cut his trip short and volunteered to take the call he'd so graciously bestowed upon me. I didn't argue. The man card that I was so vigilantly protecting was no longer an issue. I figured I'd earned a platinum membership.

"Leila and I used the next few days we had together in Sierra Lakes to really get to know each other. It gave me a chance to slightly decompress and introduce her to some friends, too. Part of getting to understand someone is finding out who they spend time with, and I had the perfect couple nearby.

"Daniel and Mirya are both amazing people. Like me, they live in Sierra Lakes part time. Mirya runs a green certification company and has been active promoting sustainable business practices for decades. Daniel is an autodidact—super curious and a self-taught expert in just about any subject that interests him. He can convert an ordinary piece of lumber into an extraordinary dresser or turned bowl.

They travel everywhere, so the pictures in their house are incredible. On top of it all, they share ownership in a winery in Napa, producing top-notch artisanal wines under the Miss Olivia Brion label. I'll get you a case. After tonight you deserve it. Needless to say, we went through a few bottles when we had dinner one of the evenings after the excitement in the Meadow.

"Daniel isn't shy, particularly when he's a little drunk. We were sitting at their table, too full to move after a delicious meal and decadent chocolate mousse dessert, talking about the storm. Out of nowhere he says, 'OK, guys, I need information. Leila, tell me about the weirdest person you ever slept with.'

"Without hesitating, Leila pointed directly at me and said, 'Was there some doubt in your mind?'

"Daniel considered momentarily and passed judgment. 'Never.' He looked in my direction. 'VJ, your turn.'

"Even three sheets to the wind, I thought answering would be a poor choice. 'Forget that—let's play Cards Against Humanity.'

"Daniel wouldn't let it go. 'We're all grown-ups here, VJ. Nobody will get offended if you tell us she was a Republican. Oh, sorry, VJ, have you become one of those?'

"Leila turned toward me and raised her eyebrows. 'Yes, VJ, why don't you tell us about whoever *that* was. It's not like we haven't shared a lot these past few days.' She gave me a knowing glance.

"I shook my head no and squeezed her hand. 'Later, sweetheart.' I decided it was better to call it a night. 'Daniel, Mirya, I love you both, but my eyes aren't going to stay open for five more minutes. Maybe we can connect on the mountain tomorrow. Is McCue's at eleven alright?' We exchanged hugs. Fortunately, the walk home is only about two blocks. On our way, the clouds parted and the stars were shining brighter than you can imagine, Orion the Hunter high in the sky aiming his mighty bow at Taurus the Bull in the eternal stance of predator and prey. The Milky Way arced overhead. It was nice to have the stars aligned on my side, if only for a short time."

Tess stopped him. "You dodged Daniel's question. I'm surprised Leila didn't push you further on it. What are you hiding from her? You know that's not a good idea early in a relationship."

VJ said, "Every conversation has a time and a place. That wasn't the time or the place."

Tess pushed: "So, how 'bout you tell *me*?"

He took a deep breath. "Tess, take my word for it. It's not worth your time."

She wouldn't take no for an answer. "Look, VJ, you've piqued my interest. You think that anything's going to faze me after what you just told me about the two assassins? Guess again.

You owe it to me. Besides, it sounds entertaining."

VJ apparently decided there was no way he was going to win this battle. "All right, Tess, feel free to cut me off any time you want. It was not on the list of things I intended to tell you about. This is sordid. Take my word for it. The person I'm going to describe to you is different. I'll keep it short.

"During my last rotation at Duke I was getting destroyed in the coronary care unit. Four of us shared call. That was before there were rules about how many hours students and residents could stay in the hospital. Thirty-six hours on, twelve hours off. I developed a moderate crush on the student I was paired with, Danika Kakikis. She was different—wouldn't take shit from anyone.

"There was a story going around that one of the attendings was hitting on her and decided it was in bounds to touch places he shouldn't. Arrogant man, poor choice. Better research would've revealed that Danika could kickbox. He nearly lost a testicle—no kidding. I can't explain it, but she intrigued me. Probably the bad-girl reputation.

"Most of the time we spoke superficially. During a call night we were just talking. I was fiddling with my stethoscope as usual because I didn't really know what else to do with it. My pathetic inability to discriminate lung, heart, and abdominal sounds makes the instrument most effective for patient care when it's draped around my neck. I decided to ask Danika more about herself. It seemed like as good an opportunity as I'd ever get. I said something innocuous like 'Where do you like to go out?'

"Danika started talking, but she seemed indifferent to my presence and the question. 'There was this off-campus frat party I went to one time,' she began. 'The place was a sewer, but everyone knew you could score anything you wanted there. Why else go? The police chose that night of all nights to conduct a raid. The neighbors had been complaining, so the cops wanted to make an example of us. Believe it or not, they showed up with a paddy wagon, walked straight into the house, then cuffed and arrested a dozen of us for underage drinking.'

"Danika was clearly on a roll, and didn't wait for my reaction. 'When they put our group in the van, a couple of the girls were bawling like five-year-olds. I think the officers were pissed because I wasn't reacting. At the station, there were two holding cells. One obviously held students; the other, town drunks and druggies. The second tank was kind of rough. That's where they put me, maybe just to see what would happen.

"'The show went differently than they expected. Some bitch got in my face and started to push me. Not cool. I broke her arm. Her radius and ulna were sticking through her skin, and she was bleeding like stuck pig. That seemed to bother the guys keeping an eye on us. One of them puked, and the other dude pissed himself. I was moved to the cell with my friends. We were held till the next morning.

"'Surprise, surprise, the house invasion was completely unconstitutional. Too many lawyer parents for the police to contend with. They miscalculated. The whole affair blew up in their face. It was in the paper for a while. Big settlement. I told my mom what happened. I might as well have told her I went to the store and boosted some ice cream. She told me to try to stay out of trouble. Thanks for that great advice, Mom. It should be really useful the next time I'm locked in a small room filled with maniacs.'"

VJ stopped for a moment to massage his knee again, then went on. "I was still processing the part about her converting the lady's forearm into matchsticks. Her tone and the expressions on her face told me that there was nothing in her story that was made up. I started to ask her something, but she just kept going. 'I did get busted once for misdemeanor possession. They gave me forty hours of community service and agreed to wipe the record clean if I swore I'd be good. My job was to rake leaves outside the Ronald McDonald House. I found a pogo stick that one of the kids left outside.

"'Why not teach myself how to do it? Certainly beats raking. The house administrator was watching me the whole time. When he called me in to talk to me about my lack of compliance, I sweet-talked him and stuck my tits in his face. My pogo career was safe. You know, Brio, I usually get what I want. Right now my boyfriend is being a total asshole. What do you say we get naked and fuck?'"

"Jeez," Tess said. "That's direct."

"Remember, that was before residency, when I still had a first name and last name. Those weren't the words I was expecting to hear. I should've known better. It's not like there weren't loud warning bells in my head. I told you before, I was completely mesmerized. Being pursued is unfamiliar territory. It's now happened exactly once.

"I did what you'd expect. I instantly agreed. Balanced impulse control is not my strongest asset. During our rotation I hadn't been subtle about letting Danika know I was interested. I still have no idea what she thought of me. The boyfriend *was* a dick, so I didn't feel any obligation to him. At that moment, we were free.

"After I got over the shock of the invitation, we searched for an empty call room and jumped into it. Danika grabbed me and *bam!* She was every male's dream and nightmare at the same time. There was never a doubt that she was

204

calling the shots. It was eye-opening. I won't say the actual sex part wasn't great—it was. The experience was very strange, though. I felt like an actor in a play. I was there to do what Danika wanted done. If it wasn't me, it would have been someone else. When we finished, she jumped in the shower, threw on her scrubs, and went back to the CCU. The fireworks were done. Within two minutes of getting back to the unit there was a code. We were successful. One family was going to keep their father for another day. The resident gave us full credit for saving the patient's life. Amazing night.

"Thirty-six hours later, I saw Danika and her man walking through the garden holding hands. To this day I can't comprehend what she saw in him. Maybe it was just because he did what Danika told him to do. A few weeks later, I returned to Sweden. It wouldn't have mattered if I'd stayed. I was nothing to her, and the encounter we'd had was strange enough that I didn't want to repeat it."

Tess raised her eyebrows. "Have to say I didn't see that coming. Did you ever cross paths again?"

VJ shook his head no. "It's not that I was emotionally scarred. Still, it's probably better that I didn't see her. I would've just been embarrassed and felt bad about myself. I hadn't thought about that night for a long time until Daniel brought up the question. Now it's stuck in my brain. Please don't judge me too harshly. Also do me a favor—be careful with the people you meet in school and at the hospital. Just because someone's wearing a white coat doesn't mean you can totally trust them. There are more predators out there than you think."

Tess said with an audible hint of sadness, "VJ, you sound like my dad, but thanks. I hate to be reminded that I should have less faith in humans. But don't worry—I stopped judging you about an hour ago."

VJ replied, "I'll take that as a compliment."

Tess looked at the window. The tree branches were still blowing wildly. "So let's get back to the story you're trying to tell me. Did you and Leila spend the rest of your week in Sierra Lakes uneventfully?"

"Actually not. While we were skiing I torqued my knee. I took a jump that my brain thought would be a terrific idea, but my body didn't. It hurt every time I turned. So instead, I thought a bike ride down in Bishop where there wasn't any snow would be fun and help clear my mind. The beginning of the ride was perfect. After my first blowout I was mildly frustrated. The second one really pissed me off. I'd checked everything and there weren't any rocks or slivers in my tire. The stem, though, had sheared off from the tube.

"'VJ, what on earth is going on with you?' Leila yelled after watching me toss the wheel about fifty feet.

"'Motherfucking asshole son of a bitch tire,' I yelled back. 'I just can't stand it! Every time I have to change this thing I kill my fingers. It drives me crazy!' Like I told you before, hurting and cursing inanimate objects gives me a unique sense of fulfillment."

Tess laughed. "I feel exactly the same way. I almost beat up the TV last week after I hit my head on the corner."

"Take it from someone who knows," VJ warned. "Don't use your hands for things like that—you need them."

She nodded obediently. "Yes, Doctor."

VJ went on, "I did finally manage to get the tire on the wheel and the wheel on the bike. My pride was at stake. This bike was not going to defeat me. We were going to have a great ride no matter what. Leila, in her infinite wisdom, placed a hand delicately on my shoulder and spoke up.

"'VJ, it's definitely time for us to get a glass of wine at Big D. Glaser's Tasting Room. Some people from the OR took me there about a month ago. You'll like it. Do you think you can be human for an hour or two?'

"Tucking my tail between my legs, I surrendered. 'I promise I'll be a good boy. Yes, I know exactly where it is. It was part of my plan to go there in the first place. I hear their Cab is *killer* good.'

"Leila groaned. With that, we set off through the back roads. I knew a couple of shortcuts. My ideas were met with protests. 'VJ, this sign says No Trespassing,' Leila pointed out. 'Does that mean anything to you?'

"I shouted, 'I like to look at signs and stoplights as suggestions. Right now, I think the owners have made a bad suggestion that we shouldn't follow. It's just about a mile farther. We have to cross a little stream. Is that OK?'

"I didn't realize until that moment that Leila has a phobia about crossing water—not being in it or surfing in it, just crossing it. She didn't reveal that information the night I asked her what she was afraid of. Her problem was much the same as my intense fear of heights. I have no difficulty with chairlifts, but put me on a cliff edge and I freak out. Completely inexplicable. I literally had to carry her over the creek."

Tess jumped in. "I knew she wasn't perfect. There's always a flaw. I bet she does something else weird, like collect Teletubby dolls."

VJ said, "Thanks, Tess, I'll be sure to be on the lookout for those. Once we got to the wine bar, the elephant wasn't just in the room—it invaded. With the Cooperative, it wouldn't be a matter of if, but when. A scene from a movie I saw a long time ago began to unspool in my head. I told myself, *It's a ridiculous idea, but maybe it'll work.*

"I looked across the table at Leila. I knew I was solidly in the it-hurts-not-to-be-with-her stage. To say I was conflicted is an understatement. I laid out my idea to Leila, and that was the beginning of our first fight.

"After hearing my words, Leila said, 'VJ, I agree with you. It sounds crazy. On another level, it's so preposterous that I think you can pull it off. My Sierra Lakes obligation is over. I built free time into my schedule to goof off. There's no reason for us not to go back to Boston together. I can help you.'

"I didn't want to hear it. 'Absolutely no way. It's dangerous. I have no idea what to expect. Who knows, maybe there's going to be a guy in Logan waiting to shoot me. I can't have you being in the middle of that.'

"She ignored me. 'VJ, I don't have to be with you to help you. There isn't a person outside of Sierra Lakes who knows we're together. That is, unless the Cooperative had someone spying on those two hit men, and that's hard for me to believe.' I opened my mouth to interrupt, then shut it. She wasn't stopping. 'We can take separate flights if you want. I'm already an accessory to this fiasco.' Her green eyes were on fire. 'If you think I'm letting you do this on your own, then you're out of your mind. Forget it. It's not even a conversation I'm willing to participate in.' The issue was decided, whether I liked it or not.

"Our discussion morphed into a strategy session. Finally, I was convinced that we had an action plan that would, I hoped, both save me and keep Leila out of harm's way.

"I enjoyed the second glass of wine a lot more than the first. Suddenly, I felt something sharp in my back. A gravelly voice said, 'Brio, move and I'll kill you!' Leila was laughing. It was the one and only Dermontti Glaser, holding a fork on me.

"I was less thrilled. 'Damn it, Big D., you about gave me a heart attack. You're going to have to comp me the wine now.'

"He was grinning from ear to ear. 'I was going to do that anyway. Thanks for fixing my hand. That collagenase injection hurt like hell, but my finger's straight and I don't catch it on stuff anymore.'

"We got some dinner to let the alcohol percolate before throwing the bikes in the truck. I'd parked near the restaurant before we went on our riding adventure. The window was fixed now. Before I took it in, I bashed it with a hammer to make it look like a break-in. I didn't need anyone asking me why my window was shot out. The forty-minute drive back to Sierra Lakes was a snap.

"Leila and I were both ready to take the next step. The following morning, I flew to San Francisco rather than route through LA. From there I headed to Boston. Leila put the flights on her card in case the Cooperative was checking mine. She drove my truck back to its Southern California base and left from there. I told her to be on the lookout for Benjamin Saito in case he was on her return flight. If by some crazy coincidence they met, I wanted to be sure she didn't say a word about working in Sierra Lakes.

"On the trip home, I could barely sit still. I felt like a tiger in a cage. Every minute seemed like an hour. The flight attendant must've thought I was hopped up on amphetamines. I kept walking up and down the aisles. Three separate times she told me to sit down because the FASTEN YOUR SEAT BELT sign was still on. I used what little charm remained to avoid getting reported to the seat belt police. It was scary to roll into Logan. The idea of bolting with Leila to whatever island would take an itinerant hand surgeon and nurse seemed very appealing. But it didn't go that way.

"Instead I had chosen to return to Boston, now for the second time. Contemplating the ongoing threat to my life forced me to think about more mundane issues like having a will. Vikka would be fine with the neighbors, but I damn sure didn't want the state to take everything I had for itself. I decided to write up something, sign it, and hope that it would pass legal muster. Seeing a lawyer immediately wasn't in the cards, though.

"I got off the plane and headed toward the exit. Not knowing what the Cooperative thought had happened or what precautions they were taking, I buried myself in a coat and cap to be as unrecognizable as possible, grabbed my stuff, and hit the T.

"Going to the townhouse seemed to be potentially dangerous, so I checked into a place in Quincy and set up shop. Elegant it wasn't. Nice would also probably be too strong a word. Functional—it was functional. The next day I got my head shaved to throw off observers. I'd also grown out as much of a beard as I was able.

"The plan Leila and I had worked out involved me not going to work. After my haircut, I picked up the phone and called my assistant Terri. 'Bad news. I crashed on the bumps big-time. Tweaked my knee. It looks like I'm going to need a few more days.'

"'You're kidding me, right?' Her desperation was audible. 'That means I've got sixty people to reschedule, plus five cases.'

"'Terri, I'll make it up to you. How does a pair of rink-side tickets to the Bruins sound? Seriously, this thing is hurting so bad that I can't stand up. I wouldn't lie to you.' Tess, does lying about a lie cancel the two out?"

212

Tess said, "In your upside-down world, VJ—absolutely."

He smiled. "Good, I was worried about that. Literally a minute after I hung up from Terri, I saw a text message from Bianka: If you're back, I still want to see you. Nothing to worry about, but call me as soon as you can. That was a message I couldn't ignore. I picked up the phone and dialed. Two rings later and I heard that distinctive, lovely voice of hers. 'Bianka, it's VJ. How are you?'

"She didn't even ask me about my trip. 'VJ, do you have any time in the next few days to take a walk?'

"'No time like the present,' I said. 'I've got time right now. Can you slip out of the lab and meet me?'

"She said, 'Let's meet at J.P. Licks in an hour.'" VJ glanced at Tess. "You may or may not know, but Bianka suffers enormously from Sweet Tooth Disease." Tess nodded.

"I got back on the T, reaching the front of the shop just in time to see Bianka walking toward me, dressed impeccably as always. She didn't recognize me and almost walked right by. I remembered to exaggerate a limp so that my story about the knee accident would stay consistent. I caught her attention with a wave. After examining me, she grabbed me and said, 'What happened to your hair? And what are you doing with that stubble on your face? Did something go wrong when you were in Sierra Lakes?'

"I wanted to tell her the truth so badly—but I didn't. 'Bianka, it's a long story. I'll tell you all about it soon.' I limped into the ice cream store with her and we got our cones. Despite the cold, we wandered down the street to a nearby bench.

"Bianka said, 'So what the hell, VJ? You look like you just got home from a war. I thought you went to Sierra Lakes to decompress.'

"I slowly straightened my knee. 'Bianka, in short, I wrecked skiing and messed up my knee. Then I had the good sense to wash my hair with green dye at a friend's house. Come to think of it, I should have kept it for St. Patty's Day. But I didn't, so I shaved it off. There you have it. Now what is it you wanted to tell me?'

"Bianka shook her head. 'Not so fast. The ski thing I understand. You go down the hill like a maniac, and it was just a matter of time. I hope it's not too bad. I'm not sure I get the dye job.'

"I readjusted myself to look her in the eye, paused, and gave a deep sigh to give myself time to think. Then I proceeded to tell her yet another fabrication. 'You're right about the crash-and-burn part. I was trying to blow by a snowboarder who passed me. I just wanted him to know I could take him anytime. Unfortunately, I caught an edge and windmilled down the run. I'm pretty sure I tore my meniscus, so I'm going to have

214

Danguerin scope it. He doesn't know that yet, but I'm going to tell him he has to. The hair story would be funny if it didn't really happen. I was cleaning up at my buddy's place where I store my truck in LA. The problem was I got some soap in my eyes just as I was grabbing what I thought was shampoo. It wasn't. It was his daughter's hair coloring. I didn't think it would be a terrific idea to parade around the office on crutches with green hair, so I cut it all off. Hopefully the beard will distract people from the bald head.'

"Bianka's face had an odd look as she started to speak. 'VJ, I need to ask you something off the wall. This is what I wanted to talk about before you left. If you recall, you were sort of out of it that morning. Have you ever donated sperm?'"

Tess protested immediately. "VJ, do not go there."

VJ raised his hands, palms up, and said, "Tess, that wasn't a question I was expecting, either. Before you get torqued out, let me get through this. I had the same response. I said, 'What kind of thing is that to ask a friend? If you mean to a sperm bank, the answer is an absolute no! Some of my friends in med school donated when they needed money. I always thought that one of me in the world was enough. Plus, how strange would it be to run into someone on the street who looks like a younger version of you and not know if it actually is?'"

Tess broke in again. "You're not kidding. One VJ in this world *is* probably enough."

He nodded. "I'd be surprised if some of your classmates haven't. Those places pay a fair bit. Remember, whether you think so or not, the men in your class represent some of the best and the brightest."

Tess snorted. "Axel had better not be doing that. If he is, I'll have to warn the mother before it's too late. Why did Bianka ask you that?"

VJ paused for a second. "I'm going to explain. I need to move this knee. One second it feels OK, and the next second it hurts like a bitch," he said, taking a deep breath, and then continued.

"So Bianka asked, 'Do you remember that you gave me that DNA sample for the study I'm doing on genetic markers for your favorite Swedish hand surgeon subject—Dupuytren's disease?' For the record, Tess, Dupuytren's occurs in up to six percent of some Caucasian populations. The nickname is 'Viking's disease' because you-know-who's countrymen are thought to be responsible for spreading it when they were raping and pillaging."

"Yeah, yeah," Tess said. "So Bianka said . . ."

VJ waited a beat. Tess rolled her eyes. "So Bianka said, 'We compared this year's samples to last year's. Anna and Susan, two of the post-docs, were curious about some of the strands

216

they saw on one of the samples. They decided to compare it to another one with possible Nordic roots. Then they looked closer because of some very interesting similarities.'"

VJ paused again. "While Bianka and I were talking, a gust of cold wind hit me in the face. I was ready to go back inside. I was suddenly beat. The travel was catching up with me." Tess motioned like she was going to pull her hair out. VJ continued. "The pigeons hunting for crumbs around us didn't seem to mind the weather. Rats with wings. I hate them."

"Enough about the fucking pigeons!" Tess poked him in the ribs with her finger. "What did Bianka *say*?"

VJ winced. "That hurt. I'm going to report you for elder abuse." Tess shifted menacingly in her chair. *"OK,"* he said. "Here it is. Bianka took my hand, squeezed it, and said, 'VJ, one of those volunteers is, without doubt, your child. Not only are you a dad, but that person is here in Boston.'"

Tess just stared. VJ shook his head and continued, "I knew there was no way Bianka was joking. Obviously, I was completely floored. If you had given me a thousand choices of what direction the conversation was going to take, fatherhood would not have been on the list. I was flabbergasted. On top of everything else, I get this news. Finally, I took a deep breath and said to Bianka, 'I really don't know what to say. In a minute, everything is different. I'm sitting here struggling to figure out what I'm supposed to do. What does someone do now? I can't for my life figure out when I made a kid. I've been a few places and don't love celibacy, but I'm usually careful. I guess if I find out the kid's birthday, the answer should be more clear.'

"We got up. Bianka walked and I limped for a few hundred yards while we said absolutely nothing."

Tess sat back, looking suddenly pensive. "So there's someone here in town who's your spawn. I know about that study. I was one of the thousand people that Bianka hit up. A lot of them were M.D. or Ph.D. students. It'd be strange if that person had you as an attending and neither of you ever knew it. Did you locate your kid?"

VJ said, "Yes, I did."

Tess added, "Wow! Are you going to tell him or her after all this time? That could be dicey."

VJ acknowledged the quandary. "Particularly right now I'm well aware of that issue. It was a huge challenge to think of the best way to present the information. I'm still not certain I worked out the most logical plan. By the way, the individual in question is a female. Bianka said I lucked out. The young woman probably favors the birth mother. Unfortunately, there is absolutely no record of who that is. Bianka checked through some back channels before she told me. She also told me a few other interesting things. Mainly that she knew the person in question."

VJ stopped again, took a deep breath, looked squarely at Tess, and said, "When your mom and dad told you that you were adopted, did you ever wonder about your birth parents?"

As he said it, he handed her the documentation from Bianka's lab to prove that what he was now claiming was true.

REVELATION

Tess' eyes lit up with scary intensity as the realization hit her. She screamed, "Are you saying what I think you're saying? *I'm* your daughter?" She jumped out of her chair and walked over to the window, muttering to herself, "Holy shit! *Holy shit!* I can't believe any of this."

Tess kept her back to VJ for several minutes, then finally turned around. Her breathing steadied. She stared at the laboratory data and shook her head. "Listen, VJ, this story is so absurd that no one in their right mind would believe a word of it. But, standing here looking at you, knowing that Bianka sent me here," she said, as she brandished the lab report, "and looking at *this*—I know all you've said is the truth. At the same time, I can't fathom that I'm actually talking to one of the two people I've wondered about since I was five.

"I pictured this scene to be a lot different. Since my parents died, I've been thinking more about trying to hunt down my biological mother and father. With everything going on in medical school, I couldn't deal with it mentally. You beat me to the punch. So, here you are. Amazing. You're definitely not who I thought you'd be, but I'll admit you're unique. I figured you were some high school punk who knocked up his girlfriend. Guess I was wrong about that." Tess walked slowly back to her chair and plopped down like a rag doll. "So you've had this information about us for how long?"

"Just a few days—and a lot has happened since I found out," VJ said. "I was totally conflicted about telling you at all. I'd desperately like you to meet the guy who existed before this all started. I've always been seriously flawed, but I certainly wasn't involved in battling a criminal syndicate."

Tess interrupted, "So you mean to say that you just got back from Sierra Lakes? That everything you've been telling me about Sierra Lakes and Leila and the assassins happened last week?"

"Exactly. My head is spinning, too. I know you've been wondering why I added so many extra details about what I do, what I think about, who the important people are in my life— basically, who I am. I wanted to give you a framework to understand everything about me, and my situation, *before* you knew about our biological connection. I've tried to be as honest as possible." She put her head in her hands.

"Tess, believe me, I know that no one can ever replace your parents. It's impossible. I wish I could change everything bad that's happened to both of us in the past year. I can't. Once I found out you existed, I wanted more than anything to meet you and find out everything about you. There are some really important details I still need to add."

Tess raised her head and stared at him like he was a rare zoo animal. Then she shook her head with disbelief. "VJ, let's switch places for a second. Imagine I just told you that I was your daughter and that, on top of everything else! Wait—let's make a list. There's a massive fraud at the hospital I'm working in, surgeons are getting their fingers cut off, people are trying to kill me, I'm killing people, and people have to think I'm dead. What would *your* response be?"

VJ answered carefully, "That would depend on the circumstances, I suppose. I will tell you this: When Bianka gave me the news, after I had a chance to digest it, I was truly excited and at the same time apprehensive. I did have the benefit of her telling me what a great person you are. To answer your question, I don't know for sure. I'd like to think I'd try my best to accept you with open arms. That's not a hint, although obviously I'd like tonight to be a beginning, not an ending."

Tess' face softened. "That's fair. It means a lot to me that at least you haven't been intentionally ignoring me for my whole life. I heard what you said—you don't know who my mother is. I assume you can narrow it down."

With slight hesitation in his voice VJ answered, "I asked Bianka about that. We couldn't determine where you were born. I don't know if you were premature or late. That leaves about a three-and-a-half-month window. It's not like I kept a black book, and, as I told Leila, I'm not usually promiscuous. That was an interesting time in my life. I've narrowed it down to four people, and yes, the arm-breaking, pogo-stick, crazy Danika is on that list. I haven't had time to try to track any of them down. But now you're really going to want to kill me. I'm not one hundred percent sure of the last names of two of them. Ideally, I would've come to you armed with this information. This other mess made that sort of hard."

Tess scowled. "Four women in three months, and two whose names you don't remember—a few years ago I wouldn't have been good with that, but VJ, I'll choose to overlook it. There are people I consider friends who've slept with more than one person in a couple of hours. It's not my thing, but I know it happens. Medical stress release. I'm going to do some digging. I'm pretty good with the computer. Unfortunately, it looks like I'll need reinforcements. I'm going to have to bury my pride and ask Axel. He can go three levels deep into the Internet. He finds things that nobody can find. I'm going to have to search for a way not to loathe him for a few minutes. But I'm not going to let this go. We're *going* to find out who *she* is!"

VJ optimistically suggested, "I promise that'll happen if I'm in a position to help. I need to finish catching you up. Can I do that?"

Tess picked up one of the dissecting scalpels sitting on the table next to her and pointed it at him, saying half-jokingly, "You'd better make this good or those fingers are coming off."

VJ nodded and crossed his heart. "Hope to die. No, scratch that. This is the first time I ever felt relieved while being threatened with a knife. When I was a kid, my sister, Kari, got so mad at me she grabbed a machete and came after me. I probably deserved it."

"That goes without saying," Tess interjected.

Relieved that Tess was staying, VJ continued, "Obviously, the problem remains the Cooperative. I assumed that the moment they saw me back in town they'd double down on the most efficient way to get rid of me.

"The night I found out about you, I did what I often do when I'm confronted with questions I don't have answers to—put on my running shoes and just go. I didn't care that it was late, where I was headed or for how long, or that my knee hurt. Remember, this was before I got it scoped. About two-thirds of the way to nowhere I decided that this meet and greet would be the best way to approach you. You might think I was oxygen-starved at the time, but I still believe this was the safest plan.

"Originally, Leila and I talked about taking the risk, sitting down with the feds here, telling them about the fraud, entering the witness protection program, and simultaneously having the police grab Anders to protect him. Unfortunately, I didn't know whether that would be a sure thing. It also meant saying goodbye to our friends, family, and any reasonable existence. And that was even before I found out about you.

"But when we were in the wine bar that day in Bishop, a different idea hit me, the one I got from the movie—one where I wouldn't always be looking over my shoulder. Dangerous, yes. Sketchy, yes. Selfish, definitely. But if it worked out, I'd be in the clear, keep Leila, and—knowing what I know now—have a daughter who can be part of my life. Conceptually, I like that outcome a lot more."

Tess stood up for a second, shook off another chill, and pulled the coat tighter. "For whatever it's worth, I'm glad you cared enough to make this happen. I honestly don't know what to say about the rest of it. You're still in the middle of a major shit-show. I might even think about helping you if I can. I have this misguided belief that I can fix things. I might get that from you. Guess you can't change genetics. I'm getting a clearer picture of why I have some of the quirks I have. When I'm doing my art, I'll change it and change it again if I'm not satisfied. I'll go over a test question twenty times in my mind if I think I got it wrong. How does it work out for you in the operating room?"

VJ answered, "Believe it or not, I'm pretty decisive there. There isn't really a lot of choice."

Tess continued, "At some point, there's a lot more family information I want to find out about. Right now, though, since all of a sudden I'm involved, tell me more about the you're-dead part."

VJ elaborated, "That night, after Bianka told me about you, I called Leila and broke the news to her. She was wonderful about it, and encouraged me to find a way to meet you. I wanted to wait and see, though, if the first part, the me-dying part, would be successful.

"The next morning—since it's morning now, then that was just two days ago—I snuck into the hospital and tracked down my anesthesiologist buddy Lige. I'd helped him get through the financial and emotional hurt of two divorces. He has listened to plenty from me, too. I consider him my best friend at MRMC. I told him my story, except Leila's name and anything about you. When I described the final part of the plan, he looked at me just the way you did a minute ago. I have that strange effect on people.

"Lige yelled. 'You want me to pretend to kill you in the OR? Perfect! Wonderful! Fantastic!

Do you have any other brilliant thoughts? Why don't we jump off the top of that construction site over there? It'll certainly make the process easier. Just how the hell am I supposed to execute you? Oh, and by the way, how is your death going to make me look? People already think I'm too much of a cowboy. Your checking out could get me thrown off the staff.'

"I stopped him. 'Lige, I've thought the whole thing through. For starters, you know damn well that you could shoot fifty people in the OR, sell their parts on the black market, declare your allegiance to Satan, and you'd still probably win a case against the hospital for firing you for undue cause. Remember that guy who had seventeen malpractice cases against him? His lawyers were very savvy. It took us two years to run him out. By the time anyone in the anesthesia department asks you an official question, I'll either be alive again to speak with them, or dead someplace. You'll have a notarized document explaining what went down and why. You'd end up taking down a multimillion-dollar criminal empire and being a local hero.'

"Lige continued to stare at me like I was giving grand rounds in my birthday suit. He obviously needed more convincing—so I pleaded with him. 'Look, Lige, if there was any other way . . . Believe me. Remember—I'm not the only one involved here. You can protect a lot of our colleagues. These people from the Cooperative are vicious, and they're out of control. Give me a chance. With more breathing room, I can figure out who's running the show and take the whole lot of them down. I've got this.'

"Lige toyed with his stethoscope—he actually puts his to use—then looked up at me again. 'So how do you know I didn't contact my buddies in the Cooperative before you came up?'

"I did a double take. 'Lige, if that's the case, go ahead and kill me for real.'

"He laughed at me. 'VJ, there's no sport in that. I think we'll try it your way. Let's hear the whole plan. Be sure to tell me again why you think all of us should put our licenses at risk and be scorned by everyone we know and care about. And by the way, does this constitute functioning in a hostile work environment? I'll have to start working on my wrongful-termination lawsuit.'

"I answered Lige seriously. 'That might be the last thing you have to worry about. If the Cooperative finds out that this is a hoax, your life isn't going to be worth two cents. Aren't you glad to have friends like me?'

"Lige said, 'I'm thinking I'll take a couple of weeks off. VJ, we have a family cabin near Sea Island. Marshes, weeping willows, Spanish moss, the whole deal. Isolated as can be. I'm the only one who'll know I'm there. We've also got some mighty fine artillery. Southern hospitality only goes so far. If one of your new friends finds

228

himself on my turf, he might not make his way back to these parts. Sort of like the guys you met at Sierra Lakes.' Lige meant every word he said. He can fieldstrip a rifle in seconds. I've seen him do it. I liked having him on my side.

"I explained Lige's part to him. 'We'll do it last case of the day tomorrow. Almost everyone will be gone. Nick's old girlfriend, Mikele, is the PACU nurse. Even though she dumped him, she still loves him. I'll let her know the whole charade's for him. It won't be too hard a sell. I need my knee scoped anyway. This freaking meniscal tear has been driving me nuts. When Danguerin looks inside he'll be perfectly satisfied that he's helping me with a real problem. Plus, Danguerin hates talking to patients and families, so he always leaves as soon as he closes. Right after he goes, you'll head to the PACU with me still tubed. We'll fake a code. You'll say I had a run of V tach and you couldn't reverse me. Mikele will be there "assisting" you.'"

Tess interrupted, "Whoa, VJ, what are you talking about? You lost me."

"Ventricular tachycardia—V tach—means that the heart's beating too fast and it can't pump blood efficiently," he explained. "The blood pressure gets very low. If it isn't reversed, it will kill a patient. Does that help?" She nodded.

"Lige said, 'You know we have to make a 911 call for any code, right?'

"I said, 'Fortunately, I planned for that. Before the EMTs get there, we'll rig the EKG leads to show a flat-line tracing and the pulse oximeter to register double goose egg. Since the ASC is technically not part of the hospital, the state requires that the EMTs do transport to the hospital. Seems absurd but it's true. When they come in, you and Mikele will tell them you've been flogging me and that I'm just plain dead—obviously with the great emotion and angst one would expect at the loss of a man of my lofty stature.'

"Lige grimaced. 'I knew there was a catch. I'm not sure I'll able to show anything but my elation that you're history. Assuming I can pretend to care, what about the base station nurse? The ambulance team will be required to call the base station. She'll have to sign off.'

"'I checked the work assignment list. Linda's in the radio room. You tell her I'm done and she'll take your word for it. After that, Pete Blasingame from the medical examiner's office will fake the post-mortem. He's an ex-patient. I spent about six hours fixing his fingers after he tried to cut them off making a beautiful cherry-wood box. Fortunately, the saw only went through the dorsal half of his digits. No flexor tendons, no digital arteries or nerves. My man Pete had a terrific result. I've got to clear it with him before I start all this. That might take some serious convincing, but I think he'll give me the green light after a heavy dose of hearing what I'm up against. Do I seem overly optimistic?'"

Tess frowned. "You did figure out that none of this would work before you did it, right? Also, it seems like all of a sudden you were telling a lot of people about the Cooperative. Why?"

VJ explained, "The short answer is that I'm selfish, and, honestly, I didn't see a better way. Self-preservation sometimes blinds reasoning. But it's also more complicated. You establish an incredibly close connection with the physicians and staff you work with and care about. All of you will face the same joys and frustrations, and only your group will truly understand them. Your outside friends will try, but believe me, they can't. It's the same reason I was willing to help Nick. Think about what soldiers do. How often do you read about one of them sacrificing their limb or life to help someone in their unit? My only leverage point was the threat I'm still facing. I consider myself to be very fortunate that people like Leila, Pete, Lige, and Mikele exist. They're all totally solid. Despite how insane the whole thing was, we decided to try to execute the plan."

Tess laughed. "Very punny indeed. VJ, so what about your brother?"

"Lige asked me the same thing. Fortunately, I had the answer. 'I've got him covered.' I arranged for Lige and me to check in with Leila separately, once I was in the clear. I included Lige in the loop in case the anesthesia was delaying my ability to talk with her. If she didn't get independent verification from both of us that everything was OK, she was going to grab Anders and take the whole story to the police. It wouldn't get the people at the top, but at least it would shut down the Cooperative at MRMC."

Tess said, "Well, here you are talking to me, so either I'm having the weirdest dream in the history of the world, or it actually did work out. Did it?"

VJ sat back and closed his eyes. "Tess, that's a curious thing you're asking." He took a deep breath. "Yesterday I sat in Chuck Danguerin's office glancing at the diplomas on the wall. All the best places."

Tess didn't give him a chance to continue. "VJ, surely you were kidding about him, of all people, doing the surgery. Wasn't that the last person on the planet you'd go to see after Sierra Lakes? For Christ's sake, he's probably running the whole show. You would have been better off sending an Instagram telling the Cooperative you were here."

"Give me a second," VJ said. "Chuck's a wizard with the arthroscope, so why not have the most skilled person do what I needed done anyway? The timeline was so short that I knew the Cooperative wouldn't have a chance to change my plan. Plus, obviously they had no idea what I intended to do. I put myself in the lion's mouth on purpose. I'm still not sure what Danguerin's up to. I can tell you he's not in charge. Whoever that is, he's probably laughing right now at the idea of me being dead. I'm counting on it. I need the Cooperative's legions to let their guard down.

"I delivered my pitch to Chuck. 'This sucker is bugging the crud out of me. I can't sit for more than fifteen minutes. It's locking. It swells when I'm up on it. I got your friend Miranda, that triathlete, radiology tech to do the MRI for me. There's a big-bucket handle lateral meniscus tear. It isn't going to heal itself. I also spoke to one of your admins, Kyle; he gave me the OK and put me on the OR schedule for late today. Don't hold it against Kyle. I leaned on him pretty hard to help me out. I know it's quick, but I'm having trouble doing anything. If you're alright with it, I just want it done.'

"Chuck manipulated my knee and started his OR speech. 'Yeah, I feel it, VJ. This one doesn't look like it's in the red zone on the MRI, so a repair is unlikely. Probably just debride it. The ACL's fine, so you're not going to have to put up with a reconstruction. I'll do it today since you already took the liberty of running my life— classic hand surgeon. You owe me for this, though. I'm supposed to meet a woman for drinks and dinner tonight. She doesn't know yet that she's making a big mistake by going out with me. If I'm late, I won't have a chance at all. I've got to be gone by five. This one's a lot classier than that Brittany chick you snaked at Anthony and Bianka's party. I still can't figure out what happened there.'

"Somewhat embarrassed I said, 'Chuck, about that. Would a bottle of Silver Oak Cabernet work for you?'

"He gave me a thumbs-up. 'Don't worry about that Brittany girl. I didn't really know her at all. I just met her at lunch the day before. She was pretty forward—just sat down at my table and started talking at me. Somehow she knew about the party and practically forced me to take her. She gave me the idea she was friends with Anthony and Bianka. I will take the wine, though. If I have to drink alone, it might as well be something good.'

"I was elated that at least the first step was successful."

DEATH OF A SURGEON

"When I checked in, my pulse and blood pressure were elevated. The pre-op nurse asked me what I was nervous about. I told her part of the truth: 'Surgery is something best done on someone else.' Then I shut up and let her start the IV.

"The wheels started to turn. The actual surgery was the least of my concerns. Lige and the circulating nurse wheeled me into lucky room four. Most of us think it's haunted. It's rare that something doesn't go wrong, whether it's a piece of equipment or that the surgery has some unforeseen complicating factor. I could tell that Lige was far from his usual self. There were no comments about my heritage, ineptitude, or anything, for that matter.

"'Lige,' I said, 'brighten up. After today you might never have to deal with me again.'

"More gruffly than he probably intended, he said, 'VJ, cap it. You're going to be perfect.'

"Ironically, Danguerin seemed to be the most upbeat of the whole group. 'VJ, you're fortunate,' he said. 'I told my dinner companion that I might be late because I'm helping out a colleague. She liked my compassion. It's a win-win. You still owe me that Silver Oak Cabernet.

I'll expect to see it on my desk at your post-op visit in two days.'

"'Sure thing, Chuck,' I said, knowing there was no way that was going to happen. I've decided to get him a case when I can show my face again—that is, if he's not in jail. About thirty seconds later it was lights out. I felt the sting of the propofol going in. It's white, so we call it milk of anesthesia.

"Lige told me a not-so-funny story afterward. Apparently, as Shoshanna, the circulating nurse, started reciting the surgical timeout Danguerin went nuts. He got on her case about her focus on fire risk and all the other useless bullshit they stuff into those nonsensical government mandates. Seems he didn't care what Vikka had for breakfast a month ago. Chuck's an impatient guy. His harangue distracted Shoshanna enough that she forgot to go over the part about me being seriously allergic to penicillin."

"You've got to be kidding," Tess blurted out.

"Afraid not. Oblivious to what was about to transpire, Danguerin did his scope magic and was sinking the last stitch. Lige simultaneously noticed I hadn't gotten my prophylactic antibiotic, so he gave it to me by IV push. Within ninety seconds my lips started to swell, my chest turned red, and my pressure bottomed out. Lige couldn't ventilate me. My oxygen saturation went

236

to shit. Shoshanna had a hard time getting the three hundred mics of epinephrine that Lige urgently needed out of the password-protected drug dispensary. He was going nuts watching me die in front of his eyes. I was about a minute from buying it. The scrub tech bashed the damn drug cabinet with a mallet that was on the back table. The drawer popped open with the life-saving epi inside. Lige grabbed it and resuscitated me from a full-blown drug-induced anaphylaxis. There's a very tiny percentage of people who demonstrate cross-reactivity between the cephalosporin antibiotic I got and penicillin. I'm one of those fortunate few. For the record, penicillin can show cross-reactivity with structurally unrelated antibiotics as well. Keep that information in your back pocket. It's always smart to have an Epipen around in the office.

"Danguerin understandably was not happy with everything that was going on. According to Lige, he sincerely tried to help out. Lige righted the ship, but I wasn't completely out of the woods. Now he was trying to make sure I stayed alive in the present. Danguerin made some crack about Lige trying to kill me with antibiotics, so he got shooed to the surgeons' lounge.

"After forty-five additional minutes and repeated visits from Danguerin, I was transferred without further incident to the PACU. Lige was not in the best spirits. Now he had to get Danguerin out of the surgical center or the game was over. Divine intervention occurred in the form of Danguerin' date. She apparently had grown tired of the delay. Chuck looked me over while I was still intubated, checked with Lige to make sure I wasn't going to jump in the box, and finally left.

"Then Lige and Mikele were able to resume the intended job of killing me. I was completely out of it for the first hour-plus that I spent in the PACU. Slowly I became aware that there was a world around me. It's the strangest feeling—very different than waking up from a deep sleep. Dreams can be so real. Anesthesia isn't like that. It's more like coming from a state of nothingness. My eyes opened, and I stared at Lige and Mikele and gave them a big smile. 'Am I dead yet?'

"Lige turned to Mikele and said, 'Should we tell him?' She nodded. Lige said, 'VJ, you're allergic to cephalosporin. You crashed in the OR. No kidding. You almost pulled off the plan for real.' After I was a little more alert, he told me the story I just told you.

"Once I got filled in, I said, 'I guess I should thank you for saving my life. Is all this going to make it harder to do what we talked about?'

"Lige sighed deeply. 'No, it's just going to make me look a hell of a lot worse. Don't let that small detail worry your little head.'"

Tess said, "You *are* truly fortunate to have such friends, VJ."

VJ nodded. "The bogus death, after almost being derailed by real death, worked to perfection. There were just the three of us left in the PACU. Mikele looked suitably distressed when the EMTs came. I was covered from head to toe in a sheet and blanket to help mask the shallow breaths I was taking. The man and woman ambulance team bought the story hook, line, and sinker, as did Linda, the radio room nurse. Who wouldn't believe that Lige, who had everything to lose by me dying, wouldn't do everything possible to keep me alive? Lige, in his state of 'despair,' insisted on riding in the back with me.

"When we got to the coroner's building, Lige continued to distract the ambulance drivers while they wheeled me in. Pete handled the post-mortem examination with panache and signed all the correct documents. I'd tipped off Anders that he'd be getting an official call from the coroner informing him of my death and requesting immediate cremation. He was directed to disregard those reports as alternative facts. His job was to play along and agree to allow me to quickly exit the planet. I told him I'd explain the details at the right time and place. As instructed, Pete made the inquiry, checked off on notification of next of kin, then bundled up a VJ mannequin and watched that sucker get toasted in the 1800 degree Fahrenheit furnace. Normally, the Jewish faith doesn't support cremation, but I

239

saw it as a necessary evil. The guy who takes care of the cremations is a little lackadaisical, like the incinerator guy in Sierra Lakes. He probably wouldn't notice something amiss if a giraffe was substituted.

"Exit me, through a back entrance. I got chauffeured by Lige to this wonderful place, and here I settled in, waiting for you. In case you're wondering, Anders and Jacques are now off to see Kari in Israel, Lige is safely ensconced in Georgia, and Mikele got an all-expenses-paid trip to Hawaii for a month. That's the least I could do. Leila received the frequent flyer points on her credit card. Even if you're six feet under, don't miss the opportunity to get points—you never know when you might need those suckers.

"I called Leila and told her only the part about the plan working, not about the allergic reaction. Lige hadn't said anything either when he'd made his call. I didn't think there was any harm in holding back the actually-almost-really-dead part. She also knows I'm here talking to you and sends her best."

Tess stood up and walked over to one of the lab stations. The room was dark, and definitely wasn't any warmer. She pointed to the cadaver wrapped in plastic sheets. "Doesn't it freak you out that you got so close to being one of these?"

VJ told her, "You know, not really. I woke up alive, and at the end of the day, that's all that

240

counts. It's not like I knew what was happening. Plus, as I've said, I trust Lige absolutely. He did everything right and it worked out. That's it—you're now one hundred percent up on the situation."

Tess shook her head. "Not quite. For the record, I'm glad you made it. I know there's still the issue of what's next. You told me you're not going to run away to hide someplace. Are you? *What is next?*" she asked.

"No, I'm not going anywhere. Anders and Jacques are headed out of Boston tomorrow. Now that I'm conveniently off the Cooperative's radar screen, their departure will be a non-issue. I'm still not in the clear. I was notified before I left that the Cooperative took the liberty to set up a bank account attached to my name complete with autodeposits and forged checks with signatures that look precisely like mine. They were smart. If I go to see law enforcement, there remains an overwhelming chance I could end up in prison for fraud. The feds might believe I was a willing partner that had a falling-out. I could plea-bargain, but who knows how that would go? And therefore, yet again, I'd be at risk to become dead at the hands of the Cooperative's stooges. I don't want to take that bet. At least not yet." VJ replied.

"Leila and I do have something very specific in mind. We've been looking for someone just like your friend Axel. I figured there wasn't much point in pursuing it until I knew this being-dead part would work. Leila got herself a traveler position at MRMC. We decided that a gig in the ICU would be most productive. People die there all the time. They also get lots of procedures. I'd be shocked if the Cooperative doesn't have their tentacles reaching deep into the unit.

"Leila is going to track actual times of death. I have a safe contact in the billing office who can identify charges associated with tests and procedures and the time they're done. Assuming some of these people get billed for things performed to them after they've actually died, there should be a computer trail to the nice folks doing it.

"Leila's also going to try to look into the comings and goings of this Rick character that Nick's thug buddies mentioned. I'd be surprised if the office Nick saw him in that very first time isn't a storage room now. Leila's going to innocently check it out. If Rick happens to be there, there should be some more information to be had about who else is involved. My guess is that anyone talking to Rick is connected to the Cooperative."

"Why not just use your OR cases?" Tess asked.

"I can't have anyone look at my surgical cases. That will raise too many red flags. We'll look at Danguerin's and clearly Milo Marconi's, though. Their profiles are a lot like Nick's. Divorced, big bills, like nice stuff. I want to examine the charges. If they're out of line, I want to trace them. It's sort of like those organized crime trees that the FBI puts together. The more people we can identify who're in the fold, the more likely we can find out who's pulling the levers. There have to be some people in the Cooperative who aren't being as careful as they should be, and that's how we'll nail them. We're counting on it."

Tess regarded VJ skeptically. "Erik 'VJ' Brio, M.D.—surgeon/detective. It sounds like a TV show pilot. You're making a lot of assumptions. What if you just track down some flunkies who lead you to a total dead end?"

He didn't have a perfect answer. "Then I'm up the creek and have to go back to plan B—witness protection."

Tess said, "That would totally suck! Seriously, I want to help. I have another idea about how to do that. Plus, if Cyrus is who we think he is . . ."

VJ laughed to himself as he gazed at the ceiling with the peeling Navajo white paint. The hue was the punch line to an off-color joke he remembered. Unfortunately, none of the individuals lying on the slabs in the room would get it. He returned his attention to Tess. "As far as Cyrus goes—the danger attached to him goes without saying. I've brought a lot more people into this morass than I intended or should've. Now you're involved. The wise thing to do is to walk away this morning and say a temporary goodbye."

Tess folded her arms with a stubborn look.

VJ said, "Connecting with me carries a lot of risk and very uncertain return. Only a few people in the world know you and I are linked in any way. I didn't tell Lige why I made him bring me here. Bianka and Leila certainly aren't going anywhere with the information. You and I aren't. What I'm saying is that you're still free and clear. Take my word for it: Having people shoot at you or try to blow you up is no way to live. I didn't come here to put you in the line of fire. That's about the last thing on the planet I want."

Tess argued, "Think about what you said, VJ. No one knows who I am. I'm just an insignificant med student. Who pays attention to us? Nobody. The nurses, the residents, the attendings—they want us to go bother someone else so they can do their work. Am I right?"

VJ laughed. "Not completely. A lot of us really enjoy teaching. But I can understand why you feel the way you do. That said, med students can get away with a lot. We never know where you're supposed to be. You guys are constantly leaving to go to lectures and God knows what. It was the same when I was where you're at now. This is different. The Cooperative is running a multimillion-dollar business. It's pretty obvious they care a lot about who's doing what."

Tess glanced at VJ rubbing his knee again, reached into her purse, and pulled out her bottle of aspirin and tossed it his way. "Looks like you need some."

He happily took three pills out. "Thanks. Stupidly, I didn't think to pick up a prescription for some narcotics before the case. A couple of Percocets would be nice. Going to get them now probably wouldn't be the best plan."

Tess said, "Can't help you with that. Guess you'll have to tough it out." Then she smiled. "Sorry, VJ, I couldn't resist. I really do feel bad for you. Look, I've been listening to your story all night. I think I've got a good idea what the Cooperative is about. Doing nothing when everything below the surface is rotten bothers me. My parents would never have accepted that choice. But I sure don't have a death wish. What's the worst that can happen? Getting my fingers chopped off. I'll just go into radiology with Nick. Like it or not, I know about you now. It'd be impossible for me just to walk away. That's not who I am."

She began to pace. "VJ, I have an idea. We have something called the Scholars in Medicine program. We're supposed to do it during the summer, but as an entrée, I can start over spring break. That'd buy me a ticket into an administration office without anyone getting suspicious. It would give me an opportunity to dig a little. Axel will help. I know he'll do anything to get on my good side. I'm pretty facile with computers, but nothing compared to him. He'll look at this as a fun challenge. Axel is insufferable, but brilliant."

VJ put up his hand. "Wait a minute there, Tess. You're getting a little ahead of yourself. I don't remember saying this is a good idea."

Tess would have none of it. "Forget it, VJ, you need me and Axel. There's no way your plan will work the way you've described it. You need a mole, and Leila's not enough. I'm not promising anything, but I know you've got a better chance to survive this with me than without me."

VJ was upset and clearly torn. "Look, Tess, I knew it would be risky to see you under the circumstances. I know you want to help, but having you get directly involved and putting you in harm's way is a whole order of magnitude worse. I really don't like this. I don't. As possibly ignorant as it sounds, I'm convinced I can find a way to beat these bastards. Hey, they think I'm dead. At the very least I'll have surprise on my side."

She looked skeptical. "That's very reassuring. Is there a vast army waiting just beyond the Boston Common, poised to attack the second you give the word?"

"How'd you guess? I contacted some of my old mates in the Swedish army. Unfortunately, the unit they intended to send just developed food poisoning from the bad herring the Finns sent over. It was meant for the Swedish national hockey team. They have a huge game coming up. Sneaky Finnish bastards. They're worse than the Norwegians. So that leaves me and Leila to *be* the Swedish, Korean, and South African armies."

Tess said, "How 'bout adding two old-fashioned American Marines?"

Part III

STRAIGHT TRIPPING

Tess wasn't going to give an inch. The look on her face and tone of her voice told VJ he'd better sit there, listen, and keep his mouth shut. She said, "I don't know whether you subliminally wanted to involve me or not, but at least, as of this moment, I'm in.

"VJ, it's either pretty late or pretty early, depending on how you look at it. Believe it or not, I have a life that predated your appearance. My closest college friend, Nicole, is walking down the aisle tomorrow—that is, today—and I'm in the wedding. Between your knee and post-anesthesia issues you're worthless from a driving perspective. So, it's your job now to keep me company and awake on the way up to Brunswick. That should give us some time to figure each other out. Maybe I'll change my mind about the Cooperative. I doubt it. I'm not giving you a choice about the trip. Besides, you're dead. My guess is that you don't have big weekend plans. You didn't mention it—what specifically did Leila say when you told her about me?"

VJ relaxed for a moment. "That was an interesting conversation. She reacted as I thought she would. She was surprised. Who wouldn't be? She asked me the same questions you did about the mother. I didn't give her much on that, other than that there were several possibilities. She really wants to meet you, if you give the OK. Speaking of Leila, I need to check in with her and tell her that there's been a small change in our plan. Can I borrow your phone? I retired mine just before my OR *accident.* I'm being paranoid, but I don't want to find out the Cooperative is hacking into my account and seeing that it's still in use. I haven't had a chance to get a burner yet."

Tess handed over her mobile. Leila picked up immediately. VJ could hear her yawning. He said, "Hey, how'd you sleep?"

"VJ, it's five in the morning! I've been tossing and turning all night. How'd it go?"

VJ glanced at Tess. "All things being equal—pretty well, I think. That's why I'm calling. We're going to take a short road trip. Tess is in her college roommate's wedding this weekend. We're headed up to Brunswick for a couple of days. Think you can live without me for that long?"

She yawned again. "Somehow I'll survive. Give me a call later. I still want to try to get some sleep. Love you."

"Love you, too," he said, and handed the phone back to Tess. She extended her hand to help VJ out of his chair and helped support him while he fiddled with his crutches.

Trying to avoid any added pain for VJ's knee, Tess got a ride share from the anatomy lab to her apartment in order to pick up her car for the drive to Maine. It was so early they were at her apartment in nothing flat. Once there she said, "VJ, as much as I'd like you to meet Jessica, I don't think now's a good time. Can you wait on the steps while I get my stuff?"

He sat dutifully, wearing a face mask against the bracing cold, with the hood of his coat pulled tightly over his head. VJ glanced through the eyeholes and saw a hulking figure walking toward him. It almost seemed like he'd been watching them, waiting for the opportunity to pounce. Just as VJ looked up, the guy said, "Hey, man, can I help you?" He looked more like he wanted to tear VJ apart.

However, before VJ had a chance to respond, Tess popped out of her front door carrying her bag. The man's eyes locked on her instantly. He growled, "Do you know this guy?" VJ saw Tess tremble for a moment, then she put her small hand on the beast's shoulder. It was suddenly clear to VJ that this was the man Tess had had dinner with and the possible fiend who had dismembered Nick.

"Hi, Cyrus. Don't worry. He's a friend of my parents. He came here to meet me just a minute ago. We're both going to the same wedding in Maine. He just got his knee operated on, so I'm driving him up. It's sort of a long story, and we're already late. Maybe I'll see you sometime soon."

Cyrus didn't look convinced. Disregarding VJ entirely, he said, "Tess, you sure everything's alright?"

Tess nodded. "Believe me, Cyrus, it's fine. I'd tell you if it wasn't. I appreciate you looking after me, though." She half-guided, half-pushed VJ into the nearby red Mini Cooper.

ENTER CYRUS

With no sleep himself, Cyrus was highly agitated. He'd spent the rest of the night casing Tess' apartment from his own place. He'd seen them get out of the ride share car together. He thought to himself, *Tess spent at least some of the night with this guy, she's lying about that part, and now she's traveling with him.* The deception rankled him enough that his resolve doubled to find out who this was and what he was doing with Tess. Cyrus decided he would make it his mission in life. That usually never worked out well for the person he was watching.

VJ didn't say anything until they hit the I-95. "I presume he was the man you had dinner with—the one you've been trying to avoid. That is, unless there's an entire stable of menacing biker-type dudes you hang out with."

Tess said, "Correct, that was Cyrus. In case you didn't pick up on the nuance of the circumstances, he's not the cuddly teddy-bear type. We have to connect with Nick and try to figure out if he's the one with the butcher knife."

The surprise encounter still had VJ on edge. "I'll agree with you there—he's kind of a scary-looking guy. I'm glad he seems to be on your side. And yes, knowing if he's working for the Cooperative is even more important."

Tess jammed the accelerator and passed a car. They didn't talk for a while—mostly because VJ passed out.

Some indeterminate time later, he felt someone prodding his ribs. It was Tess. "Hey, wake up! I need to know something. Why didn't you get married and have a kid or two that you actually know about? You might have intimacy issues, but they don't seem lethal."

VJ paused. "Tess, you and I have both had some experiences we'd prefer to forget. I had a wife for a year. Her name was Gabriella. She was from São Paulo, but came to Boston to train in pediatric oncology. The first time we met, I was consulting with her on a little boy who had the misfortune of chemo infiltrating his hand. Extremely nasty business. When that poison leaks out of an IV it can destroy all the tissue. A month later we were living together, and then boom, we were married. I—"

Tess interrupted, "What was she like? She had to be pretty patient to put up with you."

"Actually, she wasn't at all. Plus, Gabriella had a temper that makes mine seem like a gentle summer breeze. Despite that, she was one of the nicest people you could possibly know. One afternoon I asked Gabriella to meet me for lunch at the Common. She was over at Children's. I could only escape for an hour, and we hadn't been together much."

"Oh no . . . ," Tess said softly.

VJ nodded. "Some guy visiting from Nebraska was totally confused by all the one-way streets that ring the park. He never saw Gabriella crossing Beacon. I believed what he told the police. He wasn't drunk. He was just flustered and wasn't paying attention. I didn't want anyone to even press charges. What would that accomplish? That was the closest I got to a sustained meaningful relationship. I'm not telling you any of this to garner sympathy. No one escapes hardship. The issue is how we deal with what the world presents us."

A tear started down Tess' cheek. "When did . . . when was that?"

"That happened about ten years ago. After Gabriella died, I didn't function that well. I was the stereotype—working nonstop, not particularly caring if I was acting like a jerk. There's no shortage of that now, but at least I realize it when it's happening. Hey, Tess, that was supposed to get a smile."

Tears were now streaming down his daughter's cheeks. "Why did this happen to us?"

VJ gently laid a hand on Tess' knee. "There isn't any explanation at all. I used to wake up every night and think about all the different possibilities—what if I hadn't wanted to meet Gabriella for lunch? What if another car had been in line at the light, and the guy had run into that instead? What if he'd decided to visit New York instead of Boston or the aquarium instead of the Common? It was the world of 'what if,' not 'what is.' 'What if' only helps us if it permits us to change our lives in a positive way. Sorry for preaching. It's just the mantra I tell myself to help me move forward."

Tess said, "Does the pain ever go away?"

He gave her the answer she probably didn't want to hear. "It gets easier, but unfortunately not. You just find a place to put it."

Tess stared ahead. "That's what I'm working through." He saw her face change and her eyes narrow as she blew by a Porsche. "I don't know why, but I love doing that in a car like this to cars like that. Somehow it gives me a sense of power. I know it's stupid. Neither of my parents were like that. Now that I'm getting to know you, the light is starting to go on. Tell me more about your family."

VJ settled back in the seat, adjusting the belt so it would stop choking him. "Your grandfather Ari was also an extraordinary person. He was smart and really funny. Ari was a commercial architect with projects all over Europe. Occasionally he'd take one of us on a trip. It was fantastic. He was young when he died from a myocardial infarction. The post showed Ari was the victim of left main disease, the classic widow-maker. Good information for me and terrible at the same time.

"Your grandmother Ingrid died just last year. For months I've been putting off picking up some of her important things—books, jewelry, files of medical articles—the threads of her life. I don't know what to do with them. Each piece was so uniquely her. It doesn't feel right for them to be attached to anyone but her. To get the stuff means driving. The horror. Long ago, I reached the conclusion that the Boston vehicular transit system was designed to confuse Google map engineers. There's no other explanation for the absurd, random configuration of streets here. Forget the beat-up roads, terrible signage, and rabid drivers. It's the worst, don't you think?"

Tess nodded. "VJ, I didn't have a car for a reason. The one you're in right now was my mom's. She loved it. Convertibles are totally impractical here, but it was one of her few indulgences. I haven't had the heart to get rid of it yet. I know exactly what you mean about not wanting to part with the material things in life that we associate with our parents. For a change you digressed. Tell me more."

With that verbal permission slip, VJ elaborated. "Ingrid was German, not religious—definitely not Jewish. My grandfather was in the Wehrmacht and got killed early in the war. My grandmother bought the farm during an Allied bombing raid. That left my mother to fend for herself. She was a strong person and also very bright. Despite what was happening in the war, Ingrid started medical school as an eighteen-year-old. Continuing became almost impossible. The Allies kept bombing her schools. During her psychiatry rotation, the facility that she studied in was annihilated. Her professor gave her the final exam on a park bench.

"When Mom's third school got flattened, she grabbed every medical book she could salvage and hitched a ride to Göttingen. She'd heard that the school there would be willing to take on another student. That's how dedicated

258

she was. My parents met while he was working on a reconstruction project in Berlin. Dad took all of three weeks to pop the question. Do you see a pattern of rash romantic decisions from the men in the family? In any case, Ingrid's parents were gone and Germany was in ruins. Sweden represented a fresh start.

"They settled in Norrtälje, a small city just north of Stockholm. I wasn't born until Mom was further along in life. My guess is that I was a surprise. Anders and Kari are a lot older.

"Ingrid did almost everything. Her office was the first floor of our house. I used to look outside; if the patient came in on a stretcher, it was a good sign for me. In fact, the more blood the better. In Sweden, drinking and fishing are a frequent combination. Really, drinking and anything. My specialty became fishhook removal from various body parts. I could get them out in seconds. Once my task was done, it was inevitably followed by a pat on the head and 'So, you're going to be a doctor just like your mama. Good boy!'

"Nothing sugarcoated ever came from Ingrid's lips. If the patient was overweight, Mom would say, 'You're too fat. Lose twenty pounds.' It was kind of funny. The town loved my mother, but they were also afraid of her."

Tess laughed. "She sounds like a character. Clearly she's the reason you got into medicine in the first place."

VJ nodded in assent. "To me, my mom was always bigger than life. I had to do what she did. But I was involved in some other things, too. In Sweden, we have to decide when we're sixteen what path we're going to follow, and apply to *gymnasium*. I chose the natural sciences.

"After that three-year cycle, I did my year of military service. It wasn't bad. We spent a lot of time on the target range. I got assigned to a unit with Nils, the guy who took Nick. That's when we got so close. Bonds like that stay forever. Just like the medical ones between Lige, me, and Nick.

"I worked another year for the Centre Party, an environmentally focused, middle-of-the-road political group. It was a great time. I was an organizer. I don't think the experience prepared me to be prime minister, but it was valuable. As time went on I began to learn more about the politricks of politics. It doesn't matter whether it's Boston or Göteborg—the games they play are the same. I was moderately jaded when I began, but afterward, I couldn't stand the deception.

"Medical school came at the perfect time. When I applied, entrance was based exclusively on numbers. They didn't give a damn what you thought of cultural diversity, poverty in Africa, Russian hegemony, or anything else, for that matter. You either qualified or you didn't. Highly practical. Very Swedish. Karolinska was kind enough to accept me. I started there, and was really happy. Near the end of my first year, I decided that a detour to the United States was the thing to do.

"My mom reached out to her research friends at the medical school. One of them had a connection at Duke. Bam, I was on my way to the medical center for a semester of clinical science. I took pharmacokinetics, neuropathology, and extremity anatomy. I also managed to spend the time I told you about in the microvascular lab. The hand surgery bug bit me for the first time then.

"I fell in love with North Carolina. How could you not? Beautiful blue skies, people who liked me just because I was Swedish, and, of course, Southern food. There isn't a place in Stockholm that makes cheese grits, hush puppies, fried catfish, or good peach cobbler. That's also when I got to be such a big basketball fan."

"Imagine that," Tess said and yawned. "What happened when you were done?"

"Back in Sweden, all I could think about was finding a way to return to the States. It wasn't that I didn't still love my native land. I did. The U.S. had an allure I couldn't resist. Ultimately, I got my dean to approve that notorious CCU rotation that you've heard about, along with neurology and orthopaedic sub-internships.

"Tess, based on what you told me about your adventures with Jessica, you should appreciate this. One of the first nights after I got back to Durham, my buddy Magnus and I hit a local dance club. He was also doing a subinternship. We met two crazy, energetic women—Erin and Katrina. Both of them were covered head to toe in leopard outfits. You'd never know they were business students. After a couple of drinks, Erin told me that she specialized in *internationals*. She was already involved with some Nigerian diplomat's kid. Per Erin, Dikembe was *ultra benev*. In her world, people were either *benev* or *malev*—personal slang for benevolent or malevolent.

"Katrina had a boyfriend, too. His nickname was 'the Condor.' The guy's wingspan was big enough that he could practically dunk a basketball without jumping. Magnus is just under two meters himself. The pair of them ended up playing some pretty wicked one-on-one games. But that night the men were trying to finish a presentation, so they weren't along for the party. Magnus and I were fortunate enough to be both *benev* and *international*. We didn't finally roll in until six the next morning.

"Not being romantically attached made it more fun for all of us. I thought I knew Durham before we met. Erin and Katrina made it their mission to introduce us to every restaurant, bar, and club in the city. Erin's parents live in San

Diego and own a vacation house in Sierra Lakes. A crowd of us went out in the spring. That's where the connection happened. Who would have guessed that so many years later, that first ski trip would have affected my life so dramatically? It's strange when you consider the implications of the small decisions we make every day.

"All of us still keep up. Erin is an exec with Google, and Katrina runs a health care consulting group. Magnus is a big-time cardiologist in Berlin. I'll introduce you. That might be a mistake, though. They'll get you in trouble in nothing flat."

Tess nodded. "At the moment, I'm doing a good enough job on my own. All right, VJ, please tell me you stayed in the States for better reasons than sports and business exec party animals."

"In fact, I did. Once the rotations were completed, I realized I simply wasn't ready to go back. It's difficult to explain. There's life to the culture here that's hard to quantify. I checked into every option. Marriage, even a fake one, wasn't a choice. There was no woman."

Tess couldn't hold back. "That's rich! No one to fake marry, but at the same time, someone was pregnant with me, courtesy of you. You do see the irony here, I hope?"

VJ responded, "What can I say? You're totally right. But then, I didn't know what I know

now. If I did, your life would be completely different, too. We might even be sharing a drink in some Stockholm bar. After all, it is happy hour there right now. But that's not what unfolded.

"Ultimately an outreach doctor told me about a program that would work. If I could prove I'd provide care in an underserved area, my visa would be OK. So I connected with the Public Health Service. They took me on the condition that I completed a two-year surgical internship first. That was easy. I stayed at Duke. Nothing wrong with training at a powerhouse medical center. Every other night on call was not so appealing, but the comfort of the area was. And yes, there were games to be watched and friends to hang with during the three minutes a month that were free.

"When I applied to the PHS, I had visions of doing time in downtown Los Angeles, New York, Boston, Atlanta, or Chicago. The day my papers became official, I got word that a Native American reservation in North Dakota had my name on it. North Dakota has fewer seasons than Sweden—July, August, and winter. I was beside myself. The place was called Delcourier. It was odd. The reservation consisted of a mix of Native American tribes who shared blood with French trappers: Sioux, Chippewa, Metis—you name it.

"I was assigned there with four other physicians and a dentist. Walt the jawbreaker and I shared a nice two-bedroom house near the hospital. Solid man, not particularly exciting. Fortunately, he was neat. If both of us were like me, the place would have been a disaster.

"We ran the whole show. Since I'd done surgery, I was made the surgeon. Talk about proceeding by the book. Reading the book was the only way I had the slightest idea what to do at times. Our equipment was fair. We all learned to improvise. If there was a plan A, there'd better be five backups.

"The other docs were wonderful. There was a fellow in the nearby town, Rolla, who was nothing short of brilliant, Ron Gilchrist. What a mensch. He's the one who taught me that the same problem can present in different ways in different people. The key is parsing out the nuances. Evaluate and reevaluate the depth of your perception of an issue. I hope you get an opportunity like that sometime. It's a much broader exposure than what most doctors get today. The time I spent in Delcourier also gave me a finer appreciation of my mother's character. Absolute responsibility is an extraordinarily challenging burden.

"It's strange—sometimes even now, when I'm doing a case, I feel like I'm outside my own body watching myself. I float back to when I was ten, wide-eyed and amazed, seeing my mother deliver babies. I ponder how odd it is that I'm in this place cutting through tissues, drilling holes in bone, and placing sutures in people's bodies. I judge myself and rate my own performance. On some of these occasions it also occurs to me that everyone around me assumes there is a specific, perfectly correct thing to do. The answers aren't always so clear."

Tess frowned. "That's not very encouraging. So, what are you supposed to do then?"

VJ shook his head. "I usually know what the *right* answers are. But those answers don't always satisfy the needs of a particular patient. Sometimes a drill will penetrate bone like it's made of cheese. In other cases, a jackhammer could barely make a dent. As I've matured, and I do use that term loosely, I can sense potholes a little sooner. The ones cloaked in darkness and fog are more of an issue. That spun-around humerus case I told you about ultimately went fine, but for a while I was on the precipice. I hate that feeling. As a doctor, you either live with it or do something else. There aren't a lot of choices in between."

Tess hit the gas again, like she was in a stock car race. With a smirk, she said, "That or sell out and join the Cooperative. One thing I'm wondering about. How'd your mother and your brother end up here? And what about your sister?"

VJ sighed. "Kari is as happy as a clam where she is in Petah Tikvah, married with grown kids and enjoying life. Her daughter Arielle is the one who deposited Cat in my townhouse. They're the family I worry about the least. Her husband, Mark Wildstein, is a big shot with Teva, the Israeli generic pharmaceutical giant that's based there. Before that, he was part of the IDF's elite paratrooper units. Anyone the Cooperative might send their direction would be unpleasantly surprised with the result.

"My mother's circumstances were more complex. She decided to come to Boston after she had a small stroke. She had no intention of sitting around waiting for something else to happen. I was here and truly in the best position to help her out.

"Ingrid was still a completely with-it physician. She took her Massachusetts boards, blew them away, then got a license. One of the local indigent clinics took her in. I don't think they realized they were getting the equivalent of General Patton. Yes, your grandmother was quite a person. It was so sad when the blank spots started.

"I knew what was happening, but didn't want to admit that things were going south. My neurologist friend did the workup, and as gently as possible told me that she had multi-infarct dementia. Too many small hits to her brain.

"Within a year, she couldn't put together more than two words. The hardest part was watching the decay. Our society doesn't know what to do in these tragic circumstances. Was she a shell or still a real person trapped inside? It was impossible to know. Fate intervened. She developed severe pneumonia. It wasn't a painful death. We saw to it that there was plenty of morphine.

"With me and Ingrid here, Anders had ultimately decided to make the jump to the States as well. Even though Sweden is really open, where he lived he didn't feel completely comfortable being gay. I can't say I wasn't strongly encouraging Anders to join us. He has issues. The primary one is that he's tremendously talented. Anders has much, much more going on in the wonderful, artistic person department. He used to imagine a picture and then make a sketch appear. That was before he developed Stargardt macular dystrophy, an incredibly rare eye disease.

"Anders turned to his other passion, music. He loves to tell stories. When he goes on stage, the audiences eat him up. Everyone adores Anders. His husband, Jacques, jokes that living with a saint gets old."

Tess interjected, "Anders sounds incredible. How is it he inherited all the artistic, reasonable, type B genes and you didn't get any?"

VJ disregarded the sarcasm. "Nature works in mysterious ways, Tess. Maybe one of your classmates will figure those questions out one day. That's the cool thing about knowing some of the people you know. They'll make a difference."

She grinned. "I feel like I'm opening a buried treasure chest. It's a lot to think about. And now there's Leila."

VJ's mood brightened instantly. "Leila is the first woman in a long, long time that I feel I've been able to really connect with. She gets me. That's not easy for most people. I got so used to taking care of myself. I thought that was safe. I preferred to be alone, rather than take a chance and get hurt. I honestly didn't think I could be so lucky. The best part is that she doesn't need me. Leila and I both know that. Despite all the insanity, she's *choosing* to be with me. That fact makes me feel amazing."

Tess passed another car. She was driving like she was on a mission. When the road was clear of vehicles to conquer, she said, "VJ, I met you less than twenty-four hours ago. It's really peculiar, but I feel like I've known you my whole life. You're about the furthest thing from normal I've ever encountered. That's OK. I'll adjust. What about you? Are you willing to change your name to Risdall?"

He said, "As long as I don't have to change my first name, I'm good with it."

Tess slowed the Mini. "We're almost there. I forgot to ask. Do you need cash? Credit cards seem to be a bad idea."

He shook his head. "I'm set thanks. I loaded up before yesterday. There's a couple thousand dollars in my pocket. These college kids look pretty rough, though." Doing his best Laurence Olivier impression, VJ said, *"Is it safe?"*

She smiled. "In case you're wondering if I caught it—yes I did. I've seen *Marathon Man*. At the moment, my brain is barely functioning. Let's get some breakfast. Coffee is critical. There are some great places around here." With that, the car pulled into a space at the Beach Grass Café. "The red pepper–artichoke–spinach–and–cheese omelet rocks. You should get it with a piece of coffee cake. I lived on it during college."

VJ gestured to his stomach. "Do you want to turn me into a lard butt? At best, my impulse control is terrible. Once I start, it's over. I'll stick with just the entrée. I'll tell you, though, the coffee part sounds good."

In the middle of the meal, Tess blurted out, "I'm watching you eat, and all of a sudden it dawned on me why I do some of the stupid things I do. I got it from you. I saw you tie up that straw. My friends hound me about that! You're responsible. Nature versus nurture, forget it. You can't change what the DNA lottery gives us."

VJ tried to shrug it off. "Sorry—hopefully there's some good stuff, too. I'll bet you're good at remembering people's names and when and where you met them—yes?"

She backed off. "Actually, that's true. Plus, I am at least half Swedish. That's pretty cool, except I hate fish. I guess you get credit for some things."

He confessed, "On the other hand, as I've told you already, I worry about everything. I assemble my worries on a rotating carousel. When one exits, another replaces it. Is that an issue for you?"

Tess looked angry again. "That's definitely from you! People tell me I'll be gray by thirty."

All VJ could do was apologize. "Yes, genetics can be a bitch. I continue to wonder about the other half of the equation."

When the delicious food was consumed and the dishes were cleared, they solidified weekend plans. First stop was dropping VJ at the B&B she had booked when they were getting fuel. Tess looked at him dubiously. "Can I trust you to stay out of trouble? You're going to be on your own today."

"No problem," VJ said. "Free time is fine with me; I can use it. Being dead has its plus side. No one will ask me to do anything."

Tess smiled with relief. "I was afraid this might get complicated. I've decided that your code name will be Obie Rydevik. It's got a nice ring to it. Between all the wedding commitments, I'll show you around the place. If anyone I know stops us, I'll introduce you as a professor friend of my parents interviewing at Bowdoin for a position. Can you fake being a scientist for a short conversation?"

"Done! Unless the person we meet is an expert in dark matter physics, I should be fine. I'm starting to believe that subterfuge is a family trait."

Before Tess sped away, she asked, "Are you sure you don't want to just stay and set up a practice here with Dr. Saito? It's a great town. We barely register on the Boston radar."

"You have no idea how tempted I am," VJ said. "But take my word for it: The Cooperative would track me down eventually. I died to avoid hiding. I'm going to win."

REUNITED

The next day VJ got up early and decided to sit on the porch. It was cold, but clear and beautiful. He spotted Tess parking across the street and called, "Good morning, good morning."

Steadfastly using his crutches to get down the stairs outside the Brunswick Inn, he said, "Did you have the best time? This is a perfect place! It's quiet when I'm not talking, the beds are soft, and the owners are very pleasant. I stayed up late with them last night. Did you know they used to live in Silicon Valley? They made a fortune and didn't know what to do with themselves. They got tired of the travel-without-purpose lifestyle and decided to settle here. Of course, I didn't tell them that I was a zombie equivalent. I used your cover story. Thank God the two of them are on the business side."

Tess said, "Slow down, VJ, you're wired for sound. Did you just down a quadruple espresso or something? First of all, yes, I had a great time. I probably would've had more energy if supernatural forces had left me alone the night before. There's a certain symmetry that you stayed here and liked it so much. My parents always came to this place. Did yesterday work out OK? I felt slightly guilty just leaving you."

VJ sat down on the steps, beckoning Tess to follow suit. "Do you know what makes Catholics and Jews different? Catholics are guilty because they're born, and Jews are guilty because they're alive. I know you've got a dose of the latter and maybe some of the former. It's also part of the DNA. Our good friend Bianka told me guilt is X and Y linked. Very curious." Tess laughed as he continued, "The day was wonderful. I checked out your campus for an hour and then tried to keep this knee iced and elevated. Did you happen to notice it's cold? Whose idea was it to have a March wedding? Was there a shotgun involved?"

Tess said, "I have no idea why they chose this weekend," then she closed her eyes, yawned, and stretched her petite frame like a cat. "I'm trying to remember what sleep is. Let's take a walk on campus. Do you think you can handle it?"

"What's a little pain among friends?" he said. "Seriously, I need to keep the knee moving. Yesterday I saw a bunch of people hanging out by a big polar bear. That looked like the place to be."

Tess took VJ's arm to guide him. "You're talking about the Smith Student Union. If you really want some entertainment, I'll take you to the Hubbard stacks. The things that happen there are legendary. If you're up for something more sophisticated, we'll go into the Walker Art

Museum. We can take some pictures of the lions that sit out front. For such a small place, there's a lot here." VJ smiled inside at Tess' obvious pride in her school.

After a few steps, a voice rang out. "VJ! I was just thinking of you. You know you shouldn't be gimping around two days post-op." It was Benjamin Saito himself who, at the moment, seemed intent on blowing his cover. "I was really bummed this morning when I read on the ASSH Listserv that you'd died. Was that an exaggeration? You don't look dead. I assume that there's a story here."

Tess was startled, but remained quiet. VJ motioned Benjamin to keep it down and guided him to a more secluded location to sit and talk. "Benjamin Saito, star Brunswick hand surgeon, this is a close family friend and Bowdoin graduate, Riki Ostrup. How'd you recognize me? With my head shaved, *I* don't even recognize me."

"VJ, it was your voice," Benjamin explained. "I heard you talking to Riki and knew it was you right away. I don't know what you're into, but yes, I'm really curious."

"I understand why you're surprised to see me wandering in these parts—or any parts, for that matter," VJ said quietly. "Look, the business with Nick wasn't an accident, and the same people who did that to him are after me. I wanted to tell you about it on the plane to LA, but I couldn't. It's a very complicated story that you're

275

much better off not knowing too much about. I'll tell you everything over a couple of beers sometime soon, but for now, it would help me the most if you don't say anything to anyone. Honestly, that really could get me killed."

Benjamin whistled. "It sounds like evil juju if you think someone knowing you're alive will make you dead again. I'll make you a deal. You can hang out at my place till whatever this is blows over. It'll get you away from that academic ivory tower. You can do some real work and maybe learn how to rock climb. Plus, it'll be sort of nice to have someone to bounce my cases off of. I still need a partner. In a small town, it's hard to escape those midnight ER calls even when I'm supposedly off. You must know about that from your Sierra Lakes gig."

VJ was touched. "Benjamin, that's a generous offer, but I have to take care of this problem now or it'll never go away."

Benjamin said, "I wish you all the luck in the world. When we do connect, my turn to buy. I need to hear this story. Riki, nice to meet you. Watch out for this guy—sounds like he needs it. By the way, VJ, if you don't want people to recognize you, maybe you should lose the crocodile-skin cowboy boots."

Despite all of his elaborate plans, he had ignored the obvious. VJ thanked Benjamin for his counsel and watched him as he walked up the street.

Tess said, "Riki? That was weird. He seems really cool, just like my friend said."

"He is. I told you, I connected with him instantly on the flight to LA. Still, I didn't want him to know your real name. Remember, no one knows we're connected except Bianka and Leila. I don't think there's much chance Benjamin is on the Cooperative's payroll—that would suck massively—but better to play it safe."

VJ added, "Speaking of people you should stay away from, I got the tattoo information back from Nick. Does Cyrus have a murderous clown on his forearm?" The look of fright on Tess' face and the way her fingers dug into VJ's hand told him he did.

Imploringly, Tess asked, "VJ, what am I going to do when I get home?"

He thought for a moment. "Fortunately, he seems to like you a lot. From what Nick told me, the guy has some bizarre sense of honor. Obviously, it's a good idea for you to keep your distance. It's not that he doesn't worry me, too; he does. I'm glad he only saw my eyes. Having anyone, let alone the Cooperative enforcer, connecting the two of us would not be ideal. But for now, let's keep what we know about him under our hats. If he threatens you even vaguely, we'll call the police. I can't see any advantage right now in tipping them off. What are they going to get him for, felony kitchen knife possession? Who knows, maybe I can use this information."

Tess directed VJ to a shoe store to correct his oversight, and they ditched the boots.

* * * * *

On the return trip to Boston, there were no fewer high-speed passes on the highway, but Tess at least did it more fluidly. VJ tried to convince her, yet again, that helping him might not be such a brilliant idea. His arguments were no more successful than they were with Leila. They discussed where Tess could work, how she would get in, what she would investigate, and the way she would relay information back to VJ. They also determined how she, Leila, and VJ would connect.

Tess called Axel. Without knowing who or why, he saw the situation for what it was—an opportunity to show off and have fun, perhaps even score a few points with Tess. Veiled e-mails; communication code; brand-new, security-to-the-max, self-destructing, Boeing Black phones; drop points—spy movie stuff. He loved it.

The most significant challenge was avoiding suspicion. Axel mentioned a few of the latest hacking techniques, zero-day exploits that would blow through any firewall or antivirus system and remain concealed. VJ was counting on his simulated death to substantially reduce the Cooperative's alert index. They no longer had the wild-card hand surgeon to worry about.

Business for the Cooperative could return to usual. It was now up to the four conspirators to get the information to take them down.

* * * * *

Talking to Leila a few days later, VJ said, "I've decided not to attend my own funeral service. I'm interested, of course, but going would be in incredibly bad taste. I don't want to be embarrassed if only a few people show up. I can imagine the conversation. *'Thank you for being one of three people to come to my departure celebration. I'm not really dead yet. When it does happen for real, will you come back? I can use all the support I can get. By the way, try the herring. It's extraordinary.'*"

Leila did go, over VJ's objections. "I had to—morbid curiosity, I guess," she said. "Just so that you know, everyone was very complimentary, and the attendance was impressive." She then relayed in exquisite detail the good-natured jokes made at his expense. VJ acknowledged the back-handed compliment, "I guess Lige is right-- if you go dancing, you gotta pay the fiddler."

Tess approached the medical school dean and inquired about an internship with the CEO. The timing worked because of the upcoming two week spring break. No one else had expressed an interest, so it didn't take long to get it cleared. In VJ's opinion, the man's office was the perfect location to start drilling down. He knew

Summerhays. He'd fixed the CEO's kid's supracondylar fracture, and the two men had a pretty good relationship. There was no way he was in charge of the Cooperative. His family was Main Line Philadelphia; he already had everything he wanted.

PETRA GETS SUMMERHAYSED

In Petra's office, it was celebration time. The poorly executed hit on VJ had created a huge problem. What the Lucianos were doing was unclear. Neither one had attempted any communication. There wasn't any evidence they had blown themselves up in Sierra Lakes. That piece of information was gleaned in the online *Sierra Lakes Tribune* news article, the one with the huge picture of the destroyed porno king's house. Finding out anything from the Sierra Lakes Police Department was an exercise in futility.

VJ's demise at the ambulatory surgical center resolved all concerns. Petra was just picking up the Glenfiddich for a double scotch when the CEO opened her office door without knocking. It was not the first time, and it was definitely not appreciated. Petra was savvy enough to let it ride for the time being. Even James Summerhays couldn't ruin her good mood.

The man casually sat in the plush chair opposite the big desk and started talking. Petra had learned long ago to let him have his say. Interrupting would only be an exercise in not being heard. "Petra, we need to go over the new expansion plan. The fourth floor still hasn't been finished. The damn thing is just two levels above us and we can't get it done. Which union is holding up the project now? Talk with the contractor. They're three months behind. I don't care if we've had late snow. They have to complete it soon. The gala is scheduled for next month. I want to go over some numbers with you, too.

"The ambulatory surgical center revenue is down this month. They lost fifteen percent volume when Mahaffey got hurt. And now Brio goes and manages to die at the same place—our ASC! That looked great in the papers. Thank God it was buried in the back pages. Strong work. I'm sure people are going to be lining up to get procedures done there. The bottom line is going to look terrific. Maybe we'll only lose a million. By the way, be sure to send some kind of condolences on the hospital's behalf to Brio's family.

"The bean counters just sent me the update. Those hand guys are going to have to make up the lost revenue. No choice. Remind me to talk to the chief. If he can't do the job, get someone else. Oh yeah, I almost forgot. The med school dean wants to put one of her first-years in my office to do a short internship. They're trying to educate their crowd about the realities of running this place. Tag, you're it. Let Agnes know she's coming. I'll see you later. Gotta go to the MRMC Foundation meeting. Seems we've gotten into the business of providing free home care for cancer patients. The press loves it. It's costing us a ton, but Ellen Katz-Leslie, the lady who's running it, is a superstar. Used to fund-raise for Médecins Sans Frontières—you know, Doctors Without Borders, great organization. Can't keep the Foundation waiting."

In a flourish, he was gone. There was no opportunity to argue or even discuss anything said. It just had to be done. Petra knew that too well. She had skillfully made her climb up the ladder. At the London School of Economics she'd learned quite a bit about how to navigate the male-dominated business world. Petra especially prided herself on playing men to her advantage. The Cooperative was easy to build once she ascertained how to identify and manipulate the best pawns. Summerhays was a perfect example. The hospital system bottom line always looked sound with Petra pulling the strings, so he gave her free rein to run the show as she saw fit. Plus, she kept a very low profile, never taking public credit for successes. Summerhays loved that. Occasionally complaints would reach his office about strong-arm tactics, but the CEO chose to disregard them. The board was happy. Nothing else really mattered.

* * * * *

Cyrus sat at his kitchen table playing with one of his many knives. He'd shown some of his contacts the cell phone picture he'd taken of the man with the crocodile-skin boots. He'd gotten it before Tess' associate got in the Mini Cooper. A face would have been much better, but the bastard hadn't taken off his face mask even when the two of them were driving away. So far, zero hits. Cyrus was determined to be discreet. There was no way he was going to let the Cooperative become even vaguely aware of Tess' existence.

* * * * *

The day of reckoning had arrived. Now Tess fidgeted at the elevator entrance. A dedicated stair climber, she was nonplussed that the steps couldn't be easily located. She pulled a loose piece of thread on her blouse, adjusted her belt buckle. None of it helped. Her anxiety was mounting. She'd tried to find out everything she could about this person she was assigned to— Petra Lewis. The last-minute switch created a major snafu in the plan. It wasn't like she could say she wouldn't do it now. Tess just hoped that she could still get access to what they were looking for. The online bio had the usual stuff about strategic goals, business awards, association memberships. Nothing useful. Not even a picture. She thought, *Who doesn't have a picture on their website?*

The door opened and Tess got in. The elevator car was plastered with MRMC propaganda. It reminded her of Vegas. She'd been there for a bachelorette party a year earlier. There weren't any shows being touted here, but there was a big pitch for the yearly hospital fund-raiser.

Getting off on the next level, Tess identified the door to her new temporary home and walked in with trepidation. Passing her on the way out was a massive guy who looked like a Pacific Islander. He was sweaty and looked like he'd just finished a workout. The man was wearing a New England Patriots sweatshirt—the type that only real team members usually have. As he brushed by, he said, "Excuse me." The gargantuan man didn't appear happy.

Tess was flustered for a minute. When she turned to say something, he was gone. She assumed he was one of the linemen. She was mad at herself for missing the opportunity to meet an actual player. Jessica was a huge Pats fan. She probably knew everything about the guy. Tess made a mental note to ask her.

She felt unsettled. Saying she was going to do this was a lot easier than actually jumping into the ring. VJ had tried to prepare her to the greatest extent possible. He had Tess visualize the meeting and even practiced the introduction with her. However, she wryly thought, as the famous boxer Mike Tyson had observed, "Everyone has a plan until they get punched in the mouth." Then all bets are off.

Tess scanned the office. It was cold. The pale, yellow paint on the walls reminded her of the inside of a police interrogation room. There was a Picasso reproduction that made her smile inside, though.

A decaying old woman named Agnes greeted her icily. "Take a seat over there. Ms. Lewis will be with you in a bit."

It was very unclear how long "a bit" meant. Tess knew she was no one's priority. That feeling was reinforced twenty minutes later when Petra's door opened. A faint scowl creased her upper lip, even as she was cordially greeting the young woman. Petra was wearing a black pencil skirt, with a sheer beige blouse and Prada spike heels. Her long, dark hair was pulled tightly back. Tess noticed she had an extra button undone to reveal a hint of her lacy white bra. Petra's face screamed intensity, and that's the way the discussion went.

"Hi, Tess, grab a seat. Mr. Summerhays thought our office would be a good place to get your feet wet. Administration is a completely different animal from medicine. Here we make decisions that permit us to run this monstrosity. Not all of them are patient-friendly. Our mission is to serve the public, but as you will find out, that isn't necessarily an easy balance. Bills need to be paid. I reviewed your file. My connections at Bowdoin told me you're smart, you work hard, and you have a lot of energy. Tell me something about your little hacking prank—patching Bugs Bunny cartoons into the campus security monitor feed."

Tess was mortified by the question and wondered how she got those details. "Ms. Lewis, to be honest, I did it on a dare. I was mad about the parking tickets I kept getting. My roommate thought it'd be entertaining to mess with the cameras. I'm not an elite hacker. I just know a couple of things. It probably wasn't the smartest decision I've ever made."

Petra registered the explanation, but pursued the line of inquiry. "Nonetheless, I'm intrigued. How'd you get discovered? You know, doing things you shouldn't is usually only a problem if you get caught doing it. At least that's what they taught us in business school." She laughed, somewhat unpleasantly, then stopped. "Obviously, we take a different approach here at MRMC. I don't expect anything unprofessional in our office. That would reflect very badly on you, and me. Tell me how they caught you."

Everything she said was making Tess uneasy. "My roommate got drunk at a party after I hacked the system. She talked about what I'd done to someone who happened to be on the Judicial Board. Please don't get the wrong idea about me. It was a one-off. I'm here to help you and learn about hospital administration." She wondered whether she was undone already.

Petra's strong response surprised Tess. "Tess, I *didn't* get the wrong idea. I detested the campus police. Most of them pretended to be nice and helpful while they were looking down my shirt. What you did was edgy, but it didn't hurt anyone. I actually respect that. Spending your spring break here is ridiculous. Two weeks is too short a time to try to learn anything, so you can't expect much. When you come back in the summer we'll be able to accomplish a lot more. But I'll try to teach you a few things. A fair portion of what we do is mundane, but there can be some excitement, too." Petra seemed slightly more at ease, so Tess made an effort to relax enough to remember to breathe.

Petra got up and walked to her front window, staring angrily at the construction project below. "I wish they'd finish that building. It's ugly. Look at that rebar sticking out everywhere. It reminds me of some third-world country where nothing ever gets accomplished.

"Back to what I was saying—politics are paramount in every phase of our operation. I haven't really had anyone come in for an internship before. You strike me as a sensible person. I'll have you attend some of my meetings—they're endless. But I need some help with this gala. These events are not my favorite. On top of it, we're supposed to be opening the addition on the top floor soon. One of the major donors is responsible for that. She wants to show it off to her friends. There are a lot of details that need to be addressed. Responsibility means we have to get everything right. If you're going to be here, I need you to help. Are you up for that?"

Tess smiled and nodded as responsibly as she could. Petra said, "I trust you are. By the way, there are some billionaire donors we need to meet with. You need to wear a nicer outfit tomorrow. What questions can I answer for you?"

Tess' mind was going in a thousand different directions. Petra's clothing comment made her even more self-conscious. She pondered the situation. The woman sitting behind the big desk was definitely no-bullshit. Was she involved in any of the nefarious activities that VJ had told her about? Petra's personality was certainly harsh enough. If she was in the Cooperative, Tess needed to determine what was she doing for them, and how she was doing it. Petra seemed to have her hands full with everything MRMC could dish out. To Tess, everyone had to be a suspect. Agnes seemed particularly guilty. Petra's new intern resolved to be extremely careful around her.

The inquiry was repeated. "Tess, do you have any questions?"

Tess returned to the present. "No, not yet, but I know I will. I'm happy to help you with anything you need me to do. Tell me what you want me to start with and I'll get it done."

Petra responded as warmly as she seemed able. "We'll get it all figured out. If you don't mind, could you go to the coffee cart downstairs and get cups for us both? I haven't slept particularly well the last couple of weeks. Too many fires to put out. I could use the caffeine. I take mine black. Tell them to put it on my expense account."

Tess said, "Well, I can absolutely handle that." Then she thought of something else. "Ms. Lewis, my roommate's a big football fan. Was that one of the players I just saw?"

Petra did an odd thing with her mouth, pursing it, then responded, "Yes. He's making a donation, but he wants to remain anonymous, so no more about him to anyone—got it?" Tess nodded. Petra softened again. "Tess, call me Petra. I can't stand the name Lewis. I still need to use it professionally, but it reminds me of someone I detest."

While Tess was pursuing the coffee, Petra picked up her phone and dialed Rick. "Summerhays parked a med student here. Maybe he wants an unwitting spy. Who knows—I wouldn't put anything past that S.O.B. The student's name is Tess Risdall. I got her med school admissions file, and there isn't anything in it that gives her a great reason to be here. I want to know everything you can find out about her. She's sharp. I guarantee it. For now, let's keep our meetings outside the office."

* * * * *

On the T ride home that evening, Tess couldn't escape a haunting feeling. Petra was occupying her brain. She felt on edge around her, yet at the same time, oddly drawn to her, too. During the

290

course of the day, Petra had told Tess all about her own path to the COO position. Forget the glass ceiling. No one was going to hold that woman back. Petra was peculiar and familiar all at once. During the day, she made it clear that she had expectations, but equally clear that Tess was by no means going to be her slave. She'd already started to receive the "Petra Lewis Quick and Dirty How to Run a Hospital" primer. Still, she had to remind herself not to let her guard down. Tigers are beautiful animals until they rip apart their prey.

The fascination was short-lived. Within a week, Petra became more demanding and curt. In fact, the dragon lady turned out to be nice in precisely zero ways. Tess made the mistake of telling Petra she had misaligned several buttons of her blouse one morning. The comment was met with a barrage of profanity offensive even to Tess, the queen of foul language. There was a lot of yelling in Petra's office behind closed doors. She reminded Tess of a simmering pot about to explode.

That's why it gave her particular pleasure to break into Petra's office to do what needed to be done. Tess knew if Petra ever found out, she'd probably be mad enough to want to eliminate her.

* * * * *

Cyrus answered on the first ring. On the other end of the call was his childhood friend Micah.

"Hey, Cyrus, I think I've got something for you. I was showing that picture you sent me to some people. One of them works in the surgery center at MRMC. He said he's seen those crocodile boots on one of the doctors that works there. A dude named Erik Brio. You don't have to worry about him anymore, though. He died there last month."

Cyrus put down his cell and immediately went online. He found the obituary. The fact that the man had died the day *before* he saw a man with the same boots drive off with Tess did not escape Cyrus' attention.

VJ RESURFACES

Tess' short internship was half over, and VJ's ability to impotently sit and wait was wearing thin. She'd contacted him and told him she thought she'd found a window Axel could use to penetrate the system.

VJ was stewing in his run-down, off-the-beaten-track Quincy hotel room when the check-in call from Leila finally came. MRMC had lost a number of experienced nurses. Human Resources was very happy to get someone with Leila's experience in an ICU. They'd rushed her paperwork through and given her a spot in the medical intensive care unit. She'd started a week earlier. It was perfect. The sickest people in the hospital went there. Every patient was constantly undergoing tests. A shame for the patients, but very helpful for the investigation, was the fact that frequently they also died there.

VJ picked up on the first ring. "Leila, I miss you like you wouldn't believe."

She interrupted him, "That's a good thing, but it shouldn't be a problem for long." With that, there was a knock on the door.

VJ practically jumped out of his skin when he saw her through the peephole. "Leila, what are you doing here?" he asked when he let her in.

Nonchalantly she answered, "Do you think I trust you to take care of yourself? I can't have you dying twice in such a short time." With that she gave him an enormous hug.

VJ was still on edge. "Look, I can't be sure that the Cooperative doesn't know you're connected to me. Who can say what those two slimebags in Sierra Lakes saw or told their bosses? Is it impossible to think that someone's watching you?" He was worried that Leila was taking any chance whatsoever. "It's risky enough that you're working at MRMC. You do understand that this group seems to have gone from the chop-off-the-digits to the execute-all-prisoners approach."

Leila lightly traced her finger on VJ's face and kissed him. "VJ, give me some credit. The path I took to get here makes your Europe trip with Nick seem like a straight line. Believe me, there is no way the Cooperative has anyone outside. Why would anyone even look at me twice? I understand that we're playing a very dangerous game, but I just needed to see you. Talking on the phone can't replace being together to help each other."

VJ said, "You know those movies where the destroyer is hovering over the submarine, pinging, pinging, pinging? The guys in the metal tube are silently going berserk. Then the ship above starts hurling depth charges and all hell breaks loose. Gauges crack, water is spewing everywhere, and the captain is yelling orders to try to regain control. That's what we're trying to avoid. Getting blown up or drowning are both equally poor options."

She kissed him again. Holding Leila in his arms made VJ feel more human. It was hard to resist the temptation to immediately dispense with all conversation and launch into a passionate night of lovemaking. Instead, he guided Leila to sit on the threadbare, lime-green couch. "So, what's the verdict?"

She had positive news. "Believe it or not, I've already worked four twelves. Five patients have died. Axel has their identifying information and accurate times of death. Tess got him on the system. Did she tell you? He said he's been able to trace and document add-on tests and procedures done *after* the person was in the morgue. VJ, are you there?"

VJ was still thinking about the nurse-detective role Leila was playing, so it took him a second to respond. "Yes, Tess called about an hour ago. She's been working in a different office with a person I really know very little about—Petra Lewis. The CEO put her there. It sounds like the woman's a hard-ass. They've been spending time on some stupid hospital gala that the administration is hot and bothered about. According to Tess, Petra is frequently out of the office, so with Axel's help she's had latitude to work some hacking magic. Nick gave me a list of doctors he thought might be on the Cooperative payroll. Axel found a money trail, which is great. Tess has been running their names to see where intersections are popping up. I put Chuck Danguerin on the top. So far, no hits there.

"Between that and what you're doing, we're starting to get a clear picture of how big this thing really is. Tess and I have a meeting set up tomorrow morning. Now the key is finding out who's pulling the strings. If it's going to happen, I want it to be fast. Petra's a wild card I wasn't counting on. From what Tess says, she's very shrewd."

Leila spent the night. The spectacular romantic visions he had conjured in his brain didn't materialize. They both passed out in each other's arms. Before Leila left to go back to the hospital early the next morning, they agreed that she'd tell VJ in advance about their next face-to-face meeting. He longed for the opportunity to be together without threat. As she was opening the door, she turned and said, "VJ, the thing with Tess has been bothering me. Do you really think it's safe for her to do what she's doing? What if Petra herself *is* involved? That office wouldn't be the safest place on the planet to be."

VJ was already having second thoughts about Tess' role. Leila's comment struck him like a spike going through his heart. He said, "I've been wrestling with that since I found out she wasn't with Summerhays. I'm going to talk to her about pulling out today."

Leila said, "That's the answer I was looking for." She gave him a hug and kiss, and left. VJ was struck with pangs of tenderness and anxiety all at the same moment.

* * * * *

Wearing his Tufts University baseball cap with its emblazoned crossed elephant tusks pulled tightly down above his eyes, and sporting a newly dyed black goatee, VJ ventured out to the IMAX at the Boston Aquarium, the designated rendezvous location. He struggled to focus on the movie about the all-important but vanishing Great Barrier Reef sea snail. *How will we go on without them?* he mused. Tess scooted in next to him, handed him the plain manila envelope with the promised documents, and then started to get up to leave. VJ motioned for her to follow him out.

They found a relatively isolated spot near the waterfront and opened what he thought would be a low-key conversation. "Tess, Leila and I have been talking about your situation in Petra's office. Both of us think you should pull out. There's no reason that anyone should be looking at you, but I don't want to take that chance."

The conversation did not go particularly well. Tess grabbed both of his shoulders with amazing force. Her eyes became demonic. "No fucking way. I don't give a damn what you and Leila decided." The words were measured, but the cold tone sounded eerily similar to his own when he wanted there to be no doubt about the message. "You may be my father, but you're not my dad, and I'm not fourteen. I'm in, and I'm on it. I don't want to hear anything else about me quitting. Got it?" Tess released her grip.

Now she implored VJ to listen carefully. "Look at what's in that folder. It validates everything you said. The Cooperative is covering their tracks, but not well enough. To anyone sniffing from the outside, everything seems normal. But Axel is a brilliant, white-hat hacker. You were right. The reported times of death didn't correspond with the real times Leila recorded. They don't differ by more than six to eight hours, yet an amazing number of tests are squeezed into those short time frames. It's a huge revenue stream. There are multiple surgical cases on completely separate patients overloaded with bogus procedures. I've got billed charges for people who don't even exist. They did it with faked social security numbers.

"I have to talk to Leila. There is a hospital intensivist and two nurses who are tied to each of the patients. If there's someone who should be careful, it's her. This scam isn't just a Medicare fraud. They're hitting every insurance carrier the hospital contracts with. It looks like there's a tag on the fraudulent bills. We found an

'Unidentified Doctor Payment' file that has records of multiple sizable deposits. The reimbursement is routed to a separate account that's getting disbursed to banks around the world. The Cooperative has been careful. Axel did a deep-packet inspection to see if he can trace it to whoever is running the show. We don't have that yet. By the way, he's put in a logic bomb malware package that will blow their doors off the second we get everything we want. He's got it rigged so they won't even be able to collect a dollar for a box of Girl Scout cookies. This is the bonanza you wanted, we're about to decapitate them, and you're talking to me about leaving *now*?"

The rage dissipated from her face. She grabbed him again with her small, strong hands. "VJ, I'm not stupid. I'm not going to give Petra the slightest reason to believe I have any agenda other than trying to learn about administration. Remember, I didn't seek her out. She knows I was supposed to work with Summerhays. I know you feel guilty, and you should. But I really do want to do what's right. The Cooperative will disappear, and no one in charge will go down even if we report the whole thing to the police tomorrow. We're close. We'll let down a lot of people if we stop now. How many more Nicks are there going to be? How many more VJs?"

For the moment, VJ gave up the battle and removed several of the documents from the large manila folder marked "Workout Schedules." The data were amazing. He couldn't resist smiling. It was the first time he felt like the Cooperative wasn't winning. "Tess, I don't really know what a 'white-hat hacker' or a 'deep-packet inspection' is, but Axel and you are nothing less than incredible. I assume he's doing whatever he's doing in the best possible, least-easy-to-detect way?"

She looked at him like he was an idiot. "Really, VJ, are you asking me that question?"

VJ held up both hands in surrender. "By the way, did Petra give you a separate office to work in?"

Matter-of-factly, Tess said, "No, she didn't. Axel hacked her password, and it worked to get me onto her desktop. The Cooperative is using the hospital system for most of what it's doing."

VJ went berserk. "Are you out of your mind? What if she finds out? We don't know anything about her! If she's on their payroll, your life won't be worth two cents. Not even that. What was all that about being careful?"

Tess held her ground. "VJ, honestly, it's OK. Petra was out of the office all day for a meeting in Providence. Her fossil secretary has been gone for medical issues. The Cooperative probably killed her and is billing for fake procedures right now. Anyway, it gave me a perfect opportunity to do some looking. I had to pick the lock to get in, but now Axel's plugged into everything that happens on that device. Believe me, I was careful. Plus, I've only got one more day."

VJ didn't feel any better, and he didn't back down. "Great, Tess. You picked the lock and hacked the computer; it's like playing in a nuclear minefield. You need to get out of there. Axel's linked in. You've done everything you could possibly do."

Without a hint of relenting, Tess said, "OK, I promise not to do anything else to compromise myself or the plan."

VJ had to live with that. Intellectually, he knew that Tess was aware there was great danger. But he wasn't sure she truly understood it on a gut level. "I appreciate you going along with me on this. I need to talk to Axel. I want to ask him more about these data, and how deep he can go into the system."

Tess now had a look in her eyes like she was calculating her own plan. "No problem; Axel wants to speak with you, too. Not related, but I need to do my ten-mile run. Stockholm syndrome at work. Exercise is my captor. Plus, the marathon's on Monday. If you think it's stupid for me to be in Petra's office today, there's no way you should be coming out to watch me with a thousand people around that you know."

The shift in conversation allowed VJ to take a momentary break from worrying to think about the things regular people in Boston were focused on. He considered his earlier promise to show up. "You're obviously right, but I'm going completely stir-crazy. I have to get out. The forecast is for forty-six degrees and light rain. Ironically, it was exactly the same the year I did it. I can wear a hoodie, a sweatshirt, these glasses, and a new beard. I guarantee that even you and Leila won't know it's me. I can't completely explain it, but I desperately want to see you finish the race. Just qualifying in your age category is a fantastic accomplishment."

Tess finally smiled. "Thanks, VJ. How 'bout if Axel calls you at nine tonight?"

He gave her a quick hug. "Works for me." A second later she was gone. He thought about this courageous young woman with whom he was blessed to be associated. Little did the Cooperative know what a threat to them she'd become.

CYRUS DRAWS NEAR

The binoculars told Cyrus that Tess and the man she was talking to had had a big argument that they seemed to work out. It was difficult for him to be certain whether this man and Brio were one and the same, but Cyrus' instinct screamed yes. He'd already connected the dots between Brio and Mahaffey. If there was a fake death, it had to relate to the Cooperative. For his life, Cyrus could not understand what Brio and Tess had going. The way they'd hugged showed him there wasn't anything romantic.

Cyrus worried that the man he thought to be Brio had ID'd him as the one responsible for Mahaffey's hand. He had also wondered if Tess was aware. Cyrus assumed the answer to both questions was yes. He'd kicked himself a thousand times for being so impulsive and foolish that morning. Yet again, he'd blown it. Tess knew where he lived, but nothing had happened. That meant either he was wrong and they didn't know or they had no current interest in exposing him. One way or another, he had to find out.

Cyrus decided that switching reconnaissance to Brio was the smart play. After the man's liaison with Tess, he tracked him to

Quincy, but then lost him when he unexpectedly cut through an alley and into the side door of a building. Highly irritated, Cyrus said out loud, "I'll find you again."

At that same moment Cyrus heard a buzzing above his head. He looked up and saw one of those incredibly annoying drones. It was hovering with its camera trained directly on the area he was standing. A quick glance around revealed the person responsible. Cyrus charged the unsuspecting man, grabbed the controller, and smashed it on the street. The crazed look in Cyrus' eyes and the knife he flashed were enough to convince the city voyeur to stifle any protests.

* * * * *

Petra unlocked the door to her office with her personal key. Agnes was the only other person who had one. Not that there was anything important. She was too paranoid for that. She sat down in her plush swivel chair and closed her eyes for a minute. She hadn't slept well again the night before. Even though Brio was no longer a problem, she still worried about how long she could keep the whole operation functioning smoothly. There had been too many recent problems. Mahaffey. The disappearance of the Lucianos. The close call with Brio. *Is it time to get out?* Petra asked herself. Her bank accounts were close to where she thought they needed to be. Rick was worrying her, too. He seemed to be more confrontational. Pondering these dilemmas, she sat up suddenly.

Had she seen what she thought she saw? Petra stared at her keyboard. There was no doubt about it. It was off angle. She dialed Agnes at home immediately.

Without even the courtesy of a greeting, Petra interrogated her secretary. "Did you come in my office today?"

Completely used to this form of inquiry, Agnes responded in her standard blank monotone. "Of course not, Ms. Lewis. I know how much you hate that when you're gone."

Petra hung up with no goodbye. She was incensed. Agnes never lied. Out loud, Petra yelled, "That little bitch. What was she doing on my computer? How did she get in here?" Impulsively, she shoved the computer. There was a certain satisfaction she experienced with the exploding sound it made as it hit the floor.

Petra felt temporarily back in control. *Now,* she thought, *how to deal with this new problem?* She picked up the phone again and scrolled through her contacts, quickly finding the name she wanted. "Rick, I have some new concerns about this med student, Tess. I'm pretty sure she got into my office. I have no idea what she's up to, but I don't like it. Find her and watch her. *Do not* question me on this."

VJ'S TURN

VJ decided to go for a run. His knee was improved enough to tolerate a slow one. He didn't know where or how far, but it seemed like a good opportunity to clear his head and figure out his next move. It wasn't as if he had a full schedule of patients or a dinner date.

While pounding down the pavement wearing his new Hokas, a thought flew through his brain before it could even register. It had the same effect that the house creaking late at night had when he was a child. VJ was worried. Something was wrong other than the fact that his knee was barking at him. He knew it, but he wasn't even sure what it was.

He ended up at the edge of Brookline and decided to take the closest T back to the ramshackle hotel. It was late. A disheveled man, clearly blotto drunk, wandered to the end of the car, yanked his pants down, and started to take a leak on the door. One of the passengers who appeared not far from living on the street himself started screaming, "What the hell aah yah doing, yah motherfuckin' piece ah shit? Put yah fuckin' pants on and stop that!"

The drunk's head snapped around. Unfortunately, so did the spray from the source of the problem. That was all it took. The yelling man laid him out with a nice combination. "Fuckin' asshole" was all he said. Justice served. VJ had the same idea for the Cooperative.

Back at the hotel, VJ picked up the delivery he had been so eagerly awaiting. Once in the room, he studied the billing documents and names of those involved who were associated with MRMC. Axel had managed to break through multiple layers of files with strong firewalls. The scam involved strategic players in almost every surgical department, as well as the ICU. Hundreds of thousands of dollars to each. Payments were proportional to the fake charges entered. The Cooperative was making old-fashioned greed work.

VJ was saddened but not surprised to see that his urologist, Milo Marconi, was on the Cooperative payroll, as was one Brittany Jane Morgan. He winced when he saw her name. It confirmed that the one-night stand was as dumb a move as he'd thought. Chuck Danguerin's name wasn't on the list. VJ still wasn't convinced. Maybe he *was* running the whole show. It didn't make sense, but anything was possible. None of the doctors were currently married. There were a startling number who were divorced. The Cooperative did their homework to find the right type of individual for their game.

VJ passed along everything he had to Leila via the ultra-secure e-mail that Axel had set up.

If he got nailed, Leila, Tess, and Axel were now in a position to fry a lot of people. They still had nothing directly linking the doctors to the mysterious Rick and whoever else was helping to run the Cooperative. In fact, there was no Rick to be found at all. There was, however, a lot of cash being routed to someone or several someones. If Axel wasn't successful identifying him, VJ was determined to find a way to draw Rick out from the shadows.

DISCOVERED

Late in the evening several days later, Petra saw a text message from Rick asking for an emergency meeting. They agreed on a bar in the North End. The owner there would make sure no one would bother them. It was an easy sell. He was the owner.

Rick pulled his massive frame into the secluded booth Petra chose. He was even more serious than usual. No pleasantries were exchanged. "Brio's alive. I don't have to tell you that's a problem. Worse, he also seems to know Tess."

Petra smashed her fist on the table. "Jesus fucking Christ! Are you kidding me? When did you find out?"

Rick answered, "About a minute before I texted you. After Brio supposedly kicked it in the ASC, I got our IT guy to hack into the protected e-mail system. I ran a trace on everything going to or from Brio before the event. I also ran through everything his contacts sent. Brio was pretty careful. One of his friends slipped—Bianka Messi. She sent a note to your intern, Tess, but she blind-copied Brio. A meeting was arranged for Tess and the professor the night Brio supposedly died. Per your instructions Alberto has been watching her. He tailed her today to a coffee shop in Quincy—not your typical Harvard medical student hangout. He thought the guy she met looked vaguely familiar, so he took some pictures. When he ran it through the facial recognition software, Brio popped up. It can't be anyone but him.

"I sent someone to reel in the brother—Anders. He and his husband, Jacques, are gone. No trace of them. My guess is that Brio somehow found out about the hit you put on him in Sierra Lakes and got them out of Boston. The anesthesiologist and nurse who declared him dead were either incompetent or in collusion with him. Most likely the latter. Both of them are out of the city. The coroner's office independently confirmed the death. The guy in charge is gone too. Whatever happened, I don't think I have to tell you that the fact that Brio's still here in town, meeting with someone working in your office, is a major problem for both of us."

Petra glared at her accomplice with daggers. "Of course I know it. Rick—I can't stand that tone."

Rick regarded his partner with decided concern. Petra had once told him that she was guided by one principle—ruthless pragmatism. She seemed to have forgotten that basic tenet. Her decision to put the hit on Brio in the first place was a bad one. For the past several weeks she'd seemed less controlled. That meant danger for everyone around her.

Petra hissed, "Can we bring Tess in now? I'd like to have a little conversation with her."

Rick sighed. "Not yet. Alberto lost her on the T. Mr. Jeremy and Zeiger are watching her apartment. She hasn't shown up yet."

Petra said, "How did Alberto manage to lose Tess? Very sloppy. She's running the marathon tomorrow. She's probably staying at a hotel tonight. You know I'm going to have to find someone to take care of both of them."

Rick's face remained stony. He contemplated reaching across the table and strangling the small, pathological creature staring at him. He had never killed anyone. He mused that now might be the right time to start. Who would miss the she-wolf? No one. Unfortunately, even if he had the nerve, Rick knew he couldn't do it. Petra had made sure of it. The man in the corner holstering the .357 Magnum was her insurance.

Rick tried to placate his partner. "Petra, settle down. Does it make sense to threaten half the medical center? Alberto mentioned that Brio looked totally different. The connection with your intern is unclear. She just dropped into your lap, almost literally. A soft touch to find out her role in all of this would be helpful to us. Once we get to her, we'll have Brio. He can't know we're watching."

Petra finally responded, "Do not lecture me about what is or isn't a good plan. Did you get intel on this Messi lady?"

Rick handed over a folder. "Here's everything. There isn't much on the professor. She knew Tess' parents. Academia in Boston is inbred. Everyone lives around everyone else or they go to the same church or synagogue or club. Seems she was just someone Brio used to work with—no indication he was banging her. I doubt he told her anything important. Don't worry, someone will speak with Messi."

Petra wasn't feeling any happier. "All right, Rick. Keep me in the loop. I'll be patient for now."

* * * * *

The truth was Petra couldn't stand it another second. *For fuck's sake,* she thought, *Rick, what's wrong with you? This is business, pure and simple. Are you in or out? I'll take care of this, but we're going to have a serious talk about our partnership. Would she have to take care of him too?* The unlikely pair got up from the table and exited separately. Before leaving, the bouncer said, "Everything OK, boss?" Rick responded as he brushed by, "I got it."

Once home, Petra drained two shots of Death's Door White Whisky and placed the necessary call. Petra had Tess' race bib number. She'd told her she wanted to follow her progress and know exactly when Tess finished the marathon. Petra had been genuinely interested.

Taking out Tess was something she didn't really want to do. There were things about her she liked. That she was so devious made Petra respect her more. The facts were the facts, though. Having Tess or Brio continue to breathe was not something she was willing to accept.

BOSTON MARATHON, PATRIOTS' DAY

Donnie O'Sullivan woke up from another bender at four in the morning. He wasn't running the marathon. Patriots' Day wouldn't be a day off from work, because he'd lost his job. The new antidepressant the doctor gave him didn't seem to be working at all. Now his back was killing him. Donnie padded around the bathroom looking for the Toradol anti-inflammatory pills he'd gotten at some point. He couldn't find his reading glasses, so he just picked up one of the bottles that looked right; he could see a T and an L. He took three and went back to bed. Not that it worked. Donnie tossed and turned until his wife got up three hours later. From the bathroom, she yelled, "Donnie, what the hell wuh yah doing with my Ultram? I need it, and those fuckin' pain management assholes said they won't give me any moah."

Beaten down again Donnie answered, "What the fuck, the bottle says Toradol."

She yelled back, "Yah fuckin' moron—it says Tramadol. Can't yah read?"

Donnie was about to have another long day.

THE WAITING GAME

Tess and VJ walked to the Common, where she would grab the bus for the long ride to Hopkinton to the start line. It was completely overcast. The cold mist was biting. Spring would be delayed for at least a few more days. There was electricity in the crowd of people scarfing down bagels, gels, goos, salt tablets, juice, energy bars, bananas, and any other food that wasn't nailed down. Tess stared into space. She started on a short, adrenaline-fueled monologue. Having been there himself, VJ didn't interrupt.

"You know, VJ, maybe I shouldn't have gone to Pizza Craze so late on Saturday. I'm still tired. Nothing else was open and I needed a fix. The only thing available in Boston 24/7 is stupidity. Sometimes I think I have the market cornered. I was up studying for my pathology test. They scheduled it for today, the day we got back from break, on Patriot's day no less—how much sense does that make? Everyone else is taking it this morning. My professor told me there was absolutely no way I could take it early. I bribed her with double chocolate chip cookies. I think she was impressed I was willing to be so obvious. It helped that she's run the marathon before. She could relate to my stress. I snuck it in yesterday afternoon, right after you forced me to meet you at that greasy spoon in Quincy. I'm really relieved it's behind me, but now I'm going to do this race. I just want to finish in a decent time."

She took a moment and scanned the crowd. "There certainly are enough police around. I guess nobody's really interested in another bombing." VJ cringed. When it happened, he was in the operating room. The entire staff had felt powerless. It was an awful scar. Everyone in the city knew it would be impossible to erase. He snapped back to the present when Tess said, "Am I an idiot to run today?"

VJ gave her a big hug. "Tess, you're going to be fine! Just have fun. Save something for Heartbreak Hill." He walked her to the buses lined up on Boylston Street. Once she was safely in place, he took a long walk. Leila would have been there as well, but she was working/spying. The chill made him feel alive.

After wandering for a few hours, he made his way to one of the hotel lobbies near the finish line at Copley Square. He stared at the book he'd bought to pass the time, but mostly just sat observing everyone around him. One guy stood out. He was wearing a BoSox hat and wraparound shades. VJ had caught a glimpse of him outside as well. Despite being indoors, he kept the sunglasses on. The man was casually sipping coffee and reading the paper. There wasn't any real reason to be concerned, so VJ continued to quietly fidget. Finally, the clock suggested he should go outside and start looking for Tess.

Marathon crowds are joyous. The cowbells ringing, people screaming encouragement to all the runners, groups merging as a unit to achieve triumph. *So great!* he thought, then reflected back on his own experience. Gutting it out, he ultimately crossed at three hours, fifty-nine minutes, fifty-seven seconds. In the process he tore his plantar fascia with the final sprint. But, goal accomplished. He'd retire knowing he'd done a sub-four. Now here he was watching his daughter tackling the same challenge. Tess could destroy him—he liked that.

VJ walked past the library entrance. The crowd boomed. Throngs of people were making their way up the street wearing Red Sox garb. Apparently, the Patriots' Day game had ended well. He'd overheard that it was a walk-off shot over the famed Green Monster. *It's always better when Boston sports teams win,* he mused. Happy drunks fight less. The metacarpal fractures and fight bites that came in after a Red Sox loss defined VJ's practice some days. Bostonians are battlers. He was always amazed when he saw the cocky Yankees fans rev up after a victory. Those wars never ended well for them.

VJ heard a loud roar for a particularly strong runner who managed a terrific finish to conclude her day. He asked a bystander if he could check his phone app to look at Tess' progress. He was astounded. Not bad for someone running the Boston Marathon into a fourteen-mile-per-hour headwind.

VJ crossed Boylston and nestled into a spot about one hundred yards ahead of the finish line. Looking back, he briefly spotted the man wearing the BoSox hat and shades, crossing about thirty feet behind him in the crowd. Then, a moment later, VJ waved madly as he saw Tess running furiously in her bright orange shoes and lucky cloverleaf green top. She was on the other side of the street, but just at the right moment, she glanced over and their eyes met. Big smile. Tess raised her hand with a quick wave and buzzed by.

As planned, VJ met her at the hotel entrance. Draped in a Heatsheet foil wrapper and clutching her water bottle, she was beaming. Tess wanted to walk, so they passed Newbury and headed over to Comm Ave beyond where the runners were passing. He wanted to hear about every detail of the race. By not trying to set any personal records, Tess was able to do just that. Heartbreak Hill proved to be the massive pain it was expected to be, but not a deal-breaker. Tess was happy. VJ was thrilled for her. The sun broke through the clouds. God seemingly was smiling on both of them, if only for that moment.

PURSUED

The man wearing the BoSox hat and wraparound shades watched Brio and Tess from a short distance, pacing himself to keep up without alerting his quarry. He fingered the handle of the 9x19 parabellum Glock 17 beneath his coat. The suppressor was already in place. The new Trijicon RMR reflex sight assured accuracy. He smiled, visualizing the bullet penetrating Brio's brain. Petra's instructions were explicit—drop the man first, then the girl. He found the perfect location to fire the rounds without detection. The deafening noise and crowd focus on the runners was good cover.

However, at exactly the wrong moment, two plus-size tourists stopped on the sidewalk, positioning themselves in the worst possible place. He couldn't see anything. As he struggled to find a better vantage point, Brio and the girl disappeared. The assassin cursed with frustration.

He scanned the masses and thought, *Where are they?* As he filtered through the groups of runners and spectators, a malevolent smile formed. He'd spotted the targets. Brio and Tess were walking slowly toward the Back Bay. That would be an equally perfect place to do the double hit. He fingered the Glock and carefully removed it from its stealth location. The pair were his. No escape this time.

* * * * *

Donnie was barreling down the street feeling good. The medicine had kicked in big-time. At least he had his license back. He'd conned one of the mindless drones at the DMV into reissuing his. The asshole judge had said he couldn't drive for two years. Wrong—he was back on the road inside a month. All the marathon losers walking on the street were pissing him off. Every five seconds he had to stop because someone was in the road. He mused how fun it would be just to run them all down. Serve them right for thinking they were better than him.

Donnie looked up at the traffic light for the turn onto Commonwealth Avenue. He couldn't tell what color it was. He accelerated onto the ultrabusy street. Car horns sounded immediately in disapproval. Something was wrong. Donnie was feeling strange, different than he'd ever felt, even when he was dead drunk. He seemed to be separating from his own body. At the same time his head felt like it was splitting, there was a taste like burnt toast in his mouth, and his arm was tingling. The faces of the other drivers got fuzzy.

Donnie would never have the opportunity to understand that some antidepressants don't mix well with Tramadol. When the grand mal seizure began, Donnie's foot hit the gas instead of the brake. His pickup launched off the road like a rocket onto the wide pedestrian thoroughfare.

* * * * *

Shrill screams penetrated the din of the traffic. Tess wheeled around. In an instant VJ grabbed her around the waist, swept her up, and carried her to a protected site. The gray truck smashed into a tree just a few yards behind where they stood. People were knocked down like bowling pins, lying at odd angles in the newly bloodstained grass. As Tess steadied herself and assessed the surrounding carnage, the gravity of the situation became apparent. There were injured and dying everywhere.

VJ looked at his daughter with a mix of fear and urgency. "You OK?" She nodded. With that he ran to a man writhing on the ground. Tess knew she couldn't just stay there and not help. She went over to another of the fallen and did everything she possibly could before the legions of ambulances arrived.

Two runners sat huddled together, one with blood streaming down her leg. Tess approached her first, gesturing at the extremity. "Can I take a look at your leg?"

The woman was a classic marathon type—mid-twenties, blonde hair swept back in a ponytail, probably about five-three, 105 to 110 pounds. Instantly the runner dissolved in her arms. The blood wasn't the runner's. It belonged to a friend from their marathon club. No more races for that one. The magnitude of the tragedy was so obvious when viewed through the soul of this beleaguered person. Tess found a towel and gently wiped away the blood, wishing she could as simply expunge the memories that would clearly haunt both of them forever.

Tess glanced over and saw VJ attending another man wearing a red BoSox hat and wraparound shades. It struck her because she'd noticed the same guy walking close to them after the race. The 4x4's wheel was resting on his chest. No heroic medical intervention would change that indisputable fact. Curiously, sunlight was now reflecting off the black steel object in his hand. Tess wondered briefly if the man was an undercover cop. She watched for another second. The man seemed to be making a feeble attempt to raise the hand with the gun in it. Then he stopped. Tess watched as VJ knocked down the weapon and quickly moved to another victim.

In moments, an hour passed. The triage continued. Fortunately, an Israeli mass casualty guru had visited Boston a month earlier. He'd conducted seminars to help prepare the medical centers for disasters like the one they were experiencing. All the medical students were invited. That they were putting the lessons to work was fortuitous and coincidental at the same time.

A news crew had arrived on the scene at the same moment the first ambulance came. Tess did her best to duck the cameras. They were looking for anyone they could to interview. One of the teams descended on VJ. He sent them away with a glare that would melt steel. Once it was obvious the EMTs had the situation under control and there was nothing further that father and daughter could contribute, Tess nudged VJ and asked if it would be all right to leave.

About two minutes later, VJ's black phone went off.

RECONNECTING

Leila was beside herself on the other end of the call. "Is Tess OK? I just saw the TV feed and I caught a glimpse of you, but not her. Were you together? It's so awful."

"Tess is fine," VJ reassured her. "Actually, she was a superstar. I can't believe what just happened. I don't even know what happened. Did the news say anything about the driver of that truck?"

Leila calmed down. "Just speculation. Apparently, he was a regular guy from Charlestown with a bunch of DUIs. They don't know much else. No one seems to think it was intentional. The report said he died on the scene."

VJ sat down on a nearby bench. "That was one of the worst things I've ever witnessed. There's something else you need to know. I'm going to call you back soon, but find a reason to leave the hospital now and go to a private place. Trust me on this one. I love you."

With Leila placated for the moment, Tess and VJ walked to a secluded Back Bay street. It was only then that she really showed any emotion.

"VJ, I feel incredibly fortunate not to be hurt or dead, but those poor people who got hit. Oh my God. I don't think I did enough to help them."

VJ put his arm around her slender shoulders. "Tess, take my word for it. You did more than you can imagine. You were there. That situation was scary beyond belief. The comfort you gave can't be measured. I can't make sense of what we just experienced. I've seen thousands of cases. But this wasn't one or two patients lying in tidy trauma unit beds with a team of eight nurses and doctors standing by. Being in the middle of it is a totally different thing. By the way, I saw you reduce that open radius. The Norwegian orthopod was right—you're a pro."

Tess stopped walking and turned to him. "VJ, I saw a gun in the hand of that one man you were attending. What was going on there?"

He told her, "I saw him in the hotel lobby, and while we were walking, I noticed him again. I had the sense he was following us. I checked his wallet. No badge. I'm obviously not sure, but I really think the guy was there to kill me. He died about two minutes after I got to him. I can't explain how the Cooperative found out I'm still here. None of us are safe. I have to go to the police with what we've got and find protection for you and Leila."

She shook her head. "VJ, you still can't do that. If you do, you're fucked. Look, I get it.

There's no way to tell if they've connected Leila or me to you. The good news is that you spoke to Leila ten minutes ago and she's fine. I'm fine. I still think we can close the loop before you go to the feds. At least let me talk to Axel. Give me that black phone. I can't find my cell. Between the race and your stuff, my concentration sucks. I looked for it this morning, but I didn't have time to really search."

VJ couldn't help but laugh. "Tess, you're definitely related to me. There's nothing I can't lose or break in a matter of seconds."

Tess smiled faintly in return. "Thanks for that. VJ, do you have any cash? It doesn't seem like I should go home right now. What if Cyrus is hanging around? With everything going on, I just can't deal with that, too." VJ peeled off three hundred-dollar bills. She made the call to Axel, and left a message for him to meet her. Obviously frustrated, she said, "Of all the times for him not to answer. I'm going to try to run him down. For right now, call him if you need me. I'll get a burner phone and give you a heads-up when I land." She gave him a brief hug and jogged slowly back toward the T stop.

AXEL MANS UP

Once Tess got to the Red Line she headed for the Davis Square coffee shop, hoping Axel had heard her message and would be there to meet her. On the train, she scanned the passengers. No one seemed to be paying any attention to her. She was just another of the thousands of marathon runners taking the T. As an extra precaution, though, Tess got off at Central Square, then got back on just before the doors closed. If someone *was* following her, they'd be cooked.

Tess spied Axel sitting at the café munching on a raspberry scone. He greeted her with open arms and a huge grin. "You did it! You conquered the marathon. Congratulations! Man, too bad for those people on Comm Ave. Did you hear about what happened?"

She felt a rush of emotion. "Axel, I was there. I can't describe how bad it was. It was like being in the middle of those terrorist bombings you see online."

They sat down, and Axel put his hand on hers and stroked her fingers gently. Tess didn't pull away. He said, "I feel so bad for them and you. I've seen some of those broken-up trauma patients at the hospital. It's horrible. Plus, their families. You can see the tragedy in their faces. Do you want to talk about that, or what I found?"

Tess shuddered. "I don't even want to think about what just happened. Let me focus on something else. What's going on at the hospital?"

Axel said hesitantly, "I know it seems pretty insignificant right now, given what you just had to deal with, but I discovered what looks like a back door. Whoever set up the bank routing system embedded a way to get in that only he or she knows about. I wouldn't be surprised if that person is skimming some bucks. At first pass, it looks like everything is split between two accounts—one called the Beast and one called Dark Angel. But, the money is actually going three ways. The skimmer is taking an extra ten percent. I might be able to trace both of them to separate passwords that tell us who they are. That's too much right now. Let's put it on hold for a day. It can wait. You've been through more than enough."

Tess shook her head. "No, this is the best time to take care of business. I just need a short rest. This sounds weird, but it may not be a good idea for me to go home right now. I can't stay at my brother Max's. He was here for the first week of the baseball season, then left to go on a trek through South America. He gave up his apartment. Can I take a short nap on your couch?"

Axel pulled out his keys. "Take my bed. You need something more than a couch. We'll get after this when your brain has time to clear."

He was right. Tess' personal gas tank was redlining. Just as she was about to leave, she heard Axel's phone ring. It was VJ. She grabbed the phone and told him what she was doing, then handed it back to Axel. When he finished the conversation, he said, "I'm going back to the apartment with you. I have to set a trap."

VJ'S NEXT MOVE

VJ decided it wouldn't take long for the Cooperative to figure out that he still wasn't dead. He was hoping they'd be operating under the assumption that he was oblivious to their most recent assassination attempt. That gave him a slight advantage. VJ thought Axel could lock onto the data he was searching for; otherwise the chessboard was not in his favor. He desperately wanted to take Rick and his minions down. VJ had worked out a brilliant idea to use Cyrus to coax out his master. That plan was now completely in the toilet. There was no way he could show his face anywhere near St. Stephen. Enter plan B.

After Tess and VJ separated, he jumped on the Green Line and randomly decided to go to Cleveland Circle to collect his thoughts. Children ran through the park—not a care in the world, just enjoying the extra day off from school. *How lucky for them,* he thought.

VJ finally settled on the next move, and called Axel to see if he could do what was needed. VJ tasked him to send a detailed e-mail through the hospital system to his urologist buddy, Milo. In essence, it was to say that VJ was alive, that he had information linking Milo to the Cooperative, and that he wanted to make a deal. VJ asked for a meeting the next morning by the Liberty Hotel entrance—a public enough place—and said to be sure to come alone and not tell anyone. He then called Leila and told her the full story. The seriousness of the new threat was not lost on her.

About an hour and a half after the e-mail was sent, Axel called VJ back. "VJ, you were right. The urologist forwarded your message to a WCapcom6. It may be your guy. I'm also trying to see if I can link WCapcom6 to the accounts where the money is being funneled." He paused. "VJ, you're not really going to do this, are you?"

VJ said, "Axel, no chance. There's a perfect hiding place for me there. If Rick is WCapcom6 and shows up, I'm going to call the cops and tell them I just saw him try to kill someone. That should get their attention. It'll at least make them hold him. I know we don't have the proof we need yet, but time is about out. I have to make sure at least Tess and Leila are protected. Did Tess do what she said she'd do and stay at your apartment? Also, did she get a burner phone?"

Axel told VJ, "She's fine. In fact, she's passed out on my bed. It looks like the couch for me tonight. I don't think she got a phone, though; she was wiped. VJ, I'm going to keep a close eye on her."

"Axel, do whatever it takes to keep Tess there! If you find out anything else, let Leila know." After hanging up, VJ found the telephoto lens he needed at the camera shop near his newest temporary digs. Axel wasn't the only one who wasn't going to sleep well.

THE VOLCANO STIRS

Petra had come to the office to escape the noise from the party that the insufferable people next to her condo were having. Somehow she knew that she'd failed again. Jenz hadn't checked in, and it was late in the day. There was no answer to repeated texts. She paced, growing ever more impatient and angry. The beast she struggled to contain every day was emerging. An hour later, Petra decided to find out a different way if the hit was a bust. She tapped out the message: Tess, call me. No response. *Good,* she thought. *If she could, she'd get right back to me. She's always on that phone.* The anxiety diminished. Maybe it was even possible to get some work done.

Petra thought she heard a buzz and glanced across the room. On the floor by the large window she adored was something lying on the ground. She'd seen that rose-gold cover too many times in the past two weeks. Petra audibly cursed, then checked her own phone.

A news update from a local social media outlet popped up. The attached video showed the crash site near the Common. Petra was immediately drawn to the face of the determined young woman helping injured runners. The volcano inside began rising again. Her own mobile didn't survive the high-velocity impact against the wall. Feeling threatened, but not knowing how real the threat was, Petra decided she had to come up with a new plan or leave Boston and go somewhere else. She'd already set it up so Rick would take the fall if anything was exposed. She was untraceable. Her best MIT-trained computer expert had made sure of it.

An idea worked its way into her consciousness. Petra grabbed the landline and dialed Cyrus. When the conversation was over, the internal demons temporarily retreated.

* * * * *

Cyrus was standing in his kitchen, expertly chopping vegetables for the stir-fry he planned to make. He smiled at the lovely young woman sitting at the counter. Cyrus picked her up in the grocery store, of all places. He'd found the woman to be surprisingly friendly when she saw him selecting gourmet items.

This time he needed success. The constant rejection was wearing thin. Tess wasn't working out at all. He hadn't gotten any closer to figuring out what her connection to Brio was or what they were up to. Cyrus wasn't in a position to spend every waking minute trying to watch for the man. Today's adventure was a great distraction—right up to the minute the phone rang.

The last person on the planet he'd wanted to speak to was Petra, and worse, what she'd asked him to do was unacceptable. Of course, he didn't give her the slightest idea that Tess was someone he already knew, much less someone he was obsessed with. Unfortunately for Brio, Petra was after him, too. She had put them together. Petra was on the warpath. The whole thing was a disaster. But he'd sacrifice Brio in a second to protect Tess.

The cell phone vibrated again, but the new number he saw didn't make him feel any better. Cyrus feared almost nothing and no one, but Rick put him on edge. The man was the Keyser Söze of Boston. Cyrus felt he had no choice but to answer. "Hi, Rick, I already know what you want. Petra just hammered on me."

Rick listened to the recitation of what the two had discussed and then barked, "I don't care what Petra told you to do. She's going to get all of us thrown in prison. Petra stupidly forced Brio into our little enterprise. I need you to help me grab him and this girl, Tess, before Petra sends anyone else to try to kill them. We'll get Tess first, then pick up Brio. Meet at the entrance of the Liberty Hotel at nine tomorrow morning. I'm going to have you take them both to my cabin in Vermont, and keep them there till I have a chance to deal with the problems they've created. You'd better assume Brio is aware of what you did to Nick. When you take him, make sure he knows you're not going to hurt him. Otherwise, Brio's going to act like a cornered animal. When you park them at my place, tell them they'll be safe with me. Brio *will* listen and *will* disappear; otherwise I *will* kill him and the girl myself."

In a fit of rage, Cyrus stabbed the knife he was holding into the butcher block table. He was beside himself with frustration at the unfolding events. Just as he collected himself, Cyrus saw the front door closing. The wok didn't survive.

* * * * *

Tess' eyes opened slowly. She couldn't find a clock, but smelled coffee brewing. For a second she couldn't remember where she was. Then the irony of the whole thing struck her. Here she'd finally done what Jessica wanted her to do—stay overnight with Axel. That she was alone in bed was the funny part.

As Tess lay there, she contemplated what to do about her phone. What if it was in Petra's office? Tess searched her brain to think how that might have happened. She suddenly knew it was true. She had broken in again late the night before the marathon trying to check on one last item. When Tess got in, the computer was gone, but she'd heard what had sounded like gunshots outside. Instinctively she'd rushed to the window to see what was happening. It had to have happened then. If Tess was ever going to get it back, it would have to be now.

There was a knock on the door. Axel was on the other side. "Tess, hey, you awake? Hope you haven't forgotten. We're still in medical school."

Tess said, "Hold on a second," then spotted the green BRO, DO YOU EVEN LIFT? shirt and threw it on. It seemed like an eternity ago that she was abusing Axel for wearing it. That and some way-oversized scrub pants took care of the need to hide her birthday suit.

She turned the doorknob and was greeted with a steaming cup of coffee. Jessica was right. Axel really was a good person. Too bad he did such a brilliant job of hiding it. She took a sip and felt instantly better. "Axel, hope you don't mind that I borrowed these. Did Jessica text you?"

Axel took a draw of his own java and answered, "Yes, but I think she might have had the wrong idea about last night. It was painful. I had to admit that we didn't sleep together."

Tess sincerely appreciated the honesty. One more feather in the cap for him. "Thanks, Axel, that was big of you. What else did she say?"

He handed her his phone. "Here, you look at this. Huge Biker Guy from Art Class Came by Three Times Looking for Tess. Desperate to See Her!"

When she saw the words a guttural "FUCK!" erupted out of Tess' mouth. Even Axel was surprised. "Jesus, Tess, I'm not sure everyone in the building heard you. Why don't you yell that again?"

Tess sat back on his bed. "Sorry, Axel. The guy she said is trying to find me chops people up for a living. I can't go anywhere near my own

338

apartment. Regrettably, I do have to go to the office. I left my phone there. I guarantee you that hag Agnes has it."

Axel didn't look happy. "Tess, that's not a great idea. Didn't you tell me that the guy who got run over by the truck looked like he was going to try to knock off VJ? What if someone from the Cooperative has put you two together? Plus, VJ made me promise to hold you here."

Tess *needed* that phone. Her life was on it. "Axel, VJ's too paranoid. Do you have a baseball hat, a hoodie, and some shades? With these scrub pants on, I'll just look like one of the million sleep-deprived interns coming off call. I'll be in and out of that office in ten seconds flat."

Axel frowned. "I still don't like it. Let me go with you."

Tess looked directly into his hazel-green eyes. "Axel, I can take care of myself. I'll text you the second I'm out of there. If you haven't heard from me by lunch, then you can call the National Guard if you want. Trust me, I'll be fine."

* * * * *

Tess jumped on the Red Line at Harvard Square and did her entry-exit-entry trick again, just in case. No one was following her. Just as she was about to go through the sliding doors of the administration building, Tess caught sight of someone who looked a lot like Cyrus turning the corner about a block away. Jessica's text had also mentioned that she was to tell Tess to call him the first moment possible. Tess had decided to put that request on bypass, and all of a sudden here was Cyrus again. It gave her a shiver. Tess took a deep breath and quickly walked in.

CLARITY

Just as VJ was settling into his perch by the T stop across from the Liberty Hotel entryway, his black phone rang. Axel was out of breath and excited. "VJ, I nailed it! Beast is WCapcom6! The money transfers are for sure going to the person the urologist contacted yesterday. Dark Angel and one I haven't seen, GRKGODS1, are also linked. Whoever that is looks to be getting an even bigger share of the distribution. If Beast shows up, we've got him, and he should lead us to Dark Angel."

VJ was exhilarated. "Axel—you're amazing! Is Tess up? Can I talk to her?"

Axel's tone changed. "About that . . . VJ, I did everything I could to keep her here. She left for Petra's office a while ago to get her phone. Apparently, she left it there."

The revelation made VJ decidedly unhappy. "For fuck's sake. Did she really have to do that now? Axel, if she calls you, get her back to your house any way you can, then let me know." VJ hung up and dialed Tess, just in case she'd already gotten it—no response. He scanned the people walking in and out of the hotel. At that moment, Milo Marconi's face appeared. And standing in the restaurant alcove was the man

VJ was searching for—big as a tank and wearing a New England Patriots workout shirt.

The association VJ had made the day he went running, but couldn't process, hit him now like a freight train. Tess had off-handedly mentioned that she'd almost been knocked over by a Patriots player on her first internship day at Petra's office. Except it wasn't a Patriots player. It had to be Rick—WCapcom6—the guy Milo had contacted. Were Rick and Petra working together? Was she Dark Angel? VJ furiously dialed Tess' phone. His fear index blew through the roof as he started to run the two blocks to the administration building as fast as possible on his still-recovering knee.

BAD DECISION

Tess entered the outer office and checked around—nothing. Agnes wasn't in her chair, so she searched her drawers—still nothing. Tess heard a loud one-way telephone discussion behind Petra's closed door, but she couldn't make out anything clearly. *A truly bad sign,* Tess thought. *Today is going to be a terrible day for anyone who gets in her way.*

Tess went down the hall to the bathroom to see if she'd been wrong and somehow left it there. Even clandestine snooping didn't prevent nature from calling. Still no luck. Determined, Tess returned to the office for one more quick look. Petra was standing in the doorway of her inner sanctum, arms crossed, glaring. "Are you looking for this?" In her hand was the phone. Silently, Tess thanked God for password protection.

Petra continued, "Nice outfit. What is that—nouveau grunge? I figured you'd come by to get it. I had to turn the damn thing off. That constant buzzing was driving me nuts."

Tess thought to herself, *The road to Crazytown is a short drive for you.*

Petra proceeded to lecture her. "Obviously I couldn't call you when I found it. I don't know

343

how those things *ever* stay in girls' back pockets in the first place. But I'm glad you're here. Grab a seat for a minute. I want to talk to you."

Anxiously, Tess sat on the edge of the chair, facing Petra, who began a stream-of-consciousness spate. "I gave Agnes the day off today. She told me she still wasn't feeling well. I didn't want her spreading germs everywhere. I don't like sick people very much. They bother me. Believe it or not, I actually have an M.D. It was more of a four-year challenge, just to see if I could do it. I never intended to actually take care of anyone. I thought about radiology, but it was too much sitting around alone in dark rooms talking to a machine. Wasn't for me. I don't tell anyone about med school because it may mislead them into thinking they can take advantage of some inner need I have to serve others. That's not part of my DNA."

Tess thought, *Well, that's absolutely shocking.*

All at once Petra became focused. The Jekyll/Hyde conversion had happened again. With an odd quality to her voice, she asked, "Tess, would you mind going up to the fourth floor where they're doing the construction? I want to see if we can figure out how to use that outdoor space for the gala. It obviously isn't going to be ready to show off the way I intended. I know the first part of your *official* internship is finished, but it would help me a lot if we could go

344

over just a few details. Besides, it'll be nicer to talk up there. This office is stuffy, and it's a beautiful day. The sun will be good for our bones. Vitamin D and all that rot. I have to make a quick call. I'll be right behind you."

Tess felt uneasy. She wanted to exit as fast as she could, but finally decided she was just being overly paranoid. If somehow Petra had it out for her, the office would have been the place for her to do whatever she wanted to do. There really *were* major issues with the gala, as insignificant as that seemed, and from Petra's perspective, Tess *was* the one responsible for sorting them out. She felt a neurotic compulsion to follow Petra's request. Dutifully, Tess headed up the staircase to the roof where the project was under construction.

Outside, the sun warmed her face. A slight breeze tickled her hair. It was the kind of day that all days are supposed to be—totally different from only twenty-four hours earlier. Tess started to feel a little better. Before she'd left Cambridge, Axel seemed very optimistic about putting together the last piece of the puzzle. A-plus for the med school team. Tess took pleasure in thinking about her classmates trying to live up to *her* standard of accomplishment for once. She was also looking forward to meeting Leila. VJ talked about his girlfriend in such a respectful, sweet manner.

The man had many intriguing layers. He seemed completely in love with this woman he'd only recently met, and cared deeply and sincerely for his patients, but seemed at odds with himself, as well as with the practice of medicine and all its idiosyncrasies. He had the resourcefulness and wherewithal to plan and eliminate two men who posed a mortal threat. Tess hated to admit it to herself, but she admired VJ for that. Her thoughts returned to Petra—an egomaniac with seemingly unchecked power and devoid of a moral compass. It was definitely a good idea to be done with her. Her cynicism was infectious. Tess had already had a healthy enough inbred dose of that. The last thing she needed as a budding physician was Petra's constant negative attitude.

The sounds of the city below reflected the activity of all its inhabitants. Horns blowing, jackhammers pursuing endless destruction, the siren of a nearby ambulance blaring. Tess took a small tour of the work area. Why there weren't actual workers here on the fourth-floor construction site, she wasn't sure. She had heard about some type of union strike. Maybe that was it.

Tess surveyed the project. There were drills, hammers, tape measures, and just about anything a person would need for a remodel. The slight wind rippled tarps covering the heavy equipment. Sawdust littered the rooftop. The buildout was divided in halves. Most of the work had already been done to complete the offices. She was in the half that was to be a grand hall for events. The skeletons of the eighteen-foot walls were up on three of the four sides. The remaining flank had a two-foot wall that was part of the original structure. The plan there was to mount a huge glass panel to provide an unobstructed view of the river.

So far, exactly nothing had been done. Tess almost knocked over a big bag of nails while walking over to take a look. A pair of ravens perched on the short wall. When she approached, they cawed angrily, then grudgingly flew away. Next to their building was another construction project. Tess looked down. Giant clumps of rebar reaching toward the sky made the site look like a steel seagrass garden, though lacking the pretty orange caps. If the building inspectors were to come by, they'd be S.O.L.

Tess began to wonder why Petra hadn't come up yet. Going back to find her would absolutely be the wrong move. She'd interpret it as some type of personal affront and berate her. Tess had no interest in agitating the woman further.

VJ'S SURPRISE

VJ burst up the stairs and crashed into Petra's office, expecting it to be full of activity. He looked around frantically for Tess. No sign of her. The desk marked AGNES was empty. He saw the PETRA LEWIS, MBA nameplate beside the inner office. The door was open and seemed to invite him in. The person sitting at the desk was just hanging up her phone.

VJ stopped dead in his tracks and yelled, "What?" Struggling to catch his breath, he finally managed to rasp, "*You're* Petra?"

The hair was different, but the enchanting beauty remained. She just smiled, her serpent eyes dead. "And who exactly were you expecting? Cinderella's evil stepmother? I've been wondering how long it would take for you to find me. In fact, I'm shocked we haven't run into each other before. I guess we travel in different circles. I'm not really one for hanging around the hospital. I have a matter to attend to upstairs, but you're here now, so it's time to square away our business. Tess can wait for a few more minutes."

VJ remained shocked by the discovery of Petra's identity, and Tess' precarious position terrified him. The sleek revolver Petra had pulled from her desk complicated the situation further.

348

Petra had already come after him twice, and now she literally had him in her sights. But Axel held the documentation to crush the Cooperative. That was his ace in the hole. While options were filtering through his mind, the Dark Angel spoke.

"Brio, I've been at this game for a long time. You're just an amateur, though I have to say I didn't give you enough credit. Those two idiots I sent to Sierra Lakes were a mistake. What happened to those clowns, anyway? My guess is that I'm never really going to find out."

It was crystal clear that it was she, not Rick, who was pulling the levers. VJ decided to focus on getting information and trying to talk himself through the disaster at hand. Slowly and calmly, he said, "You tell me about Tess, and I'll give you the details about the Lucianos."

She laughed. "Jenz Dahl, the second man I hired, was a pro. You *know* you were amazingly lucky yesterday at the marathon. If that alcoholic, drug-abusing moron hadn't driven his truck onto the sidewalk, you'd already be dead and I wouldn't have to do what I have to do. Life certainly does take strange turns."

The look on her face reminded him of Dracula—cold, impassive, deadly. He abandoned caution and played the only card he had. "We've got detailed records of every illegal move you've engineered in the last three years. I know you've got north of ten million in protected bank accounts. My hacker will make that disappear. Don't believe for a second that he won't.

"I've got a proposition for you. Let Rick take the fall. Nobody has to know who Dark Angel is. We can easily scrub your tracks. Right now the feds will get the whole package if my people don't hear from me. I can change that. Let Tess go, and keep me under wraps as long as you need to get out of the country. I know you've got the muscle to do that. No information will be released until you're safe. I still have no interest in being dead. Take the deal. It's a good one. Walk away now and you'll still be very wealthy and free."

A hint of self-doubt seemed to crease the hydra's face, then ice again. "Brio, do you know the fable about the frog and the scorpion? The scorpion sees the frog on the side of the river and asks for a ride across. The frog asks why on earth he would do such a thing; the scorpion is just going to sting him. The scorpion says of course he won't do that because they would both then perish. The frog finally relents and agrees to carry the scorpion across the river. Midway over, the scorpion stings the frog. As they're both about to drown, the frog asks the scorpion why he stung him. The scorpion replies, 'Because that's what scorpions do.'

"Brio, you and Tess got in the way. Such a shame. We had a really good thing going here. Now I will have to take a little break. I've got my

own plan, and it doesn't include you at all."
Without any further hesitation Petra raised her
gun. "Brio, you don't have nine lives. By the way,
Tess only has one. Too bad, so sad."

Anticipating what was about to happen,
VJ lunged toward his nemesis. The effort was in
vain. Multiple shots, including two where the big
muscle pumps the blood, hit him. He couldn't
breathe at all, and his thigh and shoulder were
on fire. Then the lights went off.

ONE DOWN, ONE TO GO

Petra watched Brio's clothes turn from blue to crimson. The suppressor had done its job. No one outside the office would've heard the gunfire. She dialed. "Rick, I have a mess here at the office for you to clean up. In fact, there's going to be another one in a few minutes. Bring an extra bag."

Petra gathered herself and slowly ascended the stairs. For a second, a vague sense of remorse entered her thoughts, like the slightest brush from a feather. "Now for act two," she murmured. "It's finally time for this to end."

* * * * *

Tired of standing around, Tess found a nearby sawhorse and sat down with her back to where the big window was supposed to be. She opened her phone and turned it back on. Reading the first few texts, Tess' blood froze.

Simultaneously, Petra emerged from the door where the two halves of the roof project joined. Tess leapt to her feet, but Petra closed on her rapidly. With nowhere to go, Tess scanned the construction area, looking for any weapon, but Petra gestured with her gun and cautioned, "Tess, don't move an inch. We're going to have a discussion. Thanks for waiting up here. I had a small internal problem that needed to be cleared up. I just have to clean up one other mess and everything will be finalized. You know, this business deal has worked well for me. Fantastic money, lots of power, and I get to order people around. If they don't do what I say, they're history. The way I look at it, if you're not at the table, you're on the menu."

At this point Tess thought that Petra was speaking much less to her than to herself. Lady Macbeth popped into her mind.

Keeping an eye and the gun on Tess, Petra walked over by the short wall, looking out. She was wearing a black sleeveless three-quarter-length dress with black pointed pumps. The color motif matched the direction of the conversation. "Those bastards are never going to finish this construction. I'm leaving today, so it'll be Summerhays' problem. Serves him right."

As directed, Tess had stayed put, standing facing the doorway. Circling around, Petra turned and looked at her, directly aiming the gun barrel at Tess' chest. Tess noticed that Petra looked completely relaxed, like she'd done this kind of thing before. When she started talking, it was almost as if she was chatting with a friend, rather than holding a gun on an enemy.

"You know, I actually like you, Tess. You remind me of me somehow. Smart, plotting, devious. If you hadn't been so careless, you might have even gotten away with it. Honestly, did you think I wouldn't notice you'd been snooping around my office?"

Tess cringed. The lapse with her phone hadn't helped. But she held her tongue.

"I once had a baby," said Petra, pacing but keeping the gun pointed in Tess' direction. "It would be about your age right now. I never really liked children. Getting pregnant was sloppy on my part. I do make mistakes sometimes, not the least of which was getting knocked up, then convincing my boyfriend, Remy Lewis, to marry me. What a poor excuse for a man. But at least I came to my senses and dumped him. I didn't want Remy anywhere near me. There was a research job here with someone I knew, so I came up Boston to work before going to London for B school. Some Catholic adoption agency took the kid. I never even knew if it was a boy or girl."

Petra brushed aside an imaginary speck of dirt from her dress. "I told you the first day you walked into my office, you can't earn any respect if you get caught. You shouldn't have gotten caught, Tess."

Tess felt the phone, still in her hand, vibrate. Glancing down quickly at the updated message, she did her best to hide any reaction.

Petra's face darkened again. "By the way, if someone's threatening to kill you, it's probably a good time to stop checking your damn cell phone messages, don't you think? Is the latest Instagram so critical? Pathetic!" Petra gestured with the gun while Tess stuffed the phone in her back pocket. "Your generation drives me crazy! If you're waiting to be rescued, forget it, no one's coming. I had to take care of all this myself. Fucking Rick, I stopped being able to rely on him to deal with the tough problems. It's really a shame that you're so good at computers. You would've been much better off not knowing about our small kingdom here.

"Poor Tess—loses her adopted parents in a car crash, and now discovers that beyond today, nothing's looking assured. There are a few things you *do* need to tell me. What did you really find out about my finances? Plus, how do you know Brio, and why on earth would you help him? You're banging him, aren't you? He's a funny guy, not bad-looking, but don't you think he's a little old for you? It doesn't really matter, just curious."

Tess catalogued her options. They were simple. Bad. Clearly Petra was on the edge. She decided to push the envelope. Distract her, throw her off her game, give herself the opening she needed. Something was preventing Petra from shooting her outright. Tess wanted to keep her talking as long as she could. "How I know VJ is really none of your business. But for the record, he happens to be my biological father. I just found out. Sleeping with someone more than twenty years older is more your style Petra.

"I've got it all—the billing fraud, the payoff list, the money laundering, your bank transfers. And now VJ, who I guess you know as Brio, has it, too. You're done. Don't believe for a second you can get out of it. Guess you can forget about those bank accounts. By the way, VJ's not dead. That is, unless he's texting me from the grave."

Petra suddenly looked uncertain. One of her long brown curls fell across her face. Furiously she pushed it aside. None of this seemed to help Tess' cause, as Petra widened her stance to steady herself and said, "In that case, after I kill you I'm just going to go downstairs and blow his fucking head off. It's too bad you can't choose your parents. Seems like you struck out. Brio's not going anywhere with the bullet holes he's already got. He thought he could stop me. That was never going to happen. Now here you are, living the last day of your life."

It was Tess' turn to interrupt. "Yeah, like that'll work. You shoot me and then what? Leave me here and think the cops aren't going to come after you?"

Petra grinned maliciously. "Just a few minutes ago you e-mailed the dean, telling him that the stress from being involved in the accident at the marathon overwhelmed you. It dredged up the grief from your parents' deaths, and you're going to have to take time away to get your head straight. About a month from now, a young woman your age will be in an unfortunate car accident in Cambodia. You'll be identified by your dental records. You know, Tess, some girls like romance. I prefer vengeance. It's not fair, is it?" With extra spite she added, "I think I might even have to give your brother Max a visit later today. Do you think he'll be expecting me?"

Defiantly Tess fired back, "You can forget that. He left Boston over a week ago. *I* don't even know what country he's in. I thought you'd be better at doing your homework.

"Petra, none of this is going to fly. Do you think I found this information all by myself? I told you I'm not that good a hacker. Jail is better than the death penalty. Think about it!"

The monster three feet away was incomprehensible to her. She wondered to herself, *How does someone get to this point?* It was an answer no one would ever have. The shining barrel of the Beretta 9mm Nano didn't waiver, still aiming directly at Tess. She stared into Petra's arctic-cold eyes. *Focus, focus,* Tess reminded herself. *Find the weak spot.* She kept her eye on the doorway.

Simultaneous to Tess' decision to strike, a massive figure appeared. His deep voice boomed, "Petra, you asked me to take care of this and here I am. You don't want to get your hands dirty. I'll handle it." Slowly he moved toward the two women.

Tess was now really frightened. She'd thought she'd figured out a way to absorb a bullet and still take Petra. Now she was out of options. The weapon in the man's hand was not making her feel better. She momentarily shut her eyes and prepared for the inevitable.

Petra snarled. "You already failed me— this conniving bitch just conveniently showed up today—no, the only person I can count on is me. I'm going to do this myself." With her ally now close, Petra returned her full attention to Tess just as he raised his hand.

There were sudden popping sounds like a series of mini-explosions. Petra writhed in pain. Tess' foot caught her now impaired nemesis perfectly, forcing the banshee back toward the hulking figure. What followed was a purely savage act of fury. The behemoth picked up Petra like a rag doll and hurled her toward the short wall at the edge of the roof. It wasn't high enough to stop her momentum. Her fingers caught the edge as she struggled frantically to hold on to anything solid. There wasn't enough to grasp.

* * * * *

The surprise of flight was disorienting. The world became topsy-turvy. Petra had underestimated both of them. Brio was not the pushover she thought he'd be. The girl had intrigued her— intelligent, a good sense of humor, and at the same time so devious. If Tess wasn't the enemy, she would've recruited her. Then, for one brief moment, a veil lifted, and the irony of it all came to her. It pierced her heart.

* * * * *

Tess ran by the man who had just saved her, and literally jumped down the stairs. The suddenly beautiful sound of a Swedish accent hit her ears—VJ yelling at the EMTs to leave him alone and go help on the roof. Tess almost smacked into the pair of them as she was entering Petra's inner office. She told them she was OK and promptly turned them around so they could get back to helping VJ, who was lying on the floor by Petra's big desk. It was total chaos. She glanced at the woman dressed in scrubs hunched by VJ, visibly trying to catch her breath. "Where's Petra?" he asked.

Before Tess had a chance to answer, another voice behind her responded, "Permanently indisposed." Everyone looked his way. Tess interrupted, "VJ, Cyrus just saved my life. I know how much you appreciate that."

VJ grimaced and nodded as well as he could from a supine position. "Looks like you didn't need me after all," he said.

Tess squeezed his hand. "God was smiling on both of us. Thanks for sending the text." Then she looked at the woman. "Leila, I presume. As you probably figured out, I'm Tess. This is Cyrus. Two questions: One, how did you know to come here? Two, are you planning to do something with that scalpel?"

"Nice to finally meet you," Leila said with relief, putting down the knife. "One, VJ called and told me that Petra was on the roof threatening you with a gun. I tried to call 911, but believe it or not, they put me on hold. I ran over to the ER and told them to send an ambulance. I got here the second before you came down. Two, knowing about the gun, I grabbed the only weapon I could find. I forgot it was in my hand."

VJ's shirt was open, so Tess could see why he was still amongst the living—black body armor. "VJ, your chest plate is pretty impressive," she said. "Where'd you get it?"

He winked. "Carbon fiber nanotubes, weighs a pound, got it online—you like it?"

Tess just smiled.

* * * * *

The EMTs took VJ down to the waiting ambulance to take the short ride to MRMC. Leila climbed in next to him. Tess told them she'd be over soon and took Cyrus down the back stairs. Tess figured they had only an abbreviated time before a phalanx of Boston's finest swarmed in. She needed to speak to him. The nail gun he'd used to shoot Petra was still holstered in his pants. Fortunately, it was one of the old types that fired almost like a real handgun. Cyrus' relationship with law enforcement was tenuous at best, no doubt. That meant he had to get the hell out.

The pair talked while they walked. Tess turned and looked up to the enigma beside her.

"You probably want to make yourself scarce in a hurry, but I have to thank you, Cyrus. It's not every day that someone saves your life. How did you know to come?"

Looking weary, Cyrus explained, "That's a long story, but the short of it is that I came back looking for *you*. Petra got tipped off somehow that you and Brio were working together. She wanted me to grab you yesterday. I did everything I could to try to warn you. Didn't Jessica tell you I came by? Anyway, Petra told Rick about her plan. He ordered me to bring both of you in to try to protect you two from her. She upbraided me this morning for not finding you. When I was leaving, I thought I caught a glimpse of someone your shape and size. I kept walking, but then I couldn't shake the feeling that it *was* you, so I came back."

Tess said, "Jessica did tell me this morning that you tried to locate me. I didn't have my phone, and yesterday was almost as insane as today. I couldn't imagine what you wanted, and I was a little afraid. I've had this weird sense that you've been following me."

Obviously embarrassed, Cyrus admitted, "There's some truth to that. Sometimes I know better and other times I can't help myself. I'd never hurt you. When I returned to the building to search, I found that VJ guy. Is that his name—VJ Brio?"

Tess showed Cyrus her phone. "His name is complicated. Here, check out the text I got: not dead, help coming. I saw it while Petra was talking. I figured she wasn't the help VJ was texting me about. Then you came up and said what you said about 'handling' it. I didn't know what to believe. I was dying inside."

Cyrus nodded. "Brio was going out of his mind when I ran into the office. He sent me up to the roof the second I got here; he just wanted me to get to you as fast as I could. Once I saw you, I needed to throw Petra off enough to buy time. Otherwise, she might have shot both of us. Sorry to terrorize you, but at least it worked.

"You've been spending a lot of time with Brio. I guess you call him VJ. I know there's a hell of a lot more to the story than what you told me last month."

Tess laughed. "Petra said the same thing before you gave her that flying lesson. VJ's actually my biological father. I just met him, but events have forced us to learn a lot about each other quickly."

Cyrus looked at her, his eyes wide with questions. "No wonder he was so amped to get you help. Petra wanted to find you bad. Were you two blackmailing her? Or running some scam on the Cooperative?"

Tess shook her head no. "Us—are you out of your mind? Not even close. We were trying to take them down. I didn't know that Petra was involved, let alone in charge, until that messed-up scene on the roof. The Cooperative leaned on VJ after he helped Nick escape." She stopped suddenly, turned away, then said, "I know that you cut off Nick's fingers, Cyrus. VJ and I both figured it out. Nick seemed to remember that fanged clown tat pretty well."

Staring ahead, he said, "It'd be easy for me to lie to you and say I didn't, but you'd know I wasn't telling the truth. It wasn't personal at all. I hated doing it to him."

"Then why . . . ?" Tess said.

"Hard to explain. Petra has had something of a grip on me, I guess," he confessed. "At the beginning, she was one of the few people who was nice to me, who admired my talents—kind of enigmatic. Then, after it was too late, I realized it was just an act to get me to do what she wanted."

Tess visibly flinched thinking about the cleaver slicing through Nick's hand. She still needed to probe deeper. Quietly, but firmly she asked, "Cyrus, do you murder people?"

His face contorted. "No, I don't. Never. At least not until today. That had to be done. Petra would have found a way to come after all of us, even from prison. And she would never stop. So, in this case, I decided to make an exception. What I do is take care of *problems*—like bringing you in. Petra knew I'd never kill you. She clearly was set on doing that herself."

Tess took his hand. "Cyrus, I owe you. One day I'll treat you to the greatest meal you can imagine. If the police ask, I'm going to tell them that I have no idea who you are, that I thought you were a building employee in the right place at the right time. I'll get my friend Axel to delete anything in the computer system with your name on it. And I promise you, VJ and Leila won't give you up. They'll respect my wishes. But you have to agree that the stalking stops."

Cyrus gave her a respectful embrace, and said, "Agreed. I'm going to be moving on. We'll catch up sometime in the future, but I never want you to be afraid of me." With that he made a hasty exit.

At this point, all of Tess' fear and anxiety were gone. She was alive, and the Cooperative would soon be history. More sirens pierced the quiet. It would have been helpful for her to stay and provide the cops with information, but she couldn't deal with it. The police had two crime scenes, a live victim, and a dead body to keep them occupied. Filling in the gaps would have to wait. She quickly walked the three additional blocks to the trauma unit at MRMC.

IN THE EMERGENCY ROOM

VJ was lying in the trauma bay dressed in nothing, but he didn't give a damn. Leila was safe, Tess was safe, he was alive, and the Cooperative was finished. Or at the very least—mortally wounded.

Jason Shoemaker, the king of orthopaedic trauma, lorded over VJ. They occasionally played racquetball together, and VJ always beat him. Jason couldn't stand it. There wasn't a surgeon VJ knew who wasn't off-the-wall competitive, particularly with another surgeon. As he gently put the dressing back on VJ's thigh, he said, "VJ, now I get the chance to even the score, and you have to pay me to do it. The new EMR will take care of it. Life doesn't get any better! The distal third of your femur's dusted, so I'm going to wash it out and put in a retrograde nail. Danguerin didn't see anything too bad in your knee, did he?"

Like a recurrent nightmare, the EMR reared its ugly head again. VJ mentally scrolled through the Cooperative's on-the-take list to remind himself that his racquetball partner was clean. After reassuring himself, he answered. "The knee is fixed now. Jason, thanks in advance. I know you won't believe this, but when

I woke up this morning, I had a totally different plan for how today was going to turn out."

An anesthesiologist VJ didn't know well was whispering to the trauma nurses. He overheard part of the conversation. "Didn't this guy die in the ASC? I have to ask him how he managed to end up here."

People were floating through to get a look at him, as if he were part of the freak show at the carnival. If it weren't for the fact that there was still a bullet in his thigh, it would have been more entertaining. Finally, they packaged VJ up and rolled him into the OR. Walking on two feet wasn't in the near-term future, but living was. The OR staff was still completely unnerved. Mourning the loss of a friend, and then finding that he's really alive, albeit shot, was not anticipated on the schedule.

The propofol did its job, and he was gone to the world in seconds. Before the case started, VJ did remember to emphasize that he was allergic to cephalosporins. He didn't need another shot at getting knocked off.

* * * * *

Tess drew a deep breath. "Let me tell you a story."

Wincing from pain, VJ still laughed. She stood over him in the post-anesthesia care unit. Leila had her own hand entwined with his and seemed to have no intention of letting go. The first bullet was a through-and-through shot in

366

his left shoulder. The second one had done a nice job converting his femur into a disassembled jigsaw puzzle. At least now the top and bottom were connected, courtesy of Jason. The two more deadly ones were stopped by the nanotube vest. Petra had lost the Kill VJ game for the last time.

"I loved seeing her face when I told her you were alive," Tess crowed. "Of course, the fact that she's in the morgue makes that fact irrelevant now."

Tess explained to Leila and VJ what had happened on the roof. Leila pressed her for more details about how Petra ended up on the bullet train to the underworld. Tess gave her the concise answer. "I was playing for time. When Cyrus distracted Petra by shooting her with that nail gun, I was able to get in a good, healthy kick. I just intended to knock her down and push the gun away. Cyrus finished it. Petra's not that big. Cyrus threw her. No question it was quite a distance, maybe survivable. I think the primary problem, though, was the rebar. Without those little orange caps, Petra got skewered. Not really elegant, but certainly dramatic. Didn't do much for her outfit, either. It was so pretty. Blood red doesn't look good on Yves Saint Laurent."

Petra's reign was over. VJ knew that in the not-too-distant future, the sight of countless doctors and other personnel being led out of

MRMC in handcuffs would be quite the media spectacle. Tess was spent. She sat down by the bed and gently laid her hand on his good leg.

He was lying on the narrow hospital gurney, hopped up on morphine, feeling constricted by the starched white hospital sheets and blankets entombing him like a mummy. Leila was sitting beside him on his right. They'd put him in the isolation room usually reserved for infected patients. At least the three of them had a vague sense of privacy.

"VJ," Tess began, then paused. "Petra made it sound like she knew you. Did you sit by her at a fund-raiser or something?"

VJ waited before responding. "Afraid I did know her. Do you remember my story about Danika?" Tess nodded. "Petra is Danika," he said.

Before VJ could get another word out, Tess practically exploded. "The batshit crazy one from medical school?"

Leila glared inquisitively at him. "I was going to tell you about her, Leila. I guess the timeline just got moved up. Yes, Tess, they are one and the same. I recognized her immediately when I ran into her office. That was just before she shot me. It says a lot about my people skills. Petra must be her middle name. It was one of those things I never knew. At Duke we attached our middle initial to everything. 'Danika P. Kakikis.' I remember it very clearly."

Tess held up a hand. "For the record, her last name came from another one of her classmates—Remy Lewis. Petra gave me the rundown of her life choices before taking that BASE jump."

"I detested that guy," VJ said. "So did everyone else. I don't even think his parents liked him. Fell on his head too many times as a toddler. Danika obviously found him convenient, at least in the short term. No one who knew her would ever recognize the name Petra Lewis. That's why you couldn't find much about her background, Tess. She buried everything."

Tess interjected, "I searched the web pages and social media—no pictures, nothing about a medical school degree. That's a hard feat these days. Her team did a good scrubbing job. Petra was able to consolidate power and stay under the radar at the same time."

Leila looked puzzled. "Why go to so much trouble to hide who she was? It's not like her degrees were manufactured."

"I would guess that she left baggage wherever she went," Tess said. "As we know, Petra wasn't in line to win any Miss Personality contests. This way, she was able to carve away a whole lotta people who might come back to bite her in some way. VJ's a perfect example."

Leila asked, "VJ, you still didn't tell me anything. Did you know Petra well? You told Tess about her, so clearly she made an impression."

Tess answered the question before VJ could respond. "He slept with her!" This was not information VJ had intended to share immediately. He looked at Leila guiltily. Gesturing toward Leila, Tess said, "I think all of us can agree that your taste in women has improved."

"For the record," he pointed out, "that was a one-and-done—that *she* initiated. And yes, you're correct, she fascinated me. Nobody understood Danika, or should I say Petra, well. We have the rest of eternity to psychoanalyze her."

Leila studied VJ and said, "We're going to continue this conversation later."

He looked at her and elected to take the offensive. "By the way, what happened to you agreeing to stay away from the hospital? We just decided *that* yesterday."

Leila protested, "No, you decided that. I didn't agree to anything. There was still work to do, and I intended to do it. Don't think for a second that I'm going to do everything you say—reasonable or not."

Lacking a good response, he thought it was a good time to say what he'd really needed to say. "Tess, you and Leila are the two most extraordinary people I've ever met. I love you both, and the words 'I'm sorry' can't begin to express what I feel. I didn't connect Petra with Rick until I saw him wearing that Patriots jersey this morning. I remembered what Tess saw the first day she went to Petra's office. Suddenly everything clicked. The obvious was hitting me in the face and I'd missed it. First rule of medicine: If you hear hoofbeats in the night, think horses, not zebras—unless of course you're in medical school at Karolinska, Duke, or Harvard, where the zebra herds run thick. I was fortunate that nothing happened to either of you. Please forgive me."

Leila and Tess looked at each other. Tess said, "Not sure how we're supposed to respond to that. You ran us through the wringer, made us accessories to a variety of nefarious activities, and forced us to care about you taking a few bullets yourself. But sure, dads will be dads. Leila, what's your take?"

Leila had a look of exasperation, but tenderly said, "I guess we can give him a pass," as she gripped his hand more tightly.

VJ continued, "Thank you. I deeply and sincerely appreciate that. Tess, I was so worried. I must have called and texted you three thousand times. I've lost track of time. How long ago did this happen?" He was still fighting through the fog of the morphine. He wanted to sleep, but pushed ahead. "Now that you both realize I'm useless, I need to find something out. Leila, will you marry me? Absent a ring, I offer you this hospital name tag as a token of my unmatched love for you."

Leila regarded VJ with a jaded eye. "People are never supposed to make decisions of magnitude after extreme emotional experiences. Plus, you're high on opiates. You're physically compromised, you've killed people, and you haven't exactly established yourself as a stable breadwinner. In other words, a perfect choice. My parents expect only the best for their pampered daughter. Are you sure you'll be able to take care of me in the manner to which I'm accustomed? And by the way, just because I'm a nurse doesn't mean I have any intention of waiting hand and foot on a man who just got his femur destroyed. Perhaps we should talk about this later, maybe when you give me a little more information about your tryst with Petra?"

VJ was insistent. "No way! Tess will be the decider. Tess, what do you think? Should Leila and I agree to be married this very instant, or should we talk about it later?"

Tess responded immediately: "Leila—don't you want a man who needs you to help him? A man who keeps you interested? A man who'll drag you into impossible situations? A man who, most importantly, has an awesome kid? Leila, are you in or out? We Vikings are extremely bad at waiting."

The kiss Leila planted on his lips said everything. VJ lit up like a Little Leaguer hitting his first home run. "So what do you kids want to do now?" With that, completely emotionally and physically drained, he faded out.

* * * * *

VJ was in his hospital room experiencing a moment of peace and quiet. The door opened and a familiar face peeked in. He beckoned her to join him. She was crying as she wrapped her arms around him.

Bianka yelled at VJ, "Do you have *any idea* what you've put me through? *Any idea at all?* I'm so happy to see you alive, but I want to kill you myself! I've been devastated!"

What could he say to her? For the next two hours, he did his best. When he was done, he thought they were OK. Bianka understood he was trying to shield her, and she appreciated it. He knew it would still take a long time to fully repair the damage incurred.

While VJ was contemplating what might be lost from many of his friendships, the alien ringtone sounded on his cell phone. Leila had retrieved it from his Quincy hideout. It was his buddy Johan from Sierra Lakes.

"Hey, VJ, everything OK? I've been trying to get you for a couple of weeks. Your phone's been off even more than usual, and you haven't responded to a single e-mail. I thought we were friends."

"I'm just fine," VJ responded. "Good to hear from you. I'm getting better from a small accident. I haven't had my phone with me. Did we get any more snow? What's up?"

"No, the storms ended for the season I think," he groused. "The last good one we had is when you were out. Sorry you were hurt. You gonna be all right?"

VJ answered honestly, "Better than ever."

"Well, that's good to hear. Hey, I called to ask you about some guys named Luciano. They're from your neck of the woods. Some woman named Petra Lewis called around a month ago saying they were in Sierra Lakes on a business trip and never came back. Said she's some important player at MRMC. I told her that those guys left their hotel room empty and that it might be that they were trying to avoid her. That set her off. She started yelling at me with some words that made even me blush. Boy, I can't imagine what it must be like to work for her. She's called a few times since, and I'm sick of talking to her.

"These Lucianos were out here at the same time as that explosion across the street from your house. By the way, the porno guy still has the LAPD looking into people who might've wanted him dead. I hear the list is about the size of the entire Los Angeles population. Lucky whoever it was didn't make a mistake and go after your house by accident. Pretty crazy stuff."

VJ wondered where Johan was going with this. He said, "You have no idea. It's been pretty crazy here, too. I've got a lot to tell you, but it's going to take some time. I'll fill you in when I come back. I don't know anyone named Luciano. Have I met either of them?"

"That's the question," Johan continued. "A couple of folks said one of them was asking for you. I talked to Boston P.D. They both have rap sheets longer than my honey-do list. Armed robbery, assault, racketeering, attempted murder—don't seem like the businessmen type. Apparently, they did rent a snowmobile, then called in saying it was broken. Except I can't find any record of either of them making the call at the time Jake said they did. We found the car they rented parked by the Meadows. It was pretty trashed. We don't have the manpower to launch a big search. Do you know why they were asking about you?"

VJ internally cursed himself for forgetting about the car, but responded quickly, "I always talk up Sierra Lakes in the office. Who knows what they wanted? We do have the prison contract. It's even possible I took care of one of them one time. I'll search my records," he lied, "and let you know if I find anything. If I had to guess, the Lucianos are probably floating somewhere around Boston. Either that or they're going to show up sometime later this spring when the snow melts. At least the parts of them the bears don't eat. Sierra Lakes isn't always the kindest host for inexperienced city people."

Johan sighed. "Remember that billionaire pilot we found a couple of years ago? He was spread over two acres. VJ, don't worry too much about it. I just thought I'd ask. I'm going to have to put it on the back burner right now. Hey, man, good talking to you."

"Be sure to tell Loraine hi for me," VJ said eagerly. "Hey, Johan, I can't make the trip I planned for next month. Send me a batch of those cookies. I could use a few right now."

After VJ hung up, he wondered about Johan's questions. It wouldn't take long for Johan to hear about his Boston adventure. Johan was a very smart man, but VJ felt pretty comfortable there wasn't any evidence left behind. Petra certainly wouldn't be making any more inquiries. VJ hoped he'd decide to leave this one case alone. Scarce resources can sometimes be a good thing. In the larger picture, the demise of the Cooperative's attack dogs, Lucca and Armaceo Luciano, would make the streets a safer place.

Later that day, having had some more necessary rest, Tess came back to visit. In her arms was the special item he'd asked her to pick up. After putting it in the corner, she grabbed the chair next to his bed and tossed him one of those goofy bears dressed in surgical scrubs. "Thought you might need a friend. You should see the circus outside. They're all going to want to talk to you."

He rubbed his shoulder. "Yeah, I know. I'm going to put it off as long as possible. Maybe we should figure out what we're going to tell the police. My bet is that someone might've noticed a lady impaled on rebar at a hospital building site. What do you think?"

Tess deadpanned, "I'm relatively sure they did."

VJ wasn't in the mood to deal with insignificant problems like the men in blue. Still, it was a necessary evil. "Let's agree to give them everything they need to know. Do you think the business in Sierra Lakes falls into the need-to-know category? I spoke to the Sierra Lakes police chief earlier. He doesn't have anything, and it appears he's not going to spend any more time looking."

Tess regarded VJ seriously. "Even though those two assholes tried to blow you up and shot at you, from a legal standpoint I don't know if what ultimately happened qualifies as true self-defense. Incinerating two dead bodies definitely raises questions. Life will get pretty messy if we dredge it up, and after all, they were trying to murder you, so justice was served. If the story comes out, it makes you look guilty of something you weren't guilty of. I think the best plan is to let it ride."

VJ felt relieved. "I was thinking the same thing. I will tell them now about the threats to me and Anders in great detail. The police need to understand why I faked my death in the first place. That guy Petra sent to kill us at the marathon is tangible corroborative evidence. Petra directly admitted it. Phone calls to him can be traced. Plus, he has to have a record. That should be enough.

"I need to keep Lige, Mikele and Pete in the clear. With the shit-storm that's hitting this place, I doubt Summerhays is going to be eager to make them anything but heroes. I can see the headline: CRACK MRMC OR TEAM KILLS SURGEON TO KEEP HIM ALIVE. The tabloids will love it. I think I might even throw a Glad to Be Officially Alive Again party. We'll invite the whole staff. Even the ones who blew off my funeral."

"I'm not so sure about that," Tess objected with a grin. "There may be a few people who think it'd be better if you were still on the other side. Let's just throw a big engagement party."

VJ concurred. "Wise you are indeed, daughter. I'll see if Terri's willing to help out."

Then he asked Tess something he'd been contemplating. "I've been wondering about Petra. Did you get a sense of who she was? Like I told you before, in medical school she was a complete mystery."

Tess was forthright. "VJ, I'm not going to pretend I got some insane insight in the short time I worked with her. My impression is that Petra was a smart person who started out, how should I say this, *seriously flawed*, and ended up becoming dangerously unstable. I don't think she could handle the problems you created. Petra relied on intimidation and greed. You're a lot of things, but greedy isn't one of them. This guy Rick is obviously more level-headed. Petra cut him out of the equation in her desperation to get rid of you. Major error. Cyrus told me that Rick found out about the most recent hit attempt and even tried to get us scooped up and hidden to save us. If it means something, Petra said some positive things about you. Even when she was pointing her gun at me. I almost laughed when she accused me of sleeping with you. That's right. She thought that was why I was helping you. I mattered to her less than a bug smashed on the windshield."

"In a bizarre way, I guess that's flattering," VJ said as he grasped for Tess' hand. "Don't let it bother you. Petra's M.O. was using people. Take it from someone who knows firsthand. I think you did quite a nice job of getting in the last word."

A knock on the door interrupted the conversation. Leila said, "VJ, a friend of yours wanted to come by and say hello," and entered the room with Chuck Danguerin. For a moment, VJ wasn't sure how to react. He was truly relieved to know now that Chuck had not been compromised by the Cooperative. If Chuck had done to him what he had done to Chuck, VJ would still be furious.

Maybe Chuck saw the uncertainty in his eyes. He flashed a big smile. "That was quite a stunt you pulled off, buddy. Thank you for not letting that woman shoot you directly in the knee. If I'd had to take care of you again, I'd really have been mad." He looked around the room and spotted the box Tess had delivered on the floor. "Hey—you actually came through with my case of Silver Oak. You *are* the man."

NEW BEGINNINGS

Cyrus watched from a restaurant across the street as groups of law enforcement agents walked in and out of the administration building. He was slightly remorseful about leaving. Even though the relationship with Tess had never materialized the way he thought it might, the idea of seeing her again was attractive. Cyrus stealthily made his way to the alley off Charles Street, jumped on his Harley, and sped away. He didn't know where he'd land. Finding work was never a problem.

* * * * *

The large iron gates slowly parted, allowing the sleek town car to glide through. Once the engine stopped, the driver briskly opened the passenger door and Rick stepped out, grasped his duffel, slipped off his flip-flops, and buried his feet in the sand. Joy coursed through his body. He was free of the heinous banshee. He'd caught a glimpse of the lifeless Petra suspended by rebar, fresh crimson blood coating the iron spikes. *A perfect end,* he thought to himself. Rick had prepared for this day for several years. Beast was a small account. Most of the money he had earned was siphoned off right here, to Grand

Cayman. Petra wasn't the only one with connections at MIT.

The mansion before him sat on Seven Mile Beach, just north of Cemetery Pointe. It was exquisite, but not too attention-grabbing. He knew better than that. Completely paid for, cash on the barrelhead to the builders. They got the job done a month ahead of schedule. Rick thought they might.

He far preferred to handle matters without violence. His physical presence often was enough. What happened to Nick was over his objections. The hit Petra put on VJ and Tess was done without his knowledge.

The thriving beachside restaurant he owned would be seeing a lot more of its owner. So would the new dive shop, and his teams shuttling contraband in and out of the Caribbean. He was building this empire as a solo venture. Rick had forever sworn off partners. Grand Cayman represented a wonderful new beginning. A place where anything that happened in Boston would be meaningless. The freshly minted South African passport said it all. Good luck in the world, Mr. Robert Alan Green, the man formerly known as Rick Tuafotofoa. Fortunately, Mr. Green already had millions in his island bank accounts from years of investment.

The sun dove, lighting up the clouds in brilliant orange. One looked like a dragon breathing fire. A sailboat hung on the glistening water; three cruise liners made their exit, dotting the horizon; small aquamarine waves lapped rhythmically against the shoreline—the scene was idyllic. Robert opened the door to his house and walked in, feeling lighter than air.

HOW ABOUT THAT?

After the requisite explanations, reports, and investigations concluded, a semblance of normalcy returned. Except it didn't. Life changed. VJ was hopelessly in love with Leila, and now had an amazing grown daughter. They both seemed to think he was OK. He put work on the back burner. The staff easily survived his absence.

VJ figured, why not make a more permanent transition? He dumped call and didn't miss it for a second. Boston was so much more fun when he had the opportunity to enjoy it. When he informed Nick that the Cooperative was no more, Nick officially became the second happiest person on the planet.

One of the interesting tidbits that surfaced during the forensic audit was that all the billing with Nick's name on it was erased. Nothing from the hospital, nothing in the Medicare data bank. Poof. Like it never happened. When VJ was asked about it, he could only speculate—computer virus, sunspots, act of God. Who knew? Certainly not him. He was just a poor, innocent guy targeted by the evil empire. Nobody from the fed, state, or city would go after Nick without evidence. Nick's name also mysteriously disappeared from Tess' Cooperative doctor bribery list. Such a shame. Axel was indeed impressive. When he put that brilliant mind to a task, there was almost nothing he couldn't accomplish. VJ decided Axel needed a Ferrari, courtesy of Nick and himself. Neither of them had the bucks just yet, but it was a goal.

As expected, the hospital board rang up Summerhays and sent him back to Philadelphia. The anesthesia group had an Oh Damn He's Back soirée for Lige. Citing the public good, the governor preempted any medical board action against Pete and Lige. VJ couldn't have been happier.

Benjamin Saito checked in from his outpost in Brunswick. He offered VJ the spot that Nick tried to take. VJ declined for the immediate future, but set up a visit to just hang out. VJ told him how pleased he was when he didn't spot Benjamin's name on the Cooperative's payroll. Ben in turn ripped VJ a new one for doubting him, reneging on his offer to pay for the next round of drinks. That responsibility was placed back on VJ's shoulders.

One evening Tess came over for dinner. Fulfilling his promise, VJ had worked with her, and she'd become an anatomy whiz kid. Leila and she were tight. Shared experience. And she and Vikka were now an item, too. Vikka went nuts when Tess walked through the door. A new victim to give her the ever elusive, perfect belly rub.

Privately in the kitchen, Leila turned to face VJ and wrapped her hands delicately around him. "Are you going to tell her?"

"Tell her what?" he asked innocently.

"You know exactly what—Petra," Leila replied.

He looked in his fiancée's eyes. "Maybe sometime, definitely not now, likely never. I don't see the point."

Leila conceded, "It's your call. I just think she should know."

While they munched on Leila's dinosaur kale salad that VJ pretended to enjoy, Tess inquired, "So, are you two going to take some time away? If anybody deserves a romantic escape, it's you guys."

Leila put down her fork for a minute and peered at VJ. "VJ, that's something I've been meaning to talk to you about. I keep hearing you tell everyone how perfect Grand Cayman is. I decided that's where we're going. We can call it a pre-honeymoon trip, a vacation, or anything you want. We leave next week. I don't care if it's hot. It'll be *très romantique*! Don't worry, Terri cleared your schedule. She asked me what part of Chicago I'm from. What's that about? Nikolai, the new guy they got to replace Nick, is going to stick around. You like him, don't you?"

VJ didn't protest. "The Chicago reference is hysterical. I made up a girlfriend when I was taking Nick to Sweden. I'll tell you more about that. Grand Cayman is fabulous. Just keep me away from their TSA. They hate me! I'll tell you about that, too.

"For whatever it's worth, Nikolai goes by the Russian nickname Kolya, just like Bianka's dog. We probably shouldn't call him Koliebear, though. He's terrific. Back to what matters, Grand Cayman. Judging from the tenor of this conversation, you've already booked everything. Correct?"

Leila acknowledged his question with a nod. "You know," she said, "it's also going to be my birthday. Daily celebrations for a week. I got us a spectacular ocean-view room at Paradise Row. All the reviewers said it was the nicest place they've ever stayed. There's a grocery store nearby. We barely have to leave if we don't want to. There's another great part—one of the premier snorkeling spots on the island is just a hundred yards up the beach. It's called Cemetery Pointe."

He looked squarely at her. "Leila, there's no place I'd rather be and nobody I'd rather be with. Just us. We won't see another familiar soul."

Innocently, Tess steered the conversation to a new topic. "Not to bring up a sore subject, but I did get the test back."

Leila and VJ both refocused as he asked, "Are you telling us you're pregnant, or that the neuroanatomy went better than you thought?"

Tess smiled somewhat oddly. "Neither, actually. A different one. Don't you think it's peculiar that with all that intelligence, Petra never processed certain things—like the fact that she and I were about the same height and weight, that we shared the same facial structure, the same eye color, the same hair texture, and that our voices were so similar? Too self-absorbed, I suppose. After she went on that rant telling me about the kid she dumped, and then, when I found out that she and Danika were one in the same, the truth was pretty obvious. Your coroner friend Pete heard the Cooperative was neutralized, so he came back early from his "vacation" to do the post. Because of all the legal issues, he held the results. But he just confirmed what I knew already.

"My guess is you figured it out. And I understand why you didn't tell me. You and *that woman*, my biological parents—impossible to imagine. Please reassure me I'm more like you than her. For *your sake*, I hope so."

ACKNOWLEDGMENTS

First and foremost, I would like to thank my wonderful, always energetic wife, Ellen, who provided tremendous insight during every phase of the writing process and tolerated endless plot discussions. Her ongoing love and support made this possible. Our daughter, Erika Brown, gave brutally honest, thoughtful, and appropriate criticism of the novel. I did my best to listen. I wasn't always successful.

Tusen tack to Jessica and Benjamin Brown, our other daughter and son, for their support, insight, matchless enthusiasm, and plot inspirations. Fight On! Up the Field Big Blue! Go 'Bos!

I want to recognize my father, Dr. Leonard Brown, for his assistance, encouragement, and medical wisdom, and my mother, Ann Brown, for who she always was. Were it only true that she could still read this.

Linda Brown's herculean efforts in editing, plot development, and physically crafting the book cannot be understated. She saved me. Nancy Glaser and Sharon Reich contributed mightily to idea integration and editing. Then they did more editing. Then still more. Their devotion to this project meant so much. Toda raba.

Dr. David Dalstrom, Dr. James Blasingame, Dr. Sheila Friedlander, Jan Hudson, Nicole Kimball, Robert Glaser, Dr. Gina Fleming, Rob Kocher, Drs. Ulrika and Danny Green, Len Gregory, and Dr. Molly Siegel all spent considerable time and effort helping me. Individually, each was amazing. I cannot possibly express how grateful I remain. Should anyone ever have any questions about guns, Dr. Dalstrom is the source. Beth and Andy Brown were queried about various plot questions and were helpful shaping the content. Tack sa mychet.

While the conclusion to this story was written thirty years ago, my close friend Dr. Rob Pedowitz provided the inspiration for the central plot with an anatomy lab adventure of his own. I am indebted to him.

I would like to recognize my co–hand surgery fellows Drs. Craig Williams and Jon Ark, our fellow Godfather Dr. John Seiler, longtime hand surgery partner Dr. Robert Gelb, the physicians of Torrey Pines Orthopaedic Medical Group, along with the entire membership of the New Millennium Hand Study Group for their integrity, thoughtfulness, and leadership. Their patients are lucky to have them as doctors.

I would like to particularly thank and recognize my hand surgery mentors, Drs. Richard Gelberman, Reid Abrams, and Jesse

Jupiter. Every day their words impact me. They are role models for any practicing physician.

Walter Bode was the primary book editor. I am concerned I may have damaged his view of the medical world forever. From what I understand, an insider's view of any world can have that effect. I maintain great respect for his insights and determination to see *Scalpel's Cut* through to completion. His talents are a credit to the literary world. Thanks to the brilliant Emily Mahon for her terrific work with the book design and bookmarks, and to Phyllis DeBlanche and Dan Janeck for their hand surgeon–like diligence proofreading and editing the final document.

The institutions and characters portrayed in this book are purely fictional. The events described are also fictional, except the ones that aren't. The cadavers, the dog, the cat, and the dead plants are real.

Made in the USA
San Bernardino, CA
21 April 2018